F

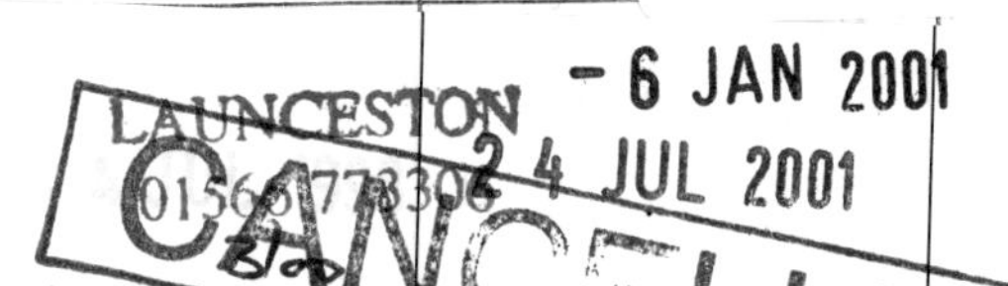
LAUNCESTON
01566 773306

- 6 JAN 2001
2 4 JUL 2001
CANCELLED
1 1 APR 2000
1 8 SEP 2001
- 6 NOV 2001
2 3 NOV 2001
18 APR 2000
- 3 MAY 2000
15th June
1 4 JUL 2000
CANCELLED
25 JAN 2002
2 4 APR 2002
12 March

RICKMAN, M.

Sarah Fowkes

185200052X

CORNWALL COUNTY COUNCIL
LIBRARIES AND ARTS DEPARTMENT

SARAH FOWKES

Sarah Fowkes

Mark Rickman

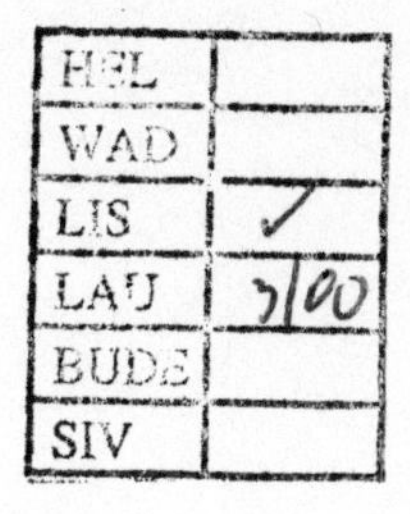

UNITED WRITERS
Cornwall

UNITED WRITERS PUBLICATIONS LTD
Ailsa, Castle Gate, Penzance, Cornwall.

All Rights Reserved. No part of this publication may be reproduced, stored in a retrieval system, or transmitted, in any form or by any means, electronic, mechanical, photocopying, recording or otherwise, without the prior permission of the Copyright owner.

British Library Cataloguing in Publication Data
A catalogue record for this book is available from the British Library.

ISBN 1 85200 052 X

Copyright (c) 1994 Mark Rickman

Printed in Great Britain by
United Writers Publications Ltd
Cornwall

for Aaron, Sam, and Dina

The letters and some of the early evidence given by Mrs Tombrin to the prosecuting counsel have some relationship with evidence given in the trial of Rachel Leverson who, in 1868, was accused of obtaining money by fraud. In all other respects the author has told the story of Sarah Fowkes, and the characters who live and die during its telling, using imagination and fiction.

Chapter One

Alice Tombrin, the last of the prosecution witnesses, took the oath in a quavery voice and, with the help of counsel, told the court she was the widow of Mr Montague Tombrin, a diplomat attached to the British Civil Service in India. She had been widowed after twenty-two years of a happy and contented married life. She first became acquainted with the female prisoner after her return to England, some four months earlier, in the December of 1880. Then she took a deep, almost sobbing breath, swore without being asked that she had escaped the dreadful fate so cruelly meted out to her dear friend, Florence Carlisle, by the skin of her teeth, and leaned over the edge of the witness-box to see what effect her words were having on the pair in the dock. To the newspaper artist sitting to one side of the accused, it seemed that her gaze passed over the man almost with a trace of wistful affection before fixing on the woman's face with the utmost hatred.

For his part, the male prisoner attempted a weak smile beneath his heavy moustaches, cleared his throat, and nodded encouragingly at the witness, as though he too was eager to have their little misunderstanding cleared up as soon as possible. The woman beside him, startlingly beautiful and impeccably dressed in a tailor made, navy blue costume over a high-necked white blouse, slowly turned her head to meet Mrs Tombrin's glittering eye with an equivalent malevolence before returning to her stony regard of William Shanklin, the prosecuting counsel.

While she watched from the dock, the fat little man stepped away from the witness and went into his, by now familiar routine of twitching at the neck of his robe, raising a hand to adjust his wig, lowering it to push his spectacles further up the bridge of his nose, and then dropping it to rustle noisily through the sheaf of papers he picked up from the table beside him. At the same time whistling tunelessly through his teeth.

Sarah Fowkes's expression remained composed but behind her façade of polite interest in the barrister's ridiculous pantomiming, she became increasingly irritated, wanting nothing better than to leap from the dock and slap his stupid hand away each time it reached one of its destinations. She was lowering her dark, heavy-lidded eyes to conceal yet another surge of rage when he coughed and took off his spectacles to polish them on the edge of his gown before popping them back on his nose and turning on his heel to glare suspiciously round the court.

It was so like a party trick that, as she stared at him, Sarah was forced to bite the inside of her cheek to prevent herself from laughing hysterically. Some days earlier, in the remand prison, her defending counsel, Arnold Roberts, told her that Willie Shanklin had one of the keenest legal minds in the country. For Sarah, none of the man's hand flapping theatricality spoke of it. She had been told to take the little mountebank seriously. Perhaps even with a touch of fear. In his opening address, Shanklin had turned his back on the dock and said he intended the jury to do its duty and find her and Charlie Bennet guilty of murder. So that the wizened and impossibly old Mr Justice Hughes could order the two of them to be taken away and hanged by the neck until they were dead.

While Sarah sat in the dock, able only to clench her fists in a fury of impotence, she tried to relieve her frustration by mentally stripping him of his wig and gown, and the tailcoat and striped trousers he wore beneath. Leaving him naked and cowering at her feet while she raised the long pointed scissors she always carried and gouged out his eyes. The pale blue, sharp little eyes that looked at her so apprais-ingly each time she was escorted into the courtroom. While Shanklin preened and Sarah's nerves were being drawn tight enough for her to jump to her feet and scream for blood, the little man startled her again by walking quickly towards the witness, coming back to gather up his notes, and turning once more to face Mrs Tombrin.

Sarah took a deep breath while she waited for him to resume questioning the witness, and glanced surreptitiously at her co-defendant. As she expected, Charlie Bennet was as twitchy as Shanklin. From the moment the trial began and they were made to sit side by side on the wooden bench of the dock, his hands had continually pulled at his moustaches, his tie, or his shirt cuffs. He was at it now, tugging at a cuff, fastening and unfastening his jacket buttons. His frightened, bewildered eyes darting from face to face. Out of his element, Charlie was cowed by the gowns and wigs, terrified of being spoken to, and terrified of what was to come. Now unrecognisable as her lover, the man was all of a fidget on the wooden bench beside her.

She glanced down at her own hands, folded them in her lap and, satisfied with their stillness, looked the other way, at the crowded courtroom. Brown and dreary, it was smelly with the mixed odours of furniture polish and unwashed people in dirty clothes who stared back at her. That smell overlaid by the ammonia and bad egg stink from the adjacent and recently set up, gentlemen's public lavatory. God almighty, what was she thinking of now? She had been brought to the court to fight for her life and all she could fasten her mind on was a bad smell. Knowing she must concentrate on the words the scraggy, red-haired woman in the witness-box meant to condemn her with, Sarah pinched the fleshy pad of her lower hand between her thumb and forefinger, winced slightly, and ordered herself for the umpteenth time to pay attention.

Alice Tombrin had more than enough reason to hate her but her whining vindictiveness meant nothing to Sarah. She knew about hatred. She could not have lived the life she had without making enemies as well as victims. Victims she had seen die, either at her own hands or Charlie's. If they had not got careless, the old bitch in the witness-box would have gone the same way as the others and the court case would never have come about. As it was, Mrs Tombrin, instead of becoming another victim, had become another of Sarah's enemies. It was she who sent the police sergeant to the shop to ask questions about Florence Carlisle. Who, she had sworn to the man, she had last seen on Sarah's premises. When Sarah denied knowing anyone called Carlisle, the sergeant brought two constables in from the street to search the building while he and another man dressed in a plain suit instead of a uniform, took her and a suddenly trembling and white-faced Charlie Bennet to the police office for questioning.

'Took me in,' she raged silently. 'Made me put the shutters of my shop up and took me to the lock-up on the word of that old toad.' Realising her mind had wandered and she was not listening to the old crone in the witness-box, she pinched herself again and resolved to concentrate. Alice Tombrin was telling of the advertisement she had seen in the *Morning Telegraph* and how it led her to Madame Sarah's establishment in Beak Street.

'Making you the latest of a long list, dearie,' Sarah was thinking sourly while Shanklin leafed through his notes and said, "A moment please, Mrs Tombrin. Will you kindly look at this advertisement and tell the court if it is identical to the one that drew you to Sarah Fowkes's shop?"

The witness had scarcely glanced at the proffered newspaper before she was nodding eagerly and saying to the counsel, "Oh yes sir, it most certainly is."

"Thank you, Mrs Tombrin. Now madam, I shall be most obliged if you will read the advertisement aloud for the benefit of his lordship and the gentlemen of the jury."

'No need to bother on my account, you old bag of bones. I thought it up.' The words flitted about Sarah's mind as the witness began to read in a high-pitched, officious voice, the advertisement which promised to make ladies beautiful for life. In the dock, Sarah's expression of polite concern did not alter while she apparently listened to Mrs Tombrin with as much interest as the rest of the court. Sarah Fowkes had learned to be careful with her face. Careful too, to avoid using words and phrases like 'dearie' and 'old bag of bones' when she spoke to people, whatever the provocation.

* * * *

She had used words like those and commoner once. Years before, when she was the girl from the laundry and old Mr Constantine would amuse himself by putting her right whenever he caught her saying something wrong. Which was often enough, God knows it was, but the old man seemed to take some pleasure in talking to her whenever he found her delivering or collecting the heavy wash at his kitchen door. She was small then and, on one of the occasions when the bundle was overly heavy and the Constantine's back way muddier than usual, her ankle turned over on the edge of his garden path and she almost fell, only to find herself caught up in the heavily bearded man's arms.

"Struth and bugger these soddin' boots!" she yelped as she sagged against him in pain, and almost dropped the clean washing on the grass verge. He laughed as he righted her and caught up the bundle. Keeping his large square hand on her shoulder, he guided her into the kitchen where she could pull off the offending boot, hitch her skirt up to her none-too-clean knee, and nurse her bare ankle. He often put in an appearance at the back garden gate after that, patting her arm and saying a few words when she came through, correcting her language whenever she said something dirty. She didn't mind him doing it if he wanted to. It pleased him and she was streetwise enough to know the old man had taken a fancy to her. He even caught a sight of her and stopped for a word on the morning he was walking his daughter across the cobblestoned Burdett Road to her wedding in St Michael's.

"Sarah," he said, putting a hand on her arm and smiling down at her. "It's Ella's wedding today. Leave your bundle with cook and ask her for a packet of bride cake. If you sleep with it under your pillow tonight, it's said you'll dream of the man you'll marry."

Fifteen-year-old Sarah, whose pillow, as often as not, was a rolled up grubby sheet from one of the big houses in the Mile End Road, said with disarming honesty, "Gerrout of it, guvnor. 'Oo the 'ell'd want me?"

Mr Constantine looked amused. "Who would want me?" he said patiently. "And the answer is, none of us know who wants us till we come down to it, do we?"

For her own answer, Sarah shrugged indifferently, turned away and for a moment, her eyes met and held the bride's. Nineteen-year-old Ella Constantine, elaborately gowned in a concoction of heavily ribboned pink and white tulle and carrying between her wildly trembling fingers, a small bouquet of orange blossom, contrasted oddly with the broken booted, raggety dressed, laundry girl, resting a bundle of washing on an out-thrust hip. Yet, had they known it, both girls shared a single wish.

Ella, prepared for her wedding night by a mother who told her there was an unpleasant duty to which a wife must submit, adding for emphasis there was no hope at all of a husband sparing his wife's finer feelings when he took his pleasure of her; and Sarah, who admired the over elaborate wedding dress enormously and still faced the long haul home to Stepney with a heavy load of dirty sheets, both fervently wished they could change places.

It was much more than a twenty minute hike that faced Sarah after the terror-stricken, white-faced Ella was led past her into the church and the solemnisation of her marriage. It was a journey back in time from the comparatively modern terraces of Bow through the labyrinth of narrow, dirty streets and alleyways that led to Broomfield Court, itself a huddle of run-down cottages surrounding an open and foetid gulley. There was no pavement to protect the raised wooden door-sills and the constantly blocked drain at the end of the gulley, ensured that the greasy cobbles she walked on were always awash with a stinking scum of refuse.

The lower floor of one of the cottages made a home and a workplace for Peter Mendel who, with the help of an apprentice and six or seven ill assorted females, made up gentlemen's waistcoats for a tailoring house in Cork Street. For more than seventy hours a week, his ladies basted out edges, felled in linings, hemmed, prickstitched, and complained. About the broken and splintered floorboards they were forced to sit or squat on while they worked. About the bad light that drove them towards the broken shutters that passed for windows and the evil smell from the broken drain that forced them back again. The most vociferous of all their complaints concerned the damp and heavy steam emanating from the laundry set up by Sarah's mother in the back room. A room that housed mother and daughter, a seemingly ever boiling copper, and a large, forbidding looking, wooden rollered mangle.

Not that the chorus of high-pitched whining from Mendel's crones troubled Aggie Fowkes who, since her scrawny, olive-skinned, husband disappeared in the murky waters of the East India Docks, compensated for her loss by taking in washing and gin in increasing quantities. It was Sarah who was made to bear the brunt of the sewing women's displeasure. When she was not delivering and collecting laundry, helping to paddle the washing in the tub, or turning the handle of the mangle with both hands, she was sitting among Mendel's workers and making buttonholes in his waistcoats. Trying, at the same time, to turn a deaf ear to being sworn at and threatened on her mother's behalf. Even, on occasion, collecting a kick or a hearty thwack across her shoulders from a seamstress irritated beyond measure by having to spend her day half-choked by a heavy cloud of stinky steam.

Late evening was the best of times for Sarah Fowkes. Everyone had gone. The sewing women to their nearby hovels and their menfolk. Holding their achy backs with both hands as they went. Their chorus of complaints dying away only when they turned the corner. Mendel and his snotty nosed, loose lipped, apprentice to their cronies and a night's gambling. Sarah's mother to the nearest gin palace.

Left to herself, her playthings the bundles of dirty washing she had to sort through and separate, Sarah could dream of sleeping between the heavy white sheets she carried home that day. She could flirt and be saucy as she liked with one of the vests or striped flannel shirts that made up part of the wash done for the single young men lodging in the neighbourhood. Some nights too, there would be a knock on Mendel's outside door and she would hand over a small bundle of clean washing, take back the dirty and the few coppers due, and now and then indulge in a little harmless banter with a personable young man.

On one such evening, a month or so after she stopped outside Mr Constantine's house to see the bride, Sarah was a little weepy over a cut finger that had earned Mendel's wrath by leaving a spot of blood on a waistcoat lining. The youngish looking man she opened the door to, noticed her red rimmed eyes and asked why she was crying. Mutely, she held out the cut finger.

"Pooh," he said derisively, "that's no more than a fleabite. Give it over and I'll kiss it better for you."

"Poison it more like," she said archly, putting the hand behind her and backing away.

"You mustn't talk to a gentleman like that, my girl. I shall think you're trying to insult me," he said half in jest, while he followed her into the room and persisted in reaching for her hand. "Give it over here when you're told."

Becoming alarmed, Sarah said as firmly as she could, " 'Ere you, bugger off. My ma'll be back in a minute and if she catches you in here with me, she'll bleeding well kill you."

"Oh no, she won't kill me, you lying little whore," the man grunted as he tried again to reach round her for her hand. "I know your ma. I just passed the old cow flopped out on the doorstep of the Queen's Head. You won't be seeing her for a long time yet."

A moment later, the girl was fighting for her life, convinced she was being murdered for the few coins she had tucked away beneath the mangle. The man's cap had fallen off, revealing an almost completely bald head, and one of his grimy hands covered her mouth, half choking her and stifling her terrified screams as he pulled her hard against him.

"Come on you little bitch, come on," he was muttering through gritted teeth as, struggling wildly, they tripped and fell heavily on to a loose bundle of unwashed sheets.

Half dazed and scarcely able to breath beneath his weight, she felt his hands scrabbling at her clothing, ripping apart the coarse fabric of her blouse and reaching down to break open the fastenings of her skirt.

"Oh my gawd, no!" she squealed as she suddenly realised his true intent. Her struggles became even more frantic but her writhing only served to inflame him further and he was too strong to be beaten off.

Again he muttered, almost pleadingly, "Come on you little bitch, come on," and at last, ignoring her scratching nails and half strangled sobs, he succeeded in holding down and raping the half naked girl before running away. Leaving Sarah bruised and semi-conscious among the twisted sheets.

Alone and trembling violently, she pulled her clothes round her legs into some semblance of modesty, dragged herself to the front door to bolt it after him and slowly crawled back on hands and knees to collapse on the pile of washing. Still dazed, she rubbed the corner of a sheet down over her belly and between her legs, trying feebly to brush the feel of him away, before dropping her head in her hands and bursting into tears. Later, when her sobs and some of the racking pain had begun to subside, she rolled over to lay on her side. Exhausted beyond thought, Sarah hiccuped and snivelled herself to sleep.

Aggie Fowkes, her over-large and shapeless black hat tipped rakishly over one eye, was sentimentally drunk and singing a bawdy song when she weaved her way along Broomfield Court to Mendel's cottage. Finding the door barred against her, she shouted good humouredly. "Sarah, my darling, come here and give your old mother a kiss." Getting no reply changed her mood and she pounded at the door with both pudgy fists until she heard some movement inside and the bolt scraped back. Grunting indignantly, she pushed past her daughter without a glance and collapsed heavily on to the sagging bed in the corner of Mendel's workroom.

"What do you think you're doing of?" she demanded petulantly. "What do you want to keep your mother standing out in the street for on a night like this?" Getting no reply, she peered at the girl standing in the shadow cast by the door and her good humour returned. Pulling a sodden, ill-wrapped package from somewhere beneath her sacking apron, she wheedled, "Look here darling, I bought us a lovely soused herring for supper. Put it on a dish and we'll share it." Again, Sarah made no move and Mrs Fowkes sat up clumsily to glare at her.

"What's the matter with you?" she bellowed. "You too good to talk to your mother all of a sudden? Come over here and take the lousy bit of herring when you're told."

Aggie screwed up her eyes to focus on Sarah while the girl limped reluctantly into the pool of light thrown by a smoky oil lamp hanging by Mendel's bed and her jaw dropped when the bruised and blood-streaked face came into view. For another moment, she continued to stare at her daughter and then, as Sarah burst into tears, she dropped the forgotten package of fish and shrieked. "For the love of God! What have you been doing to yourself?"

"I tried to stop him," Sarah wailed. "Honest I did. I thought he was trying to thieve our money but he wasn't. He knocked me down flat on the floor and done it to me."

"Done what?" roared Mrs Fowkes. "Who did? What did he do to you?"

"Took a hold of me so I couldn't move and pushed his thing into me. He kept on calling me a little bitch and whore. I couldn't hold him off, no matter what I did. First he kept on hitting me and then he pulled my skirt off and did it to me."

Mrs Fowkes, shocked into near soberness, heaved herself off the bed and pushed Sarah towards their own room. "It's all right, my darling," she said soothingly. "You stop your carry on and come in here. If that old bugger Mendel catches you in this state, he'll want to know what we get up to the minute his back is turned. Come on now, let your ma have a proper look at you."

Her hands were surprisingly gentle while she stripped Sarah of her torn garments. And, while she washed the trembling girl, she noted with tightened lips the blood and bruising on her belly and thighs. When she finished, she patted her daughter dry with one of the sheets and said quietly. "Sarah, listen to me. What that bugger did is a terrible thing but you know it happens round here. You should never have let him come in the house." Sarah flinched and her mother gave her a light smack on her bare backside. "Come on girl, I didn't say it was your fault what happened, did I? Sometimes we say something we don't mean. Sometimes we might think we're only saying a friendly word or two and one of them filthy hounds will think we mean something else."

Sarah dropped her eyes. "It wasn't my fault he came in," she snivelled, suppressing the memory of holding out her cut finger. "I didn't know what he was meaning to do to me."

"I don't suppose he knew either when he came in. Are you sure he did it right?"

"I don't know. It felt like it, but he was knocking me about all over the place. All he kept doing was hurting me."

"I know how much he hurt you. I can see the state you're in," said her mother. "What he did was supposed to give him pleasure, though what pleasure he took out of half-killing you as well as having his way, I wouldn't understand. You best lay down now and go to sleep. Maybe he hasn't done you no real harm."

"No real harm?" squealed Sarah. "I'm black and blue all over."

"Black and blue will pass off in a few days. Real harm is if he left you with a child."

Sarah's eyes widened in shock. "If he's done that to me, I'm going to end it in the river. I ain't having his bastard."

Her mother took her by the shoulders and shook her gently. "I thought I told you to lay down and go to sleep," she ordered. "If, God forbid, you are in that sort of trouble, there are better ways to get rid of it than chucking yourself off Tower Bridge. Now hush your row and go to sleep when you're told. I can hear Mendel coming in." Obediently, Sarah lay down and closed her eyes, only to open them again at the commotion coming from the next room.

"For the love of the Good God Almighty!" Mendel was shouting at the top of his voice. "Who left this lump of stinking fish on my bed?"

"It's all right, Mendel, my darling!" her mother was shrieking in return as she hurried into the next room. "You don't have to worry about it, my sweetheart. You found old Aggie's bit of supper for her, that's all." Sarah's eyes closed again of their own volition, her knees drew up to her breast, and her damaged finger went into her mouth. Unaware, as she was to discover some weeks later, that she had been made pregnant, she sighed deeply, gave a slight shudder, and slept.

On the following Sunday morning, Mr Constantine's daughter Ella, now Mrs Frank Mason, who found love-making with her husband far less formidable than her mother had prophesied, was legitimately, enjoyably, and with hardly a ruffle of the bedclothes, also made pregnant.

Chapter Two

There was a murmur of amusement when the witness, who could not be described as even remotely good looking, began to read aloud the advertisement that promised to make women beautiful for life. She faltered and looked confusedly into the well of the court when a half stifled snigger brought a warning wag of a finger from a heavily built usher. William Shanklin too, swung on his heel to stare suspiciously at the offender before returning to his witness.

"Please continue, Mrs Tombrin," he gently prompted the embarrassed woman. "You came across an advertisement describing the female prisoner as Madame Sarah, a purveyor of cosmetics, enamels, paint powders and rouge. An advertisement that also proclaimed the lady's ability to give women beauty for as long as they may live. What did you do after you read the advertisement?"

"I visited her shop in Beak Street and had some conversation with her. She asked me how much money I wished to spend. On my first visit, I spent £10 and during the course of the next two or three weeks, I had invested a further £70. I paid her various sums for cosmetics and soaps during the early part of 1881. Before I purchased the articles, I asked her to do something for my skin, which had been affected by many years spent in the Far East at my husband's side. She promised me that if I followed her course of treatments to the letter, she would ultimately succeed in making me beautiful." Mrs Tombrin paused and again a partly smothered titter made her blush to the roots of her hair.

"Oh, b-but this is hateful," she stammered through a sudden onrush of tears. "I was thought to be beautiful once. There can be nothing wrong in wanting to be made beautiful again."

At the judge's signal, the usher provided her with a glass of water. As she took it between both hands, she managed to give the man a tremulous smile of gratitude and someone clapped their hands. The murmurs became approving and the male prisoner said, "Bravo old girl. That's the ticket." Thereby earning himself a heavy dig in the ribs from the officer at his side and a cold stare from Sarah Fowkes. Charlie Bennet had only the vaguest understanding of the phrase he had used. The only ticket he was acquainted with came from a pawnbroker in Whitechapel, but he had heard Lieutenant Holland use it often enough when he was his batman.

Lord above, when he was old Holland's batman! For a moment he straightened his back and half smiled at the memory, making an artist from one of the illustrated newspapers sit up smartly and begin a new sketch. Charlie, despite his years of dissipation, was a handsome man with smoky eyes and golden hair that had been the envy of many of the women he slept with. Blessed with a good physique, he was above average height and had a military set to his square shoulders.

Twelve years earlier, when he was nineteen years of age, he'd been told the tale by a recruiting sergeant who invited him and another likely lad into a Wandsworth pub for a drink. Only half listening to the totally misleading picture of army life the sergeant painted, he enlisted in the Life Guards in preference to a life of stitching coats and breeches with his journeyman tailor father. Charlie hated stitching. He had seen it turn his father half blind and crook backed, but his own early apprenticeship in the trade had given him a dexterity in his fingers and sufficient deftness with a flat iron to make him the ideal officer's servant. As soon as his basic drilling and stamping about the barrack square was over and his military career decided upon, he was ordered to report to Lieutenant Holland and have a batman's duties explained.

Jack Holland looked up at him from the bed he was sprawled on and said crisply, "You are to bring me my mug of tea and hot shaving water at a quarter to six every duty morning. You are to get me out of this bed and standing on my two pins before six, no matter what ghastly names I call you. I must never see a mark that shouldn't be there on my kit and I mean to have the best polished boots and breastplate in the Regiment. Have you got that so far?"

"Yes sir!" snapped Charlie, standing rigidly to attention with his thumbs in line with the seams of his close fitting military overalls and his eyes on the wall before him.

Holland chuckled softly. "There's no need to be all that formal when you're in among my quarters, old man." He laughed as though he had made a private joke that Charlie should have understood, paused for a moment, and said, "By Jove, but you are a good looking young devil. Come over here and let me get a closer look at you."

"Yes sir," said Charlie, marching to the bed and standing by the side of it.

"A good looking young devil indeed," Holland said softly, stretching out a hand to run it gently down over Charlie's rump and up the inside of his thigh. "Well equipped too, I shouldn't wonder. Care to let me have a peep?"

Charlie froze. Without knowing what was expected of him, he replied cautiously, "A peep at what, sir?"

"Come on, old lad. You can't be as innocent as all that. Unburden your flies and let me see if you're a real man."

When he was his father's apprentice, Charlie had enough experience with the local girls to know all he thought there was to know about sex, but he had never before met a man who took that sort of interest in him. Beside which, Holland's hand was at his crotch and the insistent finger stroking had given him an erection that made it almost impossible to stand without wriggling.

"Yes sir, Mr Holland sir," he said, undoing his fly buttons and exposing his throbbing penis. "I'm a man right enough."

"So it would appear," said Holland, throwing back the sheet that covered his own nakedness. "Turn the key in the lock, my dear. And then come here and prove it to me."

Charlie very soon became accustomed to adding homosexual practices to his other duties, even to enjoy them. Holland was easily satisfied with a kiss or two and a hand teasing whenever he turned his plump arse to Charlie for a probing. Charlie's other duties were more arduous but he kept his officer well turned out on parade and happy in bed. Often too, he amused Holland by mimicking his posh accent. Phrases such as 'That's the ticket', 'Well done, old boy', and 'Oh I say, you are an absolute chump' began to fall from his lips as readily as they did from the officer's. And at night, his talent for mimicry added much to the laughter of his barrack-room mates.

Another practice of Holland's was to send him out on errands and it was then Charlie made the discovery that was to change his life. At first, he was aggrieved to think he was not given money to pay for the goods he purchased in Holland's name. He felt pretty certain that if he had been, he might have done himself a bit of good by haggling over the price and pocketing a few shillings for himself. Holland would have lost nothing by it and Christ knew, a soldier's pay was anything but generous. In any case, Charlie couldn't understand the officer's apparent lack of trust. Holland must know his batman was no thief since he often left money in his pockets and about his room. Money which had always been collected and returned to him.

One afternoon, after returning with three shirts from a tailor in Jermyn Street, he stripped and got into bed with a waiting Holland. Putting an arm round the man's fleshy shoulders, Charlie stroked his side whiskered cheek and said tentatively, "You know, I wouldn't have let that shopkeeper cheat you if you'd given me the money for the shirts. There's no need for you to go traipsing round after me to settle the accounts for yourself."

"Settle the accounts for myself?" repeated Holland, raising himself up on one elbow to look down at Charlie. "Why, you silly old chump, I don't settle accounts, I buy on credit. When you show my card to one of the shopkeepers who recognises my name, he knows I am the young Lieutenant Holland who will come into his fortune when the pater pegs out, bless him. Most of the rogues are quite content to wait until then. Those who aren't and choose to make a nuisance of themselves, get about a quarter of what's owing from my father and dropped like a hot cake. Does that satisfy you?"

Charlie closed his eyes and nodded, his sudden realisation of the power held by the small piece of pasteboard almost too much for him. All he had done was take the embossed card from his pocket and put it on a shop counter. After which he walked away with cigars, bottles of brandy, and clothing from shopkeepers who did not expect to get paid for years! He had even been bowed to on the strength of the card and asked to come back soon. Come back soon? God, but this wanted thinking about. Meanwhile, in answer to a murmured request from Holland, he kissed him full on the lips and trailed a hand down the man's now trembling body until it found and began to caress the erect penis.

"God, oh my dear God," shuddered Holland, heaving his buttocks upwards in a jerking ecstasy while Charlie bit deep into his neck, rubbed harder, and thought about a return visit to Jermyn Street.

'To this day, I don't know why I did it,' Charlie was thinking while he sat fidgeting in the dock next to Sarah and tried without much success, to listen to Mrs Tombrin's high whine of a voice giving the evidence intended to brand him and Sarah a pair of vicious unfeeling murderers.

Curiosity about the card had taken him back to the pebble-glass windowed tailor's shop in Jermyn Street, where he procured another quarter dozen shirts. Curiosity about their value took him from there to a Whitechapel pawnbroker, where he made the mistake of trying to raise money on the shirts without first removing the labels or even taking them from their wrappings and trying to make them look used.

"Oh yes, and what's your little game, soldier boy?" the pawnbroker said belligerently, after a cursory glance at the neatly wrapped and obviously expensive shirts. "Has that constable on the doorstep sent you in here to catch out a poor old working man?"

Charlie looked through the grubby window and saw the policeman in the street outside. Scenting danger, he turned back to the pawnbroker and using Holland's posh voice, said quietly, "Don't be such a silly chump, old boy. I happen to be a little short of the ready at the moment. They're my own shirts and I'll redeem them when my allowance comes at the end of the month."

The pawnbroker narrowed his eyes and pushed the shirts back across the counter. "Silly chump am I? Well, I'll tell you what you are, bringing these round here. You're a common thief and I shouldn't wonder if you didn't nick the uniform you're wearing too. Pick 'em up and take them out of here before I call the constable myself and give you in charge."

"Oh come on," pleaded Charlie. "Help a fellow out of a hole, will you? A couple of sovereigns will do. They're worth four times that."

"Two sov, eh?" The man screwed up his eyes to consider the shirts, and looked up at Charlie with more interest. "What have you been and done then, deserted your regiment?"

Wanting only to get out of the filthy little shop without getting caught with the shirts, Charlie was ready to agree to anything. "That's right," he said eagerly. "I'm a deserter. I'm desperate for money. I've got to get out of London somehow."

"If that's how things are, my lad, that uniform's not going to be any good to you, is it? You'll get picked up at the first railway station you try to buy a ticket at."

The pawnbroker shook his head and sighed deeply, as though pondering Charlie's problem. Then, clearly having made up his mind to be all the assistance he could without losing too much of his hard earned money over the business, he slapped the top of the rickety counter with a hand and said, "All right, soldier boy, I'll tell you what I'm going to do for you. Out of the goodness of my heart, I'm going to let you go into my shed in the backyard and take off that uniform. Then I'll give you one of my very best suits of clothes and two half crowns to set you on your way. And that's the best chance I can give you."

Fifteen minutes later, dressed in a frock coat that was more green than black, a verminous shirt, broken boots, and trousers as short in the leg as they were loose round the waist, Charlie left the pawnbroker's shop with the five shillings he had deserted the army for and no idea where to go next. It was dark, he hadn't eaten for hours, and the lighted windows of a public house invited him in. Promising himself he would soon be going back to that filthy swine of a pawnbroker and end the nightmare by getting his uniform back and a fair price for the shirts, he walked into the smoky, ill-lit bar for a glass of rum and water to give him courage, swallowed it in a gulp, and was having a second when a woman came across the sanded floor to sit on a stool beside him.

"Here, you don't want to sit there drinking that stuff on your own, my darling. Don't you know it's bad for the stomach? Get a lady a nice drop of gin and I'll have a drink with you." The prostitute's painted face swam before Charlie through the gloom, looking very like the poxy Jezebels he'd been warned against in the public houses near Knightsbridge. Charlie peered blearily at the woman and made a gesture of dismissal. "No money," he croaked. "Nowhere to go. Don't know what to do."

"Get along with you, sweetheart. A well set up young fellow like you? I bet you know what to do with a lady all right. And I bet you'll find a sov or two in your pocket if you dig for it. Come on down to my place. It's only round the corner and I'll give you a lot better time than you're having here. I'm a good clean girl and you're the first one today. Here, just for starters, cop a feel of this."

She took his limp hand and held it beneath her coat and against her bared, flabby breast. "There darling, that's a nice one, ain't it? You'd like to have a little bit more of that, wouldn't you?" In desperation, Charlie heaved himself to his feet and tried to get away by moving to the door, but she had a firm hold of his sleeve and moved with him.

"That's right, my little darling," she said encouragingly as they almost fell through the door together. "That's the way. It's just through here." Feeling dizzy in the cool night air, wanting to be left alone but unable to free his arm of her clutching hand, he stumbled after her into the nearby alley where her bully's cudgel struck his head and, as he rolled face down and bleeding, his last few shillings were stolen along with his coat and boots and he was left for dead.

"Well now, there's an egg if you like. That'll take a good sized plaster to hold it down, that will." A light was shone in Charlie's eyes and he sat up with a groan, only to lean forward again and spew between his legs, into the gutter.

"Can you stand?" asked the constable, bringing his lamp closer to Charlie's head. Before there was an answer, the officer's amused tone sharpened.

"That's a soldier's haircut," he said, "or I'm a Dutchman. You a deserter, are you? What's your regiment?"

"Life Guards, sir," Charlie confessed miserably.

"Then you'd best come along with me to the police station. We'll get you patched up and send you back where you belong. Always supposing they'll have you back, which I don't think."

The Regiment of the Life Guards would not have him back. Despite Lieutenant Holland's recommendation to the commanding officer, Trooper Bennet had lost the Queen's uniform in disgraceful circumstances and deserted his post to visit a prostitute. Crimes that were more than enough to justify the dishonourable discharge he so richly deserved. Washed and shaved but wearing only the ragged shirt and trousers the thieves had left him with, he was marched barefoot from the guardroom to the orderly office, where he stood to attention between two of the grim faced soldiers who had once been his friends. The Commanding Officer looked at him with contempt, glanced at the papers on his desk, and said sharply, "If you had deserted your post in the field, you would have been shot out of hand and a damned good riddance to you. As it is, you're very lucky not to have earned yourself a damn good flogging. If it wasn't for the good offices of Lieutenant Holland, who spoke to me on your behalf, you might well have done. Now get your filthy carcase out of my sight and never let me catch you skulking round my barracks again."

Charlie Bennet and Lieutenant Holland were near enough of a size. Partly because Charlie had kept his promise never to mention the personal side of their relationship but mostly because of his genuine affection for his young lover, Holland presented him with a suit of clothes, boots, and a coat and hat.

"I'll miss you, my dear," the officer said with tears in his eyes, "and I wish there was something more I could do about all this. Here's a fiver and keep my card by you. When the pater does decide to pop off and let me come into my inheritance, I dare say I'll hand in my papers and resign my commission. I'll need a man like you then." He touched Charlie's cheek with a forefinger and hesitated a moment, before turning smartly about and marching off. When he was out of sight, Charlie, who was as near to weeping as the officer had been, almost threw away the card that had got him into so much trouble but some instinct made him tuck it into his cuff.

Charlie was allowed by the orderly officer to change in the guardroom, though no one would speak to him. After a day that felt as though it had gone on forever, he was surprised to see it was still only early afternoon when he quit the barracks. Outside the gates, chatting to each other beneath the trees, was the usual group of nursemaids looking to hire a guardsman in uniform for an afternoon escort duty in the park, a pleasant enough duty that could pay a cavalryman as much as half a crown. Charlie crossed the street to speak to one he had walked with in the weeks before he became Holland's batman, told her he'd been unfairly discharged from the regiment, and asked how he could set about finding some clean lodgings and a situation.

"Somewhere to lodge in is easy enough," the short, snub-nosed girl said, looking up at him. "There's plenty of landladies round about Baker Street who will be only too willing to take in a single gentleman. As to a situation, I wouldn't know what to say about that one, but I'll ask my missus for you. Her husband used to be in business. Why don't you go and find a place to live first? You can meet me in the park tomorrow afternoon."

The first room offered to Charlie was small, dark and depressing, but it suited his mood and he was in no frame of mind to carry on the search. He paid the asked for two weeks rent in advance and after his ancient landlady put the money in her apron pocket and retired, he sat on the unmade bed and dropped his head in his hands. It was hard to believe he could have made such a muck of his life. Maybe the army hadn't offered much of a career but whatever it was or might have been, he'd thrown it away along with Holland and his barrack-room mates. Now there was no one he knew to talk to but that dumpy little nursemaid. Nothing to look forward to but the vague chance of a job. And he was going to need her help to get that! He drew a deep, shuddering breath and stood up, his head brushing against the low, badly plastered ceiling. Feeling lonelier than he ever remembered and having no one else in the world to talk to, he said to his reflection in the dusty, fly-blown mirror over the washstand. "Well, Mr Bennet? What are you going to do next? I know what. Let's go out and get a spot of dinner, eh old chap?"

The chop he was served was more than a touch greasy after army cooking, but he was hungry and the pint of ale that came with it washed it down well enough. Considerably cheered by the hot food and finding himself standing at the entrance to Madame Tussauds, he paid his eighteen pence to tour the exhibition, looked at the severed, blood-streaked heads of Marie Antoinette and Louis XVI below the replica of the guillotine and shivered. He hated the sight of blood, something he'd once admitted to Lieutenant Holland wasn't going to make him much of a soldier if he ever got into a battle. Holland had laughed at him and said, "The only thing you need to know about blood on a battlefield, Charlie my old cock, is if you're standing on your two feet and looking at it, it must be someone else's."

Charlie had laughed with him but the sight of the decapitated heads in the overturned basket brought the taste of the chop up in his throat and made him feel distinctly queasy. He went on to cast a cursory glance at Burke and Hare the body snatchers, and walk with the other viewers past the displays of splendour on one side and villainy on the other. Then, feeling more discomforted than entertained by what he had seen, he left and found it had come on to rain. The street-lamps had not yet been lit and the crush of passing carts and carriages pressed him against other wet pedestrians who trod on his feet and pushed him out of their path with muttered apologies. Thoroughly depressed and snappy in turn, he pushed back and in the gathering dusk, walked back to his room where he spent an almost sleepless night.

The next day being fine, he arrived at the park early and sat on the grass while he waited for Molly, scrambling to his feet when he saw her walking past the duck filled lake in his direction.

"You can come back home with me now," she told him. "The first time of asking, my missus said she couldn't recommend situations for people she don't know but when I told her how good looking and respectable you was, she said if she finds you as well set up as I say you are, she'll see what can be done for you."

Mrs Harries handed the child she was nursing in her lap to Molly and, while the girl took it to a chair in the corner, looked up at Charlie with some interest.

"Molly is quite right about your appearance," she said at last. "You certainly look well enough but the situation I am thinking of calls for a thoroughly trustworthy man. I need to know why were you discharged from the army. I want to be told no lies, Mr Bennet, please."

Charlie, unable to do anything but lie, had his story prepared and rehearsed. A natural actor, he told how a jealous sergeant had impugned a fine young officer's reputation by spreading a tale about him that was as untrue as it was scurrilous and impossible to be spoken of before a lady. He said that on hearing the wicked lies that were being spread about and laughed over in the barrack-rooms, he had been outraged and felt he must speak up in the officer's defence. The sergeant he accused to his face of lying, raised his swagger stick and struck him on the head for his impertinence and for the first time in his life, Charlie lost his temper and struck a blow in return, knocking the sergeant down to the ground.

An enthralled Mrs Harries sat with her hands clasped to her breast and her eyes fixed on Charlie's sorrowing face while in a low voice, he told of his pain and disgrace when he found himself taken and thrown into the guardroom. Where he was made to spend the night on an ice cold stone floor before being taken before his commanding officer. The colonel discharged Charlie for indiscipline and told him he'd been lucky to escape without a flogging. If it wasn't for the young officer whose reputation he defended coming to plead for him, he might well have been flogged till his back was raw. As it was, every man in the barracks knew that discharging him was unfair, but he had struck a non-commissioned officer and no one in the regiment could save him from dismissal. As for himself, all he could do was take the punishment like a man and quit the barracks without further protest.

Having more than half convinced himself he was telling the truth had given Charlie's voice a throb of sincerity that made Mrs Harries eyes fill with tears.

"Oh you poor dear man," she said after he finished. "What you have suffered. We must certainly see what can be done for you."

"Thank you very much, ma'am," he replied. "I'm only sorry that the cruel manner of my discharge has left me without a character."

"Your character is in your eyes, Mr Bennet. I too have suffered pain in my time and I know you to be a truthful man. I have an afternoon appointment but if you can come back at ten o'clock tomorrow morning, I will give you a letter to take to the manager of a shop I am well acquainted with. He is looking for a suitable man of good appearance who will greet customers at his shop door and direct them to the appropriate counters. I can think of no one better suited for the position."

Charlie thanked her again for her goodness and turned to the door, realising with a sort of wonder that she had believed every word he'd said.

'I hooked her, by God,' he was thinking exultantly while he was taking his coat and hat from the tall, oval mirrored, hall stand. 'The way she was swallowing it, I could have told her anything I liked.' His euphoria was interrupted by Molly opening the sitting-room door after him.

"Missus wants you to come back for a minute," she said abruptly enough to shatter his illusions, but when he faced her again, Mrs Harries smiled at him and said that Molly had asked if he was free to escort her and Master Jonathan while they walked in the park for an hour.

"Free and willing, ma'am," he said, politely opening

the door for Molly and the child in her arms. "And only too happy to be of service."

"I want to thank you very much for what you've done for me," he said to the girl while they walked towards the park gates. "You told me where to find my lodgings and now it seems you helped me to get a situation. I found myself a good friend in you, Molly."

"I don't know that you have," Molly said tartly. "Not after all them lies you told the missus. The state you were in when the police brought you back to the barracks and how you got thrown out of the regiment, was common knowledge all round the park yesterday afternoon. Soldiers telling the nursemaids and the nursemaids all cackling over the Guardsman who sold his uniform for a Whitechapel whore and only got a crack over his head for his trouble. I know it was you they were talking about, Charlie Bennet, so what did you have to tell all those lies for? I'm sorry I took you to see Mrs Harries now. I feel I ought to go straight back and tell her the truth about you."

Charlie, in near panic, forced himself to stay calm. "Molly," he said pleadingly, "you know what happened. I made a fool of myself and I was discharged with no character. I had to say something to explain being chucked out of the barracks. Believe me, I don't mean your missus any harm, she's a nice kind lady. If you only keep quiet and let me collect that letter tomorrow morning, she'll never see me again. And neither will you, which is a great pity."

"A pity is it?" she repeated, eyeing him suspiciously. "And what's that supposed to mean, Charlie Bennet?"

Looking deep into her eyes, he said quietly, "Molly, why do you suppose I came to you when I left the barracks? There were plenty of other nursemaids about, wasn't there? I came to you because your pretty face was wearing the first friendly smile I'd seen in two days. It lifted my heart and it reminded me of the last time we walked in the park together, you telling me about the village in Ireland you come from. Oh Mollie, I was dreaming all about you last night."

"Oh yes," she said, scornfully turning her head away. "I can just imagine the sort of dream you had about me. I know all about soldiers and their fancies."

He smiled and touched her hand. "I'd be a wicked liar if I denied it, Molly. You lay beside me in my dreams last night and I never fancied loving a girl more than I fancied loving you. Even now, when I know you can ruin me with one word to your missus, all I can think of is a kiss from those lovely red lips of yours."

Molly laughed and drew her hand away to punch him lightly on the chest. "You're a blooming natural, Charlie Bennet," she said admiringly. "If you was mine, I would never know if I'm to believe you or not."

"But you won't tell your missus, Molly?" he asked urgently. "You won't ruin me again?"

Molly shook her head. "No, the way things have turned out, I suppose you couldn't help telling all those wicked lies but I don't think there's any real harm in you. I won't tell on you. Not for now anyway."

"Come on then, my little sweetheart," a much relieved Charlie said, putting his hands on her shoulders. "Give us a kiss to seal the bargain. Just to prove I can trust you."

"Trust me? Well of all the blessed sauce. . . " Molly began when he pulled her close and dropped his hands to run as far down her back as he dared while he kissed her. After a minute or so, she pushed him away, her normally pale cheeks scarlet with embarrassment.

"Here, slow down a bit, soldier," she squealed breathlessly, "you're too hungry for it all. When was the last time you kissed a girl?"

"Good God almighty," said Charlie, thinking of Holland. "It's been so long, I swear I can't remember."

Chapter Three

"Certainly there can be nothing wrong in wishing to present oneself in the best possible manner," counsel for the prosecution told Mrs Tombrin and the jury, while the lady sat with her head bowed and a glass of water clasped tightly between her hands. "We all of us share a desire to look our best and that is the part of human vanity the pair in the dock's evil trade is meant to take full advantage of." He paused to fuss yet again with his gown, pulling it higher on his shoulders before stepping close to the witness and saying quietly, "Mrs Tombrin, if you are feeling well enough, we are now coming to a vital piece of evidence in the Crown's case. I'm quite certain his Lordship will allow you to give your evidence at your own pace if you feel you might be able to continue?"

The judge nodded briefly and Mrs Tombrin looked up and said haltingly, "On one occasion I called on Madame Sarah and she told me she had spoken to a gentleman who had fallen in love with me. When I asked his name, I was told the gentleman in question was Lord Charles Beniton. I said the name was not familiar to me and asked how he knew me. Madame Sarah told me that he knew both my husband and me for a time after our marriage but he had lost sight of me for some years. He had recently seen me leave Madame Sarah's premises in Beak Street and walk along Regent Street. Rather than attempt to speak to me in the street where I would surely not have listened to him, he spoke to Madame Sarah and asked for her help in renewing our acquaintance. She said she would introduce him to me the next day. She also told me he was a good man and he would make me a good husband. The next day I called on

Madame Sarah and she presented me to a gentleman I understood to be Lord Charles Beniton. I asked him if he was Lord Charles Beniton and he replied 'Yes madam, I am Charles Beniton. Here is my card'. He then handed me a card which I returned to him. Some small conversation took place between us and then Lord Beniton retired."

"And do you see the man you understood to be Lord Charles Beniton in court?"

"Yes sir. He is there, seated in the dock."

Shanklin ignored the stir among the patrons of the court.

"Are you quite certain that is the man, Mrs Tombrin?" he asked, pointing at Charlie. "I must remind you that his very life might hang on the evidence you give this day. There must be no room for doubt in your mind."

Mrs Tombrin nodded. "That is the gentleman I knew as Lord Charles Beniton. I have no more doubt of that than I have of knowing that in his heart, he is a good man and if he has done any wrong, it was that wicked woman who led him to it!" Mrs Tombrin raised her voice on the last few words and even Sarah had it in her to blanch when the witness's accusing finger was pointed at her heart.

'He didn't want leading so much as showing how to go about it,' she was thinking as she looked without flinching into Mrs Tombrin's vindictive eyes. Adding with a rare flash of insight. 'No more than I did once it all began happening.' As it had with the accidental death of Fanny Walsh. As it continued with the hot rush of joy that filled her heart when choosing a victim and watching her die in agony a few weeks later. As it ended with none of the victims being the hated Mrs Constantine, who cheated her by dying before she could be got to. Sarah Fowkes stopped listening to the hesitating rise and fall of Mrs Tombrin's voice, looked down at her hands, and sighed imperceptibly.

'Oh Marie,' she was thinking. 'My beautiful little Marie.'

When Aggie Fowkes was convinced that Sarah was pregnant, she insisted on her loudly protesting daughter trying all the best recommended street remedies. Beginning by making herself violently sick with a hickey pickey mixture of bitter apple, juice of aloe, and white lead and, when that didn't have the desired result in the day or two allowed, making the sadly weakened girl climb to the top of the mangle and drop like a sack of potatoes to the floor. Landing so heavily, she badly twisted her already weakened ankle. When Mrs Fowkes saw those two guaranteed remedies fail, she sighed heavily, rolled up her sleeves, and her discomforted daughter found herself trying to swallow a half pint of gin while firmly seated over an iron pot of boiling water. After which indignity, and leaning sideways on her stool in a vain effort to relieve the agony of her scalded rump, Sarah cried enough.

"I'll have no more of you trying to get rid of the thing!" she shrilled at her mother and any of Mendel's women who cared to come into the laundry to listen to her howling. "It's stuck where it is and that's where it stays till it comes down of its own choosing!"

Mrs Fowkes was forced to agree that there was no more she could do to aid nature. Piously deciding that the matter was now in the hands of the Lord God Almighty who loved fallen women, she shook her head sadly, sat on a bundle of washing with her fat legs spread wide for balance, and finished the gin herself.

With Sarah's twisted ankle so swollen after her fall she could not put any weight on it, all she could do for the next few weeks was make buttonholes for Mendel. Meantime, a loudly complaining Aggie stumped to Mile End to collect and deliver the washing she now had to do at night instead of visiting the King's Head. Despite bemoaning her fate whenever she left the laundry, she was usually good humoured enough with drink and tittle tattle by the time she rolled homewards. Most particularly, she enjoyed the pleasure of drinking the health of Ella Mason with the Mason's cook. She told Sarah the news of the young wife's pregnancy and the bad blood that had developed between Mr Mason and his mother-in-law, Mrs Constantine having practically moved into his house the moment she was told her beloved and precious daughter expected a happy event.

Cook told Mrs Fowkes of the continual rows over Mrs Ella's feeding, which Mrs Constantine wanted to come in the kitchen and supervise and cook refused to allow.

"I told Mr Mason very straight," said cook, after filling the teapot and producing two large cups. "I told him, Mr Mason sir, I've reared eight childer of me own and I don't need no supervision in my kitchen from no one. In any case, a little bit of a thing like Mrs Ella don't need a pair of mingy braised kidneys and a cup of beef tea, whatever Mrs Constantine says. What your Mrs Ella needs is a good beefy hodge podge what'll build her up for the trial she has to come."

"I should just think she does," replied Mrs Fowkes, topping up their teacups with a generous splash of gin from the bottle she kept beneath her apron. "That is exactly what a young mother needs to make her milk flow proper. And what happened to the argument then, my dear?"

"What do you think happened?" snorted the cook after a pull at her tea. "Mrs Constantine brought herself to my kitchen door and told me that Mrs Ella is definitely going to be ill and her babe will like as not be sickly as well and when it all happens it will be my fault. She said I was a disagreeable and disobedient old woman and if Mr Mason had any sense at all, he would dismiss me on the spot. Then I told her a thing or two about her interference in my duties and what with that old harridan pulling on one side of the kitchen door and me pulling just as hard on the other, Mr Mason said oh my good God, left his good dinner of rump steak and stewed kidneys and run off to the Black Swan. Then later he comes back so incapable drunk, I has to help him upstairs, undress him, and put him to bed while Mrs Ella hid herself away in the other bedroom."

Mrs Fowkes cackled and, adding another splash of gin to the cups, said, "And I bet he tried to pull you into the bed with him. I know what men are like when they've had a few glasses to raise their hopes. Go on, tell us what happened after you got in bed with him."

Cook made a dismal failure of looking offended before she laughed in turn and smoothed down her apron. "Nothing happened after I got Mr Mason into his bed, Mrs Fowkes, and don't you go thinking it could have. I didn't get into bed with him because nothing that one could do in a bed would interest me. I've had enough of men and their efforts in bed to last me a lifetime and more."

"Me and all," said Aggie, shaking her head sadly, and after pouring yet another libation. "Oh yes, my dear. Me and all." They drank their gin and gossiped on. Of poor Sarah's misfortune and how terrified she had become of men. Of what was to become of her poor fatherless babe. Of Mrs Ella and the wee blessing of God she was to bring into the world.

Sarah's ankle improved after a fortnight's rest. Now the object of sympathy from Mendel's sewing women, she went back to the delivery and collection for washing for as long as she could, carrying her bundles to Mile End and Bow and back until well into her seventh month. Some six weeks after Aggie took over again and on the day before her sixteenth birthday, the agonised girl twisted and turned on Mendel's rickety bed, pain ripping through her as both hands clenched into white knuckled, distorted fists, gripping tight to the knotted towel above her head. The elderly midwife, ignoring the girl's heart rending shrieks, shook a quantity of snuff on to the back of her bony hand and sniffed greedily, first up one capacious nostril and then the other. After which, she rocked her head from side to side and directed a vast sneeze in Sarah's direction, startling the girl into writhing even more frantically while she screamed again.

"That was a good'n," the midwife cackled approvingly. "That was God looking down on you and telling you to work harder at it, my dear."

After a pain-racked delivery, and when the baby girl had been slapped into a scarlet screaming fury, cursorily washed, and placed in the mother's arms, Sarah looked at her daughter's face and asked weakly, "What's her name?" On being told by an overcome, half drunk, and wildly sobbing Mrs Fowkes that the name was hers to choose, Sarah's eyes widened and she held her daughter's small damp head against her cheek. A moment before she fell into an exhausted sleep, she murmured. "Marie. She's my own Marie."

The following morning, in very different surroundings but with an equivalent degree of discomfort, Ella Mason was delivered of a healthy baby boy. Unhappily and almost immediately, she fulfilled the gloomiest of her mother's predictions by becoming desperately ill, though the illness had nothing to do with her diet. Looking down at her flushed, sweat-beaded face, gritted teeth, and shaking limbs, her doctor knew from long experience that even if she were to be fortunate enough to recover from the fever that gripped her, she would never be able to breast feed her baby boy. While he busied himself equalising Ella's circulation by applying leeches to her arms and cold vinegar and water to her forehead, the Constantine's housekeeper was sent in the doctor's carriage to fetch a wet-nurse.

A short time later, Sarah Fowkes, washed and agreeably full of mutton broth, was tucked up in the Mason's spare bedroom, sleepily giving suck to two contented babies. Frank Mason, arriving home to find himself barred from the sickroom by his mother-in-law, poured himself a brandy and carried it up to the bedroom to wet his son's head. Caught unawares by the opening door, a half asleep Sarah started uncontrollably and almost dropped the babies when she saw the man in the doorway, a glass of brandy in his hand, his eyes fastened on her full, naked breasts.

The girl froze in horror of what she thought was about to happen next. She had never seen the side whiskered, pointy-chinned man before and had no idea who he was, but she had no doubt of his intentions. He was going to do the same as the man did who forced his way into the laundry. He was going to take no notice of her condition, snatch the babies out of her arms, and beat her into submitting to him. The thought of being raped again, less than forty-eight hours after giving birth, was so horrific she cringed back against the pillows and closed her eyes. Feeling tears start running down her cheeks, she knew he would have no more mercy than the other one had and this time she would die of it. With not a hope in the world for herself, she licked her suddenly dry lips and was preparing to promise anything if he'd leave her be now for the sake of the two babes.

She was about to stammer something, when she heard him say in a strained voice. "Excuse me. You must be Sarah Fowkes. I'm sorry to have walked in on you without knocking at the door. My mother-in-law, Mrs Constantine, told me my son was in here but I hadn't thought you might be nursing him. I'll come back when you are finished."

Hearing the door close, she opened her eyes to find him gone and, as her fit of trembling passed, she once more gathered the loudly protesting babies to her breasts. She was holding his son, he'd said, so he was Mr Mason and he had let her off this time. She didn't know why, she supposed it must be for his baby boy's sake, but she'd seen the way he looked at her titties and knew bleeding well it wasn't for hers. With a strong sense of impending doom, she put the babies down in the cradle beside the bed and fastened the flannel nightgown cook had given her, as high as she could tie it under her chin.

About fifteen minutes later, she heard a light tap on the door and a voice she now recognised said, "Sarah, this is Mr Mason. Are you finished with nursing the babies? May I come in?"

She pulled her mother's shawl round her shoulders and, keeping herself upright against her pillows, replied with a hesitant, "Yes sir."

"Thank you." Again, he had a glass of brandy in his hand and he was, if anything, drunker than when he first stood in the doorway looking at her, but his legs were steady when he walked over to look into the cradle and say, "Good heavens, Sarah, what a pair of little monkeys they are. Which one is which?"

"This one is yours, sir."

"Ah, is he now. Do you know, Sarah, I think I prefer the look of yours. A girl isn't it?"

Realising, despite her terror of him, that he was trying to put her at her ease, Sarah managed a wan smile. "Yes sir. But your son is a beautiful baby too."

"My son? Yes, I suppose he is mine. I must say being a father takes some getting used to."

He looked up from the cradle to meet her eyes. "Sarah, I think I must have given you something of a shock when I came in earlier. It was thoughtless of me not to knock. I'm sorry."

Sarah, not knowing what to make of him or his unexpected apology, did not give a direct answer. Instead, she lowered her head and mumbled, "I am a good girl, sir. I didn't ought to be looked at like that by a gentleman."

Frank reddened and did his best to manage a reassuring smile. "I'm quite sure you are a good girl, my dear," he said quietly. "Forgive me for staring at you earlier. I couldn't help but watch you nursing. With the babies in your arms, you made a delightful sight, but I promise I meant no harm by it."

He put out a hand to pat her shoulder and seeing her shrink away from him, protested, "But my dear girl, I may be a little drunk but I'm not going to touch you. Not if you don't want me to." He paused to swallow more brandy and almost under his breath, added, "The plain truth is, Sarah, I'm already more than a little envious of my son. His lips have kissed your breast. I would gladly give a guinea if mine could do the same."

"Sir!" Sarah gasped. He smiled, tipped his glass at her, and lurched towards the door.

"A guinea each to kiss the pair," he said as he went out of the room.

'Gawd love us,' thought Sarah, watching the door close behind him. 'What's his blessed game?' First he pulled away from putting his hand on her and then he offered her all that money to kiss her titties! He must think she was one of them women who hang round the docks, trying to wheedle a half crown or two from a piddled up sailor. And willing to let the dirty pig take what liberties he liked for it. Suddenly, her fear of Frank Mason turned to self-pity and she began to weep copiously. He must have reckoned she got her baby that way and that gave him the right to talk to her like she was a common whore. It was too much on top of everything else she had to put up with and the next time he came into the bedroom to insult her that way, she was going to say if he didn't keep off her, she was going to tell Mrs Constantine all about him and what he wanted to do.

But when Mr Mason did come back into the room after cook had brought up her supper, he was so maudlin she thought he must be as stewed as her mother got on Saturday nights. In point of fact, he was not very drunk. He had been drinking more than usual, but what was happening to Ella downstairs had shocked him into near sobriety.

"Sarah, I'm sorry to trouble you again," he told her, "but I'm not myself at all. The doctor has told me my wife is very ill. My mother-in-law and the doctor's nurse are battling over who should care for her and they both turn on the cook every time she puts her face near the sickroom. I tell you, my dear Sarah, my house is fast becoming a bear garden and this is the only room I can escape to where I do not feel like an animal at bay. At least, I hope I can?"

It was a question and Sarah's tone was resentful when she replied, "You said you want to give me money to kiss my titties. I was brought here to look after your baby, Mr Mason sir. I done nothing to make you think I would do those sort of favours."

"I know you did not and I am sorry I said what I did. You look so rosy and beautiful sitting in the bed I was carried away. The brandy spoke for me."

Only part mollified but sensing he wouldn't try to do anything to her, at least while she was feeding his son, she said, "Them two babies are going to wake up in a few minutes and then I'll have to give them another feed. I don't want any company when I'm feeding babies. It's private."

"Of course it is."

Despite his words, the memory of his eyes on her breasts was still fresh and she expected him to say he wanted to stay and watch her, but he got to his feet obediently enough and walked to the door. Pausing as he opened it, he said, "I am a very lonely man at the moment, Sarah. I hope you won't object to my spending a little time with you in the evenings."

He was gone before she could answer, even if she had known what she was supposed to say to him. He was a man, wasn't he? How was she to stop him going where he liked in his own home? Or doing what he liked with the people in it? Men liked touching young girls. Mr Constantine had stroked her arm every time he met her. Even old Mendel, who must be near enough to seventy years old, had his dirty hand up her skirts whenever she got too close, and looked away as though his fingers were straying between her plump cheeks by accident. This Mr Mason didn't look as hard natured as the swine who threw her down on the floor in the laundry but she knew he was after the same thing. When he got up the nerve a drop or two of rum would give him, he'd be back for it. She was so convinced of his intentions that the next time the door opened she braced herself to scream for help, but it was only Mrs Constantine, come to fuss over her grandson and to warn Sarah against giving her own child the lion's share of her milk.

"You are being cared for and well paid for your services," Mrs Constantine said acidly. "And I won't be cheated. If my grandson falls short of your child in size or any other particular, you may be sure I will know the reason for it."

"But he was littler than her to start with," protested Sarah, "and he falls asleep when he sucks. You ask Mr Mason. He saw him."

"Mr Mason saw him at the breast?" Mrs Constantine thundered. "How dare you allow a gentleman to watch you nurse a baby? Have you no shame, girl?"

"I couldn't help it, ma'am," Sarah snivelled. "Mr Mason walked straight in to the room and looked at me while they was both feeding."

"Did he, indeed. I will see about that. Meantime, you see to it that my grandson receives sufficient nourishment or it will be the worse for you."

Sarah had eaten and was dozing when cook came to take the supper tray. It was only having the tray in her hands that stopped Cook rubbing them together in glee.

"You started something my girl, my word you did," she told a wide-eyed Sarah. "What with that Mrs Constantine coming downstairs and leading off at Mr Mason about what filthy pigs men are and the way we poor women is taken advantage of and how dare he stick his lecherous whiskers through this door while you had his very own son at your breast? It was enough to curdle your milk! Then she starts on about what he must have done to poor Mrs Ella to bring on such a terrible fever, his poor wife has to be leeched for it. And then he got his rag out and banged his fist on the dining-room table and started to shout back at her that he would bar her from the house if she didn't stop upsetting everybody and that she was more likely responsible than him for Mrs Ella's illness with her fads about what she should eat and what she shouldn't eat while she was expecting his son.

And Mrs Constantine tells him she had warned Mrs Ella on the night before her wedding about the unpleasant duty her husband would expect of her and he shouts back that it's a husband's duty to instruct his wife in these matters and Mrs Ella had been so afraid of him on their wedding night, she jumped out of the bed the minute he got in it and swore she needed to pee in the chamber pot, only she couldn't use it with him in the room so he had to wait outside."

At that, the cook dropped the tray on the foot of Sarah's bed and let out such a whoop of laughter, both babies jumped and began to cry. Sarah picked them up and held them close against her breast, as much for her own protection as theirs.

"I wasn't trying to make no trouble," she whispered, the tremble in her voice revealing her fear. "It just came out when she said I was giving my own baby better feeding than her grandson. They ain't going to chuck me out of here, are they?"

The cook chuckled and picked up the tray. "You've got nothing to worry about there, my girl. You've got milk in plenty for both them babbies and the doctor says you're healthy enough to feed 'em till Kingdom come. They ain't going to bother searching out another wet-nurse for their little boy now. Anyway, if Mr Mason has taken a fancy to you, it's all to the good. He told the old lady that he means to come up here and see his son whenever he wants to and she can keep her nasty suspicious thinkings to herself."

About half an hour after cook had left her, Sarah was sitting on the side of the bed and cooing at the babies while she changed their clothes. She had all but finished when there came a hesitant tap at the door and a red-eyed Frank Mason walked into the room clutching a large damp handkerchief in his hand.

"God Almighty sir," said the startled girl. "Whatever is it? Surely Mrs Ella hasn't gone and copped it?"

"No Sarah, it's nothing like that," he answered wearily as he sat beside her on the bed and put out a finger to stroke his baby son's cheek. "The doctor tells me there is some slight improvement in Mrs Mason. He says it will be a matter of time and careful nursing."

"Then whatever is it?"

Frank sighed heavily, tucked the handkerchief into his top pocket, and before she knew he meant to do it, took Sarah's hand in his own.

"It's Mrs Constantine," he confessed, looking down at the girl's captured fingers. He went on to tell her how his mother-in-law continually insulted and harassed him, how little defence he could put up, since his father-in-law, who he respected and admired, was his employer and that made Mrs Constantine think of herself as his employer too. The strain of coming home from the office evening after evening to find that woman in charge of his house and preventing him from visiting his wife, was driving him insane. The situation had become impossible and only she, Sarah, and the babies made him realise it could be bearable again. To the girl's astonishment he fell to his knees beside her, tears streaming down his face. "Be kind to me, Sarah," he begged, "Please help me."

"No I won't," said Sarah, pulling her hand away. "You want to do what that other one did to me. I've only just had a baby. It'd tear me guts out."

"I don't want to hurt you. I swear it. I just want to lay my head on your sweet breast and have you put your arms round me."

Sixteen-year-old Sarah Fowkes looked down at Frank Mason's bowed head and wondered what she was supposed to do with him. He was a big man. He could break her in half if he chose but it seemed he wouldn't lay a finger on her if she didn't want him to. She knew what he wanted to do to her, she wasn't stupid, but it wasn't going to be a rut on a pile of sheets like the dirty pig who came in the laundry did. It wasn't even the same as old Mendel's twitchy fingers up her skirts. Even so, he was on his knees and waiting for her to do something. Remembering what cook had told her about him, she said softly. "Oh come on then, Mr Mason, you're not much more than a baby yourself. You can put your head on me if you must." Trembling with the sudden knowledge of the power she had over him, she opened the front of her nightgown, put her arms round him and laid his head against her breast.

"Oh Sarah," he shuddered after his lips had touched each of her nipples. "You wonderful girl."

"That's enough now," she whispered gently, feeling his hands slide down to her thighs. "I ain't fit for nothing like that, honest I ain't. Else I expect I wouldn't mind. Not with a real gentleman like you."

"Wouldn't you mind, Sarah?" he asked eagerly.

"I expect I mightn't," she said demurely, hearing his quickened urgency. "When I'm properly myself again. You'd better leave off and go now, Mr Mason. Mrs Constantine said she's coming up here to have another look at her grandson before she goes home tonight."

Frank Mason looked back at her from the doorway and kissed his hand in farewell. Sarah thought he must have gone barmy but she fully expected him to have his way with her one day and if she had to let him do it, she might as well have some of them sovereigns he was talking about. Maybe she could have one of Mrs Ella's old dresses, too. It wasn't as though Sarah had anything of her own to put on her back. She had been brought into the house wearing one of cook's patched nightgowns and her mother's old woollen shawl and all she had since was a change of the nightgown.

'The next time he comes in here,' she prophesied while she composed herself for sleep and let her thumb find its way into her mouth, 'I'll ask him for one of Mrs Ella's dresses. And a pair of corsets. I always wanted a pair of corsets.' The babies let her sleep till very near midnight. Feeding them with her eyes more than half closed, she thought she heard a footstep in the passage, but when she put the children down, the sound had stopped and she drifted off to sleep without knowing that Frank Mason sat on the floor outside, a brandy bottle in his hand and with his back against her door.

It was three days later, when cook said it was high time she put up a couch for Sarah and the babies in the sitting-room and saved herself the blessed trouble of climbing up and down the blessed stairs all blessed day long, that Sarah summoned up the courage to ask Frank for a dress. As had become his habit in the late evenings, he was sitting beside her on the bed, alternately rubbing his cheek against her bare shoulder and kissing her neck, his hand cupping her naked breast, when she covered his hand with her own.

"Frank," she said hesitantly, "cook wants me to sit downstairs with the babies during the day but I've got nothing to wear outside the bedroom. Do you think Mrs Ella might give me one of her dresses? It can be as old as she likes. I only want to look respectable."

"Of course you can have a dress to wear in the sitting-room," Frank said. "Ella's dresses are in the master bedroom next to this one. When you are ready to come down, go in there and choose any one you like."

The dress Sarah chose was a deep red velvet with a low cut bodice and satin bows, but she had more sense than to go downstairs wearing it. Instead, she put on a simple yellow and green striped day dress that was obviously well worn and rubbed about the seams and elbows. Casting a last envious eye on the red velvet gown that Ella had never dared wear, she closed the wardrobe and went downstairs to present herself and the babies to Mrs Constantine.

"Mr Mason told me I can wear one of Mrs Mason's oldest dresses, ma'am," she piped respectfully. "Mr Mason says he wouldn't want to see me sitting downstairs in one of cook's old nightgowns and a shawl. I hope this dress is all right for me to wear, madam?"

Mrs Constantine narrowed her eyes and as Sarah expected, considered ordering her to take her daughter's dress off at once, but because the old lady did not relish the thought of Sarah sitting about the house in a patched nightgown any more than her son-in-law seemed to, and because Ella's dress was not merely well worn, it was outgrown, she inclined her head stiffly and said it would do but it was a very expensive gown and must be kept from getting soiled.

"Rotten old sow," Sarah sniffed as Mrs Constantine walked past her and into the darkened sick room. "You ought to see me in the red velvet. That'd make you sit up and look twice." The thought of wearing the red velvet gown and swanning about Frank Mason's house like a lady, made her smile secretly to herself. One day she would put it on and look at herself in the full length oval mirror standing by Mrs Ella's wardrobe, she would have to.

The day, or rather the evening, came sooner than Sarah expected. The babies were asleep and the doctor had come to shake his head yet again over Mrs Ella, which would keep Mrs Constantine busy questioning him for an hour. Leaving the sleeping babies, she ran upstairs to have another look at the dress and this time, holding it against herself wasn't enough. Quickly, she let the despised day dress drop to the floor and put on the velvet gown, fastening as many of the small black hooks as she could reach.

Gazing at herself in the mirror, she saw the perfection of a young and beautiful woman. Her dark eyes glowing, she forgot everyone else in the house and was dreamily brushing her long black hair with one of Ella's silver backed brushes when she heard a horrified gasp and raised her eyes to see the reflection of Mrs Constantine standing behind her. Dropping the hair-brush, she turned sharply, received the full force of Mrs Constantine's slap on her face, and fell back on the bed, the dress fastenings bursting open to expose her naked breasts. Once more she saw Mrs Constantine raise her hand and shrank back as the old woman spluttered. "Y-you wicked creature. How dare you come in here like a sneak thief and steal my poor daughter's clothes?"

On the bed, Sarah hunched her shoulders and crouched low, covering her face with her hands, but the expected second blow did not fall. Instead, Mrs Constantine was pulled sharply away and Frank Mason was shouting, "Leave the girl alone, you old hag! I won't have her hurt. I told her she could wear any damned dress she wants to."

In the shocked silence that followed, Sarah whimpered, "Don't let her hit me again, Frank. I didn't mean no harm by it."

"So it's Frank, is it?" Mrs Constantine hissed. Her back was pressed against the wardrobe and she looked from one to the other of them with her small glittering eyes. "Well sir, you are dismissed from my husband's service and you may get out of this house and take your cheap whore with you."

Sarah watched goggle-eyed as Frank Mason, chalk-faced and breathing as hard as his mother-in-law, declared that he was employed by Mr Constantine and until that gentleman saw fit to dispense with his services, he was not dismissed and that Mrs Constantine had ruined his marriage and she was far more responsible for the consequences of that ruin than he was. And, since the house was his, she was the one who should get out at once and leave him to manage his own affairs.

"Leave my daughter with you and your whore?" Mrs Constantine shrilled. "I would fear for her safety."

"Then take her with you!" Frank Mason said hoarsely. "Let her lie in a darkened room till she dies in your house, for she's dying here and I can't bear to watch it happening any more!"

"May God forgive you," said Mrs Constantine as she left the room. "I know I never shall. I will make the necessary arrangements for my daughter and my grandson's removal to my home and you Miss, do not touch my grandson again. I will arrange for another wet-nurse immediately."

Sarah and Frank stood without speaking at the bedroom window and watched the wickerwork invalid carriage, with Ella Mason wrapped in a blanket and strapped securely to it, carried down the front steps and wheeled along the street, Mrs Constantine walking on one side and an unsmiling, square bodied nurse carrying her grandson on the other. When the party had disappeared round the corner of Tredegar Square, Sarah smiled winningly up at Frank and asked, "Can I keep the dress now, Frank? If Mrs Ella's going to die in their house, can I have all of her dresses?"

Slowly, Frank Mason turned his head to look at the dishevelled girl in the opulent red dress, her breasts exposed and her tear stained face still bearing the clear imprint of Mrs Constantine's hand. Then he turned his eyes back to the street corner around which his wife and child had disappeared.

"God knows I must be gone mad," he said quietly. "You can take anything you like, Sarah. What does it matter to me now. My life is ended." His voice sounded so strange to her, she dared not speak as he walked out of the room. It was only when she heard cook begin to scream and scream again, she ran to the head of the stairs and saw that he was dead.

Chapter Four

"Mrs Tombrin," said William Shanklin, "you have told this court that the gentleman you knew as Lord Charles Beniton handed you his card and you returned it. Did you study the card with any particular care before you gave it back to him?"

Alice Tombrin shook her head apologetically. "No, I did not look at the card very closely, sir. At the time, I saw no reason for a close inspection."

"Quite so. But you glanced at it. What do you remember seeing?"

"Only that it had Lord Charles Beniton written in script across the centre and the name of a London club printed in a corner. There was no other address."

"I see. Do you remember the name of the club?"

"I'm not sure. Greville's, Piccadilly, or something very like it."

For the benefit of the packed court, William Shanklin made a show of looking distressed before he went on with: "I am sorry to have to tell you this, Mrs Tombrin, but no such club as Greville's exists in London's Piccadilly. Do you think you might be as mistaken in the name of the gentleman's club as you were in the name of Lord Charles Beniton?"

Mrs Tombrin flushed. "I may have been misled by the card, sir," she replied stiffly. "I do not believe I am mistaken in what I was told."

Shanklin bowed. "I am quite certain you were misled, Mrs Tombrin, but let us go a little further along this road. You returned the card and after some conversation, Lord Beniton retired. What happened next?"

"I went with Madame Sarah to her parlour. While we had tea, she told me Lord Charles Beniton would make me a very good husband."

"I see," said Shanklin, after a significant glance at the jurymen. "And was this the first time marriage had been mentioned?"

"It was the first time any such suggestion was made to me."

Prosecuting counsel turned on his heel to look directly at the female prisoner. "And you are telling the court," he asked the witness, "that the suggestion came from Sarah Fowkes alone? Lord Beniton had not broached the subject in any way?"

Sarah met the barrister's eyes and gave a small shrug when Mrs Tombrin replied, "Lord Beniton had said nothing at all on the subject of marriage and the idea had not occurred to me. It was Madame Sarah who first put the idea of my becoming married to Lord Beniton into my mind."

Shanklin turned back to face his witness and said mildly, "Thank you, Mrs Tombrin, and then what happened?"

"I met Lord Beniton in Madame Sarah's establishment on several subsequent occasions. On one such evening, Sarah told me to go upstairs and take a bath as part of the course of treatments I was paying for. I took the bath and on my return to the shop parlour, I found Lord Beniton sitting drinking coffee. Madame Sarah again introduced him to me. He made a bow but I forget the conversation we had. After he retired, she again said he would make me a good husband but it was necessary to go through an extra process of being made beautiful for the rest of my life. She told me Lord Beniton would write me a letter that would say the process was to be gone through at his express wish. He wanted me to be the envy of his friends and fellow officers when I stood by his side as his bride."

The witness paused to dab at her eyes with a crumpled lace handkerchief and William Shanklin took the opportunity to take off his spectacles and polish them vigorously on the hem of his gown. When they were cleaned to his satisfaction, he popped them back on his nose and said drily, "This extra process, Mrs Tombrin. No doubt it entailed some considerable extra expense?"

"Oh yes sir," Mrs Tombrin shot a glance of pure hatred at Sarah. "The sum I was to pay for the treatments amounted to £1,000. I went with Madame Sarah to my bankers in Fenchurch Street to sell out money in the Funds amounting to £963. I then went back with Sarah to her establishment, where I saw a solicitor named Mr Barry. The £963 was never handed over to me but I gave an order to the solicitor. It said: 'Mr Barry, I request you to pay Madame Sarah £800 on account of £963 received this day."

Shanklin raised a hand. "Bear with me, Mrs Tombrin, please. You wrote out the order?"

"No sir. The order was prepared in advance for me to sign and I did so."

"I see. And then?"

"Mr Barry asked me for a receipt, Madame Sarah told me how to word it, and I wrote out a receipt for £800. It was the balance of £1,000 received from me for bath preparations, spices, powders, sponges, perfumes and attendance, to be continued until I was finished by the process. Madame Sarah said that Lord Beniton and I were to be married by proxy and that it was to be done by letter writings. She said she had married two parties before by proxy and she was delighted that I should be the third. She also told me I should need jewellery for the marriage and that it would cost £1,400. She said that the letters I was to receive from Lord Beniton would be signed Thomas in case they were left about. I knew at that time that his Christian name is Charles . . . Charles," she repeated piteously, her damp eyes meeting the male prisoner's for a moment before tears began again to steal down her cheeks. "She told me his name was Charles."

Charlie Bennet's dread of the court proceedings, the grim faced judge, and the wigs and gowns of the advocates had already brought him to a highly charged state of emotion and when Mrs Tombrin began to weep, he too felt hot tears welling up in his eyes and had to turn his head away from her gaze. That morning he awoke with tears on his cheeks and looked round the bare prison cell, not knowing where he was or what he had been dreaming. The gaoler, who had shaken him into consciousness, told him gruffly he was returning to the court and when he got there, he was to stop snivelling and take his medicine like a man.

"What medicine?" Charlie returned with a faint show of defiance. "I ain't been found guilty of nothing yet. I might not have killed the old woman for all you know."

But the gaoler's slaty grey eyes showed nothing but contempt when he replied, "If you're so bleeding innocent there ain't no need to be laying down there sobbing and shitting your dirty self, is there."

'If I'm so bleeding innocent?' Charlie Bennet sat in the dock and, rather than watch the proceedings of the court, which he felt were all directed against him, looked down at his unpolished, unlaced boots, the laces having been removed with his braces and necktie in case he contemplated suicide. He was not a bit bleeding innocent. He had not been innocent since the first night he met Sarah Fowkes.

Listening to Mrs Tombrin give evidence, and with the spectre of being sent back to Wandsworth prison under sentence of death hanging over him, his mind stretched back to a time before he met Sarah. When he was involved with Mrs Harries and Molly, who watched over Mrs Harries's baby.

'I could twist women round my little finger in those days,' he thought wistfully. 'I could do what I liked with every woman I ever met until I came across Sarah Fowkes.'

He might have got fond of Mrs Harries. She was fond enough of him, as she lost little time in showing when he went back to her house to collect the letter of introduction she had promised him. She opened the front door herself and invited him in, saying in a flustered manner, "I'm so sorry, Mr Bennet, I haven't found time to write your letter yet. You can come back for it later or, if you don't mind waiting in the drawing-room, Molly is out with the baby and tea is made. I can pour you a cup and write the note while you drink it."

Charlie took off his hat. "If it's not going to be any trouble to you, ma'am, a cup of tea while I'm waiting would go down very well."

"Oh good, that's very good of you. This way then." She smiled up at him a little nervously, looked to be reassured by the breadth of the grin he returned, and led the way into the room she had interviewed him in the previous evening.

Sitting on a chair close by the door and sipping at the tea she poured, Charlie watched her cross the blue carpeted floor to sit at a small writing desk, let down the flap, and take out her writing materials.

"I'm very grateful to you for going to all this trouble, Mrs Harries," he said apologetically. "I imagined you were just going to mention my name to Mr Harries and ask him to oblige me."

"I am a widow, Mr Bennet," she said quietly, as she selected a pen and prepared to dip it in the inkwell. "I am made to keep my own promises. However, I can assure you that Mr Montague, the owner of the shop I am sending you to, knows me very well. He will respect my judgement."

Charlie put his cup down on a side table and scrambled to his feet. "I meant no disrespect, ma'am," he said hastily. "I just didn't realise I was putting you to so much trouble."

"I am quite sure you did not, Mr Bennet. Being alone creates problems for a woman, a young man like you can hardly be aware of."

"Being a man don't stop you getting lonely at night," Charlie said without thinking. "I've got used to sleeping in a barrack-room with a lot of other men. Last night was the first I spent on my own for I don't know how long and I couldn't sleep at all, ma'am. I spent the whole night watching the lamp smoke and counting the cracks in the ceiling. I'll tell you the honest truth, Mrs Harries. If I was a bit younger, I might have blubbed into my pillow for the loneliness of it."

Mrs Harries's face was pink when she turned her head to look at him. "I was not speaking of that sort of difficulty, Mr Bennet. I was speaking of the problems a single woman has in dealing with tradesmen and others who know she is not protected."

Charlie squared his shoulders. "Not protected?" he said indignantly. "You can let them know you're protected now, Mrs Harries. You're being very good to me and I can deal with any trouble that sort are likely to give you, believe you me I can."

Livvie Harries laughed aloud. "Mr Bennet," she pleaded, "won't you please sit down and stop looking so fierce, you are frightening me. As to what you have said, while your way of dealing with people might give me some personal satisfaction, having you strike my bank manager every time he asks me to get a gentleman to guarantee my transactions, I think will only add to my problems. Especially when he gives you in charge and I have to send Molly to visit you in prison."

"Send Molly?" Charlie smiled broadly and resumed his seat. "I'll only promise to punch your bank manager in the eye if I can be sure of a visit from you, Mrs Harries."

"Now stop it at once, Mr Bennet. That's more than enough flattery for one morning. Kindly drink your tea and I will finish the letter for you."

A delicate flush continued to stain her cheeks and, as she concentrated on writing the note, the pointed tip of her tongue protruded from the corner of her mouth and strayed between her soft lips until it reached the other corner and wandered back again, the childish action making her look younger than her thirty some years. Charlie, watching her, wondered how long it had been since she last shared her bed with a man. God, but she looked ripe for it and she was a pretty little thing with her fair ringlets and those round blue eyes. He took a deep and slightly shaky breath. The fumbling embrace and kiss he shared with Molly in the park had made him keenly aware of what he had been missing during his homosexual adventures with Lieutenant Holland. Charlie Bennet decided at that moment he was more than ready to be the man for the widowed Mrs Harries if only she would go for him. With his eyes on her lowered head and his thoughts running on what it might feel like to hold her slight body close in his arms and touch the tip of that clean little tongue with his own, he couldn't resist the slight tremor that ran through him. She, catching the movement, looked up.

"Are you feeling the cold, Mr Bennet?" she asked. "My husband used to complain that this is a very draughty room."

"Well now," said an embarrassed Charlie. "Perhaps I did

feel a bit of a draught at that, ma'am."

"Then please come and sit by the fire while you drink your tea. I'm very nearly finished."

Not trusting himself to say any more, he nodded, walked across to the low seat by the fireplace and made himself stare into the flames. He could no longer see her from where he sat but, at the desk, she was nearer to him and the smell of her perfume was enough to drive his imaginings wild. He closed his eyes and was almost caught out when, after a few more minutes, she came to stand before him with the letter in her hand.

"Here it is at last," she said, smiling as she held it out to him. "The address is on the front and if you ask for Mr Harold Montague to spare you a moment when he is free, I am quite certain that the situation will be yours."

"Thank you, Mrs Harries. It's very good of you to take all this trouble," Charlie replied as formally as he could. He was about to take the letter and get to his feet when she said softly.

"There is one more thing I would like to say before you go, Mr Bennet. What you were telling me about not being able to sleep last night for your loneliness. I was not speaking of that when I told you of a widow's problems but I do know what you mean and I feel very sorry for you. I too have suffered much from that kind of loneliness and there is little hope of a cure for me. I wish I could be of some help to you."

Her small waist was inches away, below it her skirts belled out to brush his knees, and the sweet smell of her scented body filled his nostrils. It was all much too much for Charlie Bennet.

"B-but you can help me," he stammered. "Of course you can help me. Oh Mrs Harries, I've been thinking about nothing else since I came in here. Honest, I'm just busting to put my arms round you and steal a kiss."

"Mr Bennet," she said in a shocked voice, backing away until she reached a low couch with the backs of her legs and plumped down with less grace and more ankle than she would usually show.

In an instant, he was kneeling beside her, his arms close around her legs and his face buried in her lap. Above him,

Mrs Harries licked her soft lips, smiled gently, and allowed her fingers to caress the back of his strong neck.

"Mr Bennet," she asked demurely. "What is it you want of me?"

"What do I want of you?" he repeated hoarsely, his hands up among her petticoats and scrabbling at her thighs. "I want loving. I want loving before I bust of it."

"Stop it!" squealed Livvie Harries, all pretence of modesty forgotten. "For the love of Heaven, will you stop it? You'll be tearing my drawers to shreds. Stop and I'll do it myself. Come upstairs, you naughty man."

A red faced and over excited Charlie followed close behind her up the stairs, laughing like a loon as she slapped his hands away from her rump and said, "Stop pushing me for goodness sake and for the love of God, will you stop making all that noise! Molly will be back with the baby any time. She'll hear you!"

Molly did bring the baby back while her mistress and Charlie Bennet were rumpling the covers on the bed upstairs. Coming into the sitting-room, she put the child down on the couch and let him kick while she looked round, her eyes narrowing when she found the discarded letter to Mr Montague on the floor by the low sofa. With a grimace of distaste, she picked it up between two fingers and dropped it on top of the writing desk before going back to the baby. She knew what was happening in the bedroom. If she was to be honest with herself, she could have expected nothing less, since the missus was one of those women who could never be satisfied in that way, no matter how much of it they got.

But somehow, with Charlie Bennet, Molly had let herself hope things might be different. After all, he might be handsome looking but he wasn't any class compared to the sort of gentlemen the missus usually went for and she might not have demeaned herself with him. So far as Molly was concerned, after all the lies he told her, she knew he couldn't be trusted. But even so, she had taken a fancy to him. In the park, when he held her and she felt the strength of his arms round her, she had let herself believe his need was for her alone and here was a man she might marry.

Well, she knew better now. Mrs Harries had her hooks in him. There was no chance now of Molly taking Charlie Bennet back to Cork and showing off her tall, golden-haired, English husband. Giving herself the pleasure of making her five sisters go green with envy of her. Perhaps the worst of it was that he was a trickster. He had made up to her in the park so she would keep quiet about his lies and then he took the first chance he got to jump into bed with the missus and play the jack rabbit for her doe. Filthy animals so they were, the pair of them.

Molly sniffed virtuously and began taking off the baby's coat and bonnet. "That Charlie Bennet has done me a bad turn," she told the child when it stopped crying and began sucking on her red and sugared knuckle. "And if I should ever come on a chance to get back at him for it, I'll do him down, so I will."

In the meantime, Charlie had tasted the tip and more of Livvie Harries's tongue and felt her nipples harden and her buttocks begin to move restlessly beneath his exploring fingers. He heard her uneven breathing sharpen into a half suppressed scream as he entered her hard and all the way before beginning to thrust and saw back and forwards while she heaved and bucked in response, their comings together becoming even more frenzied as their heat rose until the moment when they clung to each other in open-mouthed, simultaneous climax before collapsing among the bedclothes in a tumbling heap.

Completely spent by the experience, Charlie Bennet was lying face down when he felt Livvie's sharp nails dig into his rump. Hearing her shrill demand for more of his attentions, he remembered with some nostalgia, Lieutenant Holland's deep comforting voice and that after he climaxed, he would give Charlie a tobacco laden kiss for a job well done and go to sleep. Feeling the dig of her sharp nails score his rump again, he groaned and propped himself up on one elbow to look down at his tumble haired and rosy faced lover.

"Don't you think I ought to go to Mr Montague's shop and secure my position first, ma'am," he asked politely as he made to swing his legs to the floor. "I wouldn't want to lose the chance of decent employment and I can come back as soon as I can."

Livvie's eyes narrowed. "Have I been a disappointment to you? Did you not enjoy doing what you did with me?" she countered. "You acted the ram eagerly enough when you were busy among my skirts downstairs."

"Enjoy doing it with you?" Charlie dismissed all thought of Montague's shop and a gently snoring Lieutenant Holland as he traced two fingers down from her slim shoulder to follow the curve of her breast and then down the length of her belly until her legs came hard together to grip his hand. Feeling his own response growing, he murmured. "Oh yes Mrs Harries, I enjoy doing it with you. I like you very much."

"Well then?"

"Well then, Mrs Harries, how's this for a start off?"

When at last he went downstairs, he tried not to see the accusation in Molly's eyes and said as casually as he could, "Oh hello Molly, my dear, we knew you were back. Your missus says she'll be down in a couple of shakes and you're to set an extra place at the lunch table for me. She's written a letter for me to take to Mr Montague's shop and I'm to be there to see him at two o'clock sharp."

Molly's immediate response was a toss of the head and a meaningful look at the staircase. He shrugged awkwardly and blushed to the roots of his hair when she turned away and muttered, "I'll be surprised if you can walk that far after what you been up to with her all morning."

"Now, you look here . . . " he began angrily, but before he could say anything more, she had disappeared into the dining-room.

Charlie Bennet spent two more exhausting afternoons with Mrs Harries and took up his position at the main entrance of 'Montagues' on the following Monday morning. Quick to learn the work and by nature courteous, he bowed the patrons, who were mostly female, into the store, asked what they wished to see – he was on no account allowed to utter the word 'buy' – and led, or directed them to the appropriate counter or staircase. When they had finished their business and returned to the tall, glass paned door, he held it open and bowed them out. Charlie seldom knew if they bought anything. The House of Montague's customers rarely took their purchases with them and from his position at the main door, he never saw money change hands. Which reminded him rather uncomfortably of Lieutenant Holland's card and made him wonder if all the members of the upper classes waited for someone to die before giving a thought to paying their bills. A thought that also planted in him the vague ambition that one day, he too might find a way to live on credit.

In the meantime, he was kept busy at the shop door and, after his first month's trial, he was told by Mr Montague that he was satisfactory. When he was also offered an opportunity to boost his modest income by going out with the carrier in the evenings and helping with after hours deliveries, he jumped at the chance. Partly for the extra money and the sharing of an occasional threepenny or sixpenny tip, partly to avoid the ever more demanding attentions of Mrs Harries. He hadn't known what he was about when he started making up to that one, God knew he hadn't. The long red weals her nails raked across his shoulders and backside almost every night, showed that only too clearly.

Now, when he stood at the shop door and some of the less disdainful ladies favoured the tall, gravely handsome, young man with a smile, he hardly dared return it in case something more might be expected of him. Not that he could always prevent himself from grinning down at a pretty face and letting his imagination run rife over a shapely bosom and narrow waist. His great weakness was women, and he knew it. Not the grasping, over eager sort like Livvie Harries who never allowed a man any peace. Or the nasty sly piece Molly had become, staring waspy eyed at him every time he came down from the bedroom and turning her head away rather than answer a gentleman civilly when he asked her to set another place for dinner. Little Annie Barnes was a very different case.

The first time he saw the tiny girl was when she followed her mistress into the store and rewarded him with an impish grin as he opened the door with a salute and a bow. The next time they met was the following evening when she opened the door of her mistress's home to him, returned a parody of his salute and added a deep curtsey. Caught by the impudence of her grin when she accepted the small parcel he delivered, Charlie was still laughing when he got back to the carrier's van. So captivated was he by the girl's smile and neat little shape, he hardly noticed her mistress the first few times they came into the store, but as their visits and his deliveries to the house in Maiden Lane became more frequent, he saw that Mrs Avery was not young and that she had a plain, long nosed face and a poor complexion. She was not in his thoughts at all on the evening when, with Annie's connivance, he persuaded the van driver to make the house in Maiden Lane their last delivery and told him he would make his own way home.

To his chagrin, Annie proved to be a complete disappointment. Over the weeks, while they exchanged confidential little whispers on the doorstep, she made him think she was ripe for any sort of game he wanted to play, but when he followed her through the door and put out a hand to lift her skirt and tickle her pretty little backside, she let out a squeal and told him to leave off.

"I'm fourteen year old," she told him succinctly. "I don't mind a kiss or two if you want it but I won't have any of that. Besides, my Mrs Avery is still indoors, so you better come into the kitchen and behave yourself. I'll give you a cup of tea to drink."

Charlie stopped at the kitchen door and looked down at her. "Mrs Avery here? I thought you said they were going out tonight."

"I know what I said. They were going to the theatre for seven o'clock but when Mr Avery asked her why she wasn't wearing her pearls and her rings, she said there'd been a spate of burglaries round here and she put her jewellery in the bank for safe-keeping. She said she meant to bring them back for tonight but she quite forgot. Mr Avery acted like he didn't believe her and wanted to see the receipt. She said she couldn't lay her hands on it at the minute but she was quite certain that the man at the bank would recognise her and return the jewels in the morning. Then Mr Avery started shouting at her like he does. He told her that he wasn't going to take her to the theatre. He said she was an ugly enough sight when she was wearing her jewels. Without them he wouldn't inflict her on his friends and business associates. Then he said he was too flaming angry with her and her stupid behaviour to stay in the house tonight. He was going off to his club and when he comes back tomorrow she had best have the jewellery or a damn good reason for not having the jewellery and then it was good evening, madam, and he marched out. She's been sitting up in the bedroom sobbing her eyes out ever since."

Intrigued by the story, Charlie sat down at the table. "Go on," he said. "What happened to the jewels? Were they pinched?"

"How should I know?" the girl asked indignantly. "You ain't saying I stole them, are you?"

"Of course I'm not saying you stole them . . . " Charlie began when the kitchen door opened wide and a red-eyed Mrs Avery stood in the doorway. He scrambled to his feet but she ignored him.

Glaring at Annie, she snapped, "I knew I could hear voices in here. I've a good mind to turn you out on the spot. You know perfectly well you are not allowed to bring strangers into my house without permission."

"But I'm not really a stranger, ma'am," Charlie broke in. "I'm the doorman from Montague's. Your parcel was the last delivery I had to make tonight and because my throat was dry, I took the liberty of asking your maidservant for a glass of water. She very kindly offered me a cup of tea because she had one in the pot. I should be very sorry if she got into any sort of trouble through her kindness to me, Mrs Avery ma'am."

"Oh, is that what it is." Mrs Avery favoured him with a watery smile and turned back to Annie. "It will be all right this once. Pour the gentleman a cup of tea for his dry throat. I only wish my troubles could be cured as easily."

As she spoke the words, her shoulders drooped and she began to cry. In an instant, Charlie was beside her and guiding her to a chair. "Please sit down ma'am," he said. "I can see you've had an upset. I'd best be going."

"Thank you but you must have your tea. I am sorry for making such a scene, but my nerves are truly all to pieces.

I don't know what I am do to." Charlie could see she was bursting to pour out her troubles and he listened sympathetically while she told him of her acquaintanceship with a certain Madame Sarah, who sold soaps and perfumes and was also an expert in helping women to regain and keep a youthful appearance.

"I have been in the habit of taking treatments in her shop and the last time I went there, I foolishly wore a number of valuable rings and my pearl earrings and necklace. Madame Sarah sent me upstairs to take a bath and while I prepared myself for it, I took my ornaments off and put them in a drawer. After I finished my toilet and returned to the dressing-room, I opened the drawer and found my jewellery had disappeared. I rang the bell and when Madame Sarah came into the room, I told her of my loss and she at once flew into a terrible rage. She swore there had been no jewellery left in the drawer and she accused me of lying. Then she said she knew all about me and the disgraceful way I behaved. She asked how my husband would like to know about my assignations with a certain gentleman who visited me in her shop. I was so horrified by what she was saying, I hurried away from the shop and have not been back there since. As for what I can say to my husband tomorrow, I simply do not know."

She began to weep again and Charlie put out a hand to touch her on the shoulder. "You should have faced her down and called a constable, ma'am, you really should. I know about these cheats who deal in ointments and cures. There's an embrocation merchant who makes up a muck of lard and peppermint and travels the markets selling it as a rub for bad backs. I gave him a bad back for himself when the packet he sold me turned rancid and worms came crawling out of it. I do wish I'd known about your trouble, Mrs Avery. Charlie Bennet would have been more than happy to get the better of one of those merchants for you." He took his hand from her shoulder and, thumping his other fist into the palm, saw she was sitting up straight, her eyes fixed on him in sudden hope.

"Would you, Mr Bennet? I would gladly give you £100 if you could recover my jewellery tonight."

"Well now," said Charlie, who had done nothing about the embrocation pedlar apart from hoping he would choke on the tuppence he gave him. "Ordinarily ma'am, I'd be glad to go and see to the matter for you . . . "

"I understand," interrupted Mrs Avery, her voice dull. "Ordinarily you would be pleased to help me but tonight you are engaged upon another matter and I am ruined."

Charlie swallowed and took the plunge. "Hold hard, ma'am, you're going a bit too fast for me. I'm saying that this cheat is a woman and I can't treat her the way I would a man. I might even have to offer her money to get the goods back. I don't have any money with me at present.

"But I do," said Mrs Avery. "Oh Mr Bennet, if that is your only reason, I'll give you money to take with you and a £100 for yourself when you bring my jewellery back to me."

Charlie stood up and put his hand over his heart. "In that case, Mrs Avery, you can rely on me."

A few minutes later, furnished with £150 and a description of the rings and necklace, Charlie Bennet went to the door with a wide-eyed Annie at his side.

"Here, you be careful," she warned as she opened it for him. "You don't know what sort of a spiteful woman you might be having to deal with."

Charlie laughed with a confidence he was far from feeling. "Go on with you," he said, tapping himself on the chest. "If there's one thing this young fellow has learned during his lifetime, it's how to handle a woman."

Chapter Five

William Shanklin pushed back his wig to scratch his head and gently patted the grey wool back in place before saying patiently, "Mrs Tombrin, you have told the court that you knew Lord Beniton had the Christian name of Charles. Now you are saying that Sarah Fowkes told you his letters would be signed Thomas. Did she tell you why?"

"Madame Sarah said it was in case they were left about, sir," said Mrs Tombrin. "She told me that personal letters have been known to cause great harm when they fall into the wrong hands and that members of the aristocracy must be particularly careful."

"Members of the aristocracy must be particularly careful," Shanklin repeated slowly. "Very well, I can understand that. And did you receive any of the promised letters?"

Mrs Tombrin nodded. "Yes sir, I did. They began arriving about three weeks after I paid Madame Sarah and she began to give me my treatments."

"Did the man you knew as Lord Beniton send his letters to you direct?"

"No sir, each of his letters was handed to me by Madame Sarah. After I read them, she took them back for safe-keeping."

Shanklin leafed through the papers in his hand as though searching for some piece of information, shook his head to indicate to the world at large and the jury in particular, that it was not to be found, and dropped the papers on the table beside him before resuming his questioning with, "Lord Beniton, I presume, is an educated man. Did his letters reveal an educated hand?"

Mrs Tombrin frowned. "No sir, they did not. On at least two occasions I had reason to remark that the spelling of his letters was very bad and Sarah said his manservant must have written them on his behalf. She also said that was why some of the letters were signed William."

Again there was some sniggering in the well of the court and prosecuting counsel allowed himself a bleak smile before asking for the general purport of the letters.

"The letters told me that he loved me dearly and wished for no happier fate than to be allowed to spend the rest of his life at my side as my husband and protector. He hoped we would be married very soon and promised me that when we were married and I became the new Lady Beniton, I should be given his mother's coronet and other pieces of jewellery of great antiquity and value. In the meantime, Lord Beniton sent me as a token, a small perfume box and pencil case which had belonged to his mother. He told me in his letter that she had died with them in her hand. He also told me to obey Madame Sarah's instructions in every particular because it was to her we owed our future happiness. Lord Beniton told me not to worry about any slight expense I might be put to. When certain of his business affairs were taken care of, we should be extremely wealthy and those expenses would seem trifling."

In the dock, Sarah Fowkes couldn't resist a slight nod of agreement.

She had taken a deal of trouble over the letters. They were good and whatever the old crow chose to say about them now, when she first read them she was ready for the plucking and willing to pay the cost of it. They were all the same when it came to rumpling. Starting with Frank Mason. What had he got for his money other than a hand on her tit and a kiss or two. Twelve sovereigns she had out of him before the stupid swine hanged himself from a banister rail and choked to death with his eyes bulging and his tongue poked out. Twenty sovereigns more she found tucked away in a drawer when she went back in the bedroom, put on Ella's yellow and green dress, and packed a bag with as many of her clothes as she could carry and the two small bottles of perfume she found on the dressing-table. She had the good sense not to take Ella's hairbrushes. A girl like her might get away with a bag of second-hand clothes and a half full bottle of scent but if she was caught with those silver backed hairbrushes, she was a goner for sure.

After one horrified glance at his face, she kept her eyes averted as she crept past the knotted scarf supporting the weight of Frank Mason's body and down the stairs, carrying her sleeping baby and the heavy bag. In the hall, she ignored the din of cook's shrieking from the kitchen and swung open the front door. Almost collapsing with shock when she found herself face to face with a distraught Mr Constantine, come to see if he could repair the damage done between his son-in-law and his wife.

"Sarah?" he said, putting out a hand to steady her after their near collision. "My dear child, what in the world is happening in this house? Why is the cook making that dreadful noise?"

Sarah, dressed in his daughter's clothes and caught in the business of carrying away more of them, thought she was lost. Dropping the bag to the floor and holding Marie close to her breast, she began to sob.

"Oh, Mr Constantine," she wailed through her tears. "Mr Mason is dead and I was so frightened, I was trying to run away."

"Frank dead?" repeated Mr Constantine. "But how can he be dead, you silly child? Take me to him and for the love of God, stop that confounded woman screaming before she drives me demented with her noise. Go and fetch her to me."

Sarah pushed the bag behind the door with a foot and led the way back to the hall before going into the kitchen and telling cook that Mr Constantine had come to take charge and said she was to stop her bleeding racketing at once. By the time cook had quietened sufficiently to accompany Sarah, they found the old man had taken off his hat and was standing before Frank Mason's body with tears in his eyes.

Turning to them as they approached, he patted cook

gently on the shoulder and said, "This is a bad business, my dear, but it must be dealt with. Will you put your coat on and fetch a constable for me?"

"Yes sir," said the weeping cook and, after she put her coat on and, still sobbing wildly, left by the front door, Mr Constantine asked Sarah to sit with him in the drawing-room and tell him what had happened and why she was running away.

"It was Mrs Constantine having such a down on me, sir," Sarah whined pathetically. "Mr Mason told me I could wear Mrs Ella's clothes to sit downstairs in and when Mrs Constantine caught me putting one of the dresses on, she said I was stealing it and clouted me so hard across the face, I fell over on the bed. Then she was coming after me to give me another clout when Mr Mason heard the row and came in to stop her. He told her to leave me be and she started to scream terrible things at him. She said I was his whore and he was dismissed from your company and he was to get out and take me with him. Then she went off to get another wet-nurse for your little grandson Timothy and took him and Mrs Ella away. Mr Mason was very down when he saw what she did, Mr Constantine. He watched them go from the bedroom window and told me to take whatever clothes I wanted and to get out of the house. He said nothing wouldn't matter any more, he was finished. Then he went out of the room and did that to himself. Mrs Constantine shouldn't have called me his whore, Mr Constantine. I never done whoring for no one and Mr Mason was only being good to me because I was nursing his little boy."

She put her damp, flushed cheek down on her own baby's head and despite what had happened, Mr Constantine was scarcely able to resist putting an arm round her shoulders and smoothing her tumbled hair back from her forehead. God, but even in her misery, the girl was a vision of loveliness. If Mrs Constantine was right and poor Frank had lost his head over her, he could hardly blame him for it. Mr Constantine was over 60 years of age and his experience of marital sex with an unforgivingly frigid Mrs Constantine had soon enough made him find a lover to keep him happy through the years. Even so, he could not fail to be stirred by Sarah's youth and beauty.

"But where did you think you were going at this time of night?" he asked, dropping his half raised hand. "Surely you were not going back to Stepney?"

"I didn't know where I should go, Mr Constantine. I thought I might find a cheap lodging house for the night and go back to my mother tomorrow."

"That won't do at all, Sarah. Typhoid has broken out all over the Aldgate and Whitechapel districts. You can't possibly take your child there."

"I can't stop here, sir. Mrs Constantine will come back and flay the skin off my back. I know she will."

"No," Mr Constantine agreed. "You'll do no good here." He pondered for a moment and then said quietly, "Listen to me, my dear. Close by my warehouse in Covent Garden, I have a small house which I use as an office. There is no one there at night and you had better take some food with you. You'll find a couch in one of the lower rooms which will serve as a bed. A cab will get you there in fifteen minutes from here. Have you any money?"

Sarah, not daring to let him see one of her stolen sovereigns, dumbly shook her head and he produced some coins from his purse.

"Take this money and the key to the house. When you find a cab, tell the driver to take you to 31 Windell Street and I will see you in the morning. Perhaps you had best go now, before cook comes back with a constable. I will look after my poor son-in-law."

He went back into the hall and stood by Frank's body, seeming not to notice Sarah or the loosely tied bag she carried, when she passed by on her way to the kitchen. She helped herself to a small parcel of food, left the house by the kitchen door, and at the top of the area steps, hailed a passing cab. When the driver reined his horse in and looked down at her doubtfully, she called up at him, "Here you, take me to Mr Constantine's house at 31 Windell Street. You don't have to worry about your fare. I've got it here in my hand." On arrival, she carefully counted out the exact money, ignored the cabbie's sniff of disapproval, and let herself into the house. The lamp she lit, showed her a drawing-room, sparsely furnished and not very clean, but good enough for the night. Totally worn out by the events of the day, she explored no further but woke and fed Marie before falling asleep on the sofa with her baby in her arms.

It was not until the following morning, with sunlight streaming through the partly curtained window on to her face, that she woke to remember the horror of Frank Mason's body suspended from the banister and the money and clothes she had stolen. As soon as Mrs Constantine knew Frank Mason was dead and Sarah was gone from the house, the old crone was bound to look in Mrs Ella's wardrobe and find it emptied. By now, she would have told Mr Constantine and he must be on his way with the police. No one was going to believe a girl like her, no matter how many times she swore Mr Mason told her she could have the dresses. She had to get away from the house, but where could she go?

Before she could think it out, Marie woke with a start and began to howl. Automatically, she fed and changed her and, when the howling continued unabated, scowled at the baby and muttered, "Why don't you shut up, you little cow? Can't you see I'm trying to think?" Marie quietened instantly, burped loudly, and smiled. Despite her troubles, Sarah laughed and kissed her head. She was telling her daughter she was sorry for being an old crab, when she heard a key turn in the front door lock and shrugged. Knowing she couldn't run far carrying a baby, she was resigned to her fate. Whatever was going to happen to the pair of them was no longer in her hands but they would be together. She got to her feet, and was facing the door with Marie in her arms when it opened. She caught her breath in relief when she saw Mr Constantine enter and he had no policeman with him.

"I hope you managed to get some sleep, my dear," he said, taking off his hat and sitting heavily on the sofa. Sarah contented herself with a wary nod and he went on almost as though speaking to himself. "God in Heaven, what a time I've had of it. I hope I never have to go through another night like that as long as I live. But there it is. They brought him down and took him away at last. Poor, poor Frank."

He blew his nose loudly and turned to look at Sarah. "Sit down, my dear. I have something I want to tell you.

My son-in-law has been taken from the house this morning and I've closed the place up. I hope there's nothing of yours there?"

Sarah shook her head and said there was nothing there she wanted. The elderly man managed a brief smile and nodded. "That's good. I've no wish to go back there, I promise you. Now tell me, how are you and little Marie?"

"We're all right sir, but I don't know what I must do. Are the police coming after me for running away?"

"No my dear. I told the officers you were dismissed by my wife for no good reason and that my unhappy son-in-law gave you some of my daughter's old dresses by way of compensation. I told them I sent you and your baby away from the premises as soon as I knew of the unfortunate incident and that, since the quarrel was between Mr Mason and his mother-in-law, you could know nothing that would help them. The fact that Frank killed himself is not in any doubt and Mrs Constantine was sufficiently chastened by her own part in the affair to be not sorry to know you are gone. The question now is, what is to become of Sarah Fowkes and her daughter?"

"I-I don't know sir."

Sarah's voice broke and she dropped her head. Again resisting the temptation to take her in his arms and comfort her, he said, "Well, you can't make a career of being a wet-nurse and even if typhoid was not rampant throughout the Whitechapel district, I've no wish to see you back in that wretched laundry. Tell me, can you read and write? Can you reckon up your money?"

"I can read and reckon a little. Enough to count the cost of the washing and give the right change and suchlike."

Mr Constantine gave her a mock frown. "Try not to say suchlike, Sarah. If I am to find you a place, and with your good looks, I am quite sure I can, you'll have to speak considerably better than you do now."

Sarah held Marie closer. "Find me a place, Mr Constantine?"

The elderly man put out a hand to touch her shoulder and raised it to let his fingers rest against her cheek. "You have the promise of becoming a very beautiful woman, Sarah. I am an importer of soaps and perfumes. I have not yet spoken to her but I think I might be able to place you with a good friend of mine, who deals in beauty products and treatment for afflictions of the skin. If you become useful in the shop and her customers think they can be made to look as you do by the use of my products, it can do nothing but good to Mrs Pendleton's business and my own. It will also provide you with a roof over your head and a splendid opportunity to learn the business of shopkeeping. Do you think you would like working with perfumes and soaps, Sarah? I can tell you now that the perfume you took from Ella's dressing-table and are wearing rather too much of at the moment is one of my products."

Sarah blushed furiously but raised her head to meet his eyes. "They was only bottles of scent, Mr Constantine. I thought they were too little to be worth much. I didn't touch Mrs Ella's hairbrushes."

Mr Constantine chuckled. "You'll be surprised when you learn how much a bottle of good perfume is worth, but never mind that for now. Just thank your stars you did not take the hairbrushes with you. Leaving them behind made Mrs Constantine think you are too foolish to recognise their worth and probably took nothing else of value. Actually, my own inclination is to think quite the opposite. Anyway, my dear, there it is. When you are ready, come down to the warehouse with your baby and we will take breakfast together. After we have eaten, I will accompany you to Mrs Pendleton's shop in Beak Street and introduce you to the lady. She is a very good soul and we'll see what she can make of Sarah Fowkes."

"God in Heaven, how dreadful for you both," Mrs Pendleton exclaimed when she was told of Frank's suicide and Mr Constantine's reason for bringing Sarah to her. "Come and sit down, my child. Let me have a look at you." She walked round the gold painted chair Sarah perched on with her feet not quite touching the carpeted floor, and studied her thoughtfully before returning to Mr Constantine and saying, "You're quite right, of course. Her complexion could be a little higher and we'll have to do something with that hair, but there is no doubt she'll adorn my little shop. Have you thought where she is to live?"

"I hoped we might come to an arrangement whereby she could live here with you. At least for the time being."

"I'll be pleased to have her and her beautiful baby if it promises to stay as quiet as it is at the moment."

Sarah's sudden smile transformed her face. "She's ever so good, ma'am," she said eagerly. "When I put her down after a feed, she goes to sleep just like a little angel."

Mrs Pendleton returned the smile cautiously. "That's all right for now, my dear. It's when she becomes a bigger little angel and starts crawling about the place and climbing up the stairs, we might have to find someone to keep an eye on her." Sarah's eyes rounded at the thought of Marie getting bigger and crawling.

Mrs Pendleton laughed aloud and kissed Marie's head. "Oh they do grow, believe me," she said, "but never mind all that for now, my dear. I'll be happy to have you both. I expect the three of us will get along beautifully."

"And knowing that will be a great relief to me," said Mr Constantine, getting up and reaching for his hat. "Thanks to my good wife, the girl has had a very hard time lately. I think she deserves the chance of a better one now."

Together, Sarah and Mrs Pendleton watched Mr Constantine leave and when the door closed behind him, Mrs Pendleton said, "Poor soul, but he's aged. You should have known him in his prime." She sighed and turned away from the door. "Listen my girl. There's one matter I didn't want to go into with Mr Constantine here. I would rather you did not let the baby's father know where you are living. I don't want followers coming into the shop. They can make trouble."

The girl blanched. "That man knocked me down on the laundry floor and half killed me," she said bitterly. "He ran away after he done what he wanted and he's never been near me since. He would have got a pair of old Mendel's tailor scissors in his guts if he did."

Mrs Pendleton laid a sympathetic hand on Sarah's arm. "So it was like that, was it? If he's one of those swine, I know a better place than his guts for those scissors, my dear. Castration is what he wants. It's what any man of that filthy nature wants to teach him a lesson once and for all."

Sarah gave her a puzzled look. "What's castration do to

them then?" she asked and her jaw dropped as Mrs Pendleton told her, sketching the motion with the long pair of scissors she took from her pocket and laughing at the expression on the girl's face.

"Go on with you," she said, "and stop looking so shocked. I'm quite sure you wouldn't mind busying yourself between his legs with a sharp pair of these. Not after what he did to you. You can have this pair in case you ever meet him again." Nora Pendleton laughed again and even Sarah couldn't stop the reluctant smile that spread across her face as her hand closed over the blades. The older woman glanced away to look up at the clock over the shop counter.

"Heavens, will you look at that," she fussed. "Come on, my girl, it's almost time to open the shop and you can't help me wearing a dress like that. And you've got too much perfume on. Come upstairs and I'll find you a black dress that will do for now. When I open for business, look at what I do, take the pots and bottles off the shelves for me when I ask for them and make sure you put the unsold ones back on the shelf and out of harm's way. You wouldn't believe how light fingered some of these ladies can be and the richer they get the more eccentric they become. You look like a sharp enough girl to me. You'll learn."

Over the weeks and months that followed, Sarah did learn. First to copy Mrs Pendleton's manner of speaking to the clients and then to adopt the smooth, virtually expressionless face that did not show resentment at the way she was spoken to by the apparently wealthy ladies who patronised the shop. Not to be too obvious either, in her admiration of their many ringed fingers when they presented the inside of a thin, blue veined wrist for her to dab a touch of perfume on to. Especially after the incident when a customer swore she had taken off a valuable ring while she was inspecting a box of soaps and when she turned back to the counter to pick it up, it had gone and she was going to fetch a constable.

"My ring is worth more than £200," she declared loudly. "I am not leaving this establishment until it is found and returned."

"Or you receive adequate compensation, madam?" Mrs Pendleton asked smoothly, while Sarah, as the accused, paled and shrank back against the shelves behind the counter.

"I suppose I might accept the value in money if it will save you some embarrassment," the woman said, smiling acidly.

"Oh no, madam," Nora Pendleton replied. "If your ring is missing, I agree with you. We must have a constable in no matter what embarrassment I may suffer. A member of my staff is accused of theft and while I believe her to be a good girl and innocent, you tell me she is guilty. I shall have to insist on you both being taken to the police cells where you can be stripped and searched by a matron. Unless, of course, you would like to have another look in your handbag in case you inadvertently dropped it in there while you were looking at the soaps?"

"Well, really," snapped the woman as she made for the door without looking in her bag. "I have been treated most abominably in this shop. I shall buy my soaps and perfumes elsewhere in future and I will see to it that my friends do the same."

"Thank you madam," Nora Pendleton said when she closed the door firmly behind the woman. Turning back to the frightened girl, she smiled at her. "Come along my dear, put the kettle on and make us a cup of tea. You mustn't let a woman like her worry you. Give back as good as you get is my motto. When that sort think a constable is really coming into the shop, they clear out of here fast enough."

Nora Pendleton's shop was popular and in addition to the goods for sale, she offered treatments in the rooms upstairs for a variety of skin and hair conditions. Nora liked Sarah and after the girl had been with her a few months, encouraged her to address customers direct and ask how she might help them. And as she judged, the customers took to the earnest young woman with the Madonna-like beauty and let her advise them. In the hope, no doubt, that the paints and powders she persuaded them to buy, would in some way shorten their noses, flesh out their hollowed cheeks, and straighten their frizzy hair, making their indifferent husbands find them desirable. Perhaps as desirable as they found them on their wedding nights.

It was Sarah who coined the phrase 'beautiful for life'.

Nora Pendleton was afraid of making any such claim, considering the flap breasted, pot bellied, old women they often attended to in the treatment rooms upstairs but, when the suggestion was put to Mr Constantine, who was a regular visitor, he was delighted with the idea.

"I like it very much and I am going to incorporate it in my advertising," he said in answer to the demurring Nora. "Use Constantine's enamels and soaps and be beautiful all your life is no more of an exaggeration than the advertisement next to it that promises to grow hair on a billiard ball." He laughed a little ruefully and patted his own bald crown. "No one need ever know how much money and time I have wasted on that preparation."

He smiled again, if a little ruefully, and accepted the cup of tea Sarah poured for him. Studying her face over the rim of the cup, he said, "You're a bright child as well as being a beauty. One of these days some young man will come along and want to marry you. Then Mrs Pendleton and I will lose you and we'll both be sorry for it." Sarah shook her head and swore it would never happen. To her, the great advantage of working in a soap and perfume shop was that she had so little contact with men. Apart from Mr Constantine, who had shown her nothing but kindness, the memory of the man who raped her and the lunatic behaviour of Frank Mason kept her afraid of the creatures and wary. Despite her love for Marie, who had grown pretty and curly haired and was always being spoiled and dandled by the customers, the memory of how the child was conceived still made her shudder and wake up in a cold sweat at night, reaching for the scissors Mrs Pendleton had given her to protect herself with.

"Oh no, Mr Constantine sir, that'll never happen to me. I won't let it," she assured Mr Constantine with a firm shake of the head and a hug for Marie. At that period in her life, she was determined never to speak to a man again, far less marry one.

Mr Constantine rarely mentioned his family or Sarah's mother on his weekly visits to the shop but when, one morning, he came in much earlier than usual, his face was drawn and pale and the moment he saw her, he put his hand over Sarah's.

"My dear," he said quietly. "We both have troubles at the moment. My grandson Timothy is gravely ill and I am afraid your mother too, is near death after a bad fall in the street." He sat down heavily and, after a glance at Marie who was smiling up at him and clutching his finger, went on blindly. "Oh Sarah, if my wife hadn't been so full of hate for my son-in-law, you would have kept nursing Timothy and he would have remained as healthy and as strong as your own dear little one. As things are, I fear he is too sickly to manage yet another illness. Whatever the doctor says, I think we have lost him."

"Oh Mr Constantine," Mrs Pendleton said softly, "I do hope not."

"Hope is all I have, Nora," he replied, "and very little of it, but that isn't what I came here to speak about. Sarah, I am sorry to have to tell you about your mother's ill health. I must go home now but I'll send my carriage back to collect you. The coachman will take you to Stepney and stay until you have completed your visit."

The carriage got as near as it could to the iron posts at the end of Broomfield Court, leaving Sarah to hold up her skirts with a delicately gloved hand and pick her way across the greasy cobbles, her nose wrinkled in disdain of the half-remembered stink. She put a hand on her hat and lowered her head to duck into Mendel's workshop, where she found nothing changed. Mendel and his apprentice cut and ironed and handed out work in the corner by the bed. The women sat on the splintered floor and, seemingly dressed in the same rags they had on their backs when she last saw them, stitched at gentlemen's waistcoats and bickered among themselves; though they dropped their work sharp enough to stare at Sarah when she came through the doorway. For a moment she returned stare for stare, remembering with as much surprise as disgust that she had once sat among Mendel's stitchers and was more than likely indistinguishable from any one of them. Before anyone spoke, there came a low moan from the back room and the women made way for her to go through to where her mother lay on a cot set beside the unlit boiler. Aggie's sickness since the fall had left her stale smelling and saggy-cheeked and Sarah hardly knew her mother when she held out a grubby, claw like hand.

Aggie Fowkes was barely forty years old but her wispy grey hair and blotched face suggested a woman of twice that age. She was too ill to speak but her eyes were on her daughter's face and she tried to smile when Sarah took her hand and told her she worked in a shop, earned quite good wages, and was going to leave some money with Mendel so he could get her some better food and attention.

"I'll come back and see you again soon," she said in her new, Mrs Pendleton like, voice. "And when you're feeling better, I'll bring your granddaughter to see you."

'It's a safe enough story to tell a dying woman.' Sarah was thinking as she leaned forward to brush her mother's forehead with her soft lips. Even knowing she would never see Aggie alive again, she could feel no emotion for the hollow-eyed stranger her mother had become and the sooner it was over and done with, the better. Going back into Mendel's room, she gave him five pounds and asked him to see to her mother's comfort and the funeral arrangements when it became necessary.

"Oh certainly ma'am," said Mendel, the man whose dirty fingers used to busy themselves about her backside. He clasped his hands and bowed deferentially. "I'm sorry about your dear mother and of course, I'll let you know when she is being laid to rest."

"Thank you, Mr Mendel. A letter to Mr Constantine's house will find me."

He bowed again. "Before you go, Miss Sarah, it so happens there's another party here wishing to have a few words with you."

Sarah shook her head. "I'm sorry Mr Mendel," she began, "I really don't think there's anyone else I could talk to today . . ."

The voice that interrupted from the doorway behind her was harsh and hatefully familiar. "Don't you come the high and mighty with me, my little sweetheart," it rasped. "I've had it in you and don't tell me you wasn't loving it, the way you was waggling your little arse. Now you listen here. I've been told you've got a child I can lay claim to and I've a mind to do it if we don't come to an agreement to suit us both." Stunned, Sarah could not turn, nor could she interrupt the man who had raped her for the icy thrill of fear that shot through her heart. When she felt she must say something or she would lose her head and scream, Sarah remembered the way Mrs Pendleton had faced down the woman who swore she left a valuable ring on the shop counter and had it stolen. Keeping her eyes on Mendel's inane and toothless smirk, she willed herself to breathe slowly and keep her voice steady when she said, "If you are the man who attacked me, you are the child's father. Tell me where you live. I will bring her and a constable to you this afternoon."

"Now you hold hard," said the man, putting a hand on her shoulder. Infuriated by his touch, she swung to face him and in the instant of doing so, knew that the years of good food and decent living had made her taller and much stronger than she had been when he was able to throw her on the floor of the laundry.

Angrily striking his hand from her shoulder, she gritted, "No, it's your turn to hold hard, you filthy swine. You knocked me down and rutted on me like a dog. You ain't getting my baby and you ain't getting a penny out of me either, but I'll tell you what you are going to get before you leave here. Do you know what a castration is?" The man took a pace back, shook his head, and Sarah went on. "Then I'll show you what a castration is. A lady taught me and I've seen it done lots of times. These nice ladies are going to pull your trousers down and hold you still while I get hold of Mendel's biggest pair of scissors and cut your stinking bollocks off."

"Gaw on. I'd like to see you try it on," blustered the man as he retreated hastily through the group of sniggering women.

" 'Ere you are, Sarah darling," said one, catching at his ankle as he passed and making him stagger. "I got 'im for you. You get your hands on Mendel's scissors while we pull 'is trousers off. We could do with a bit of a lark round here."

The laughter increased as the man clapped his hands over his crotch and struck his head on the lintel over the low doorway in his hurry to get away.

"We might have lost one of the buggers," said the scrawny, red-headed woman who tripped the man, "but there's always old Mendel. Losing his scraggy bits and pieces might cure him of being so free with his hands."

"Now come on, ladies," Mendel said hastily, while he retreated to the filthy old bed and sat down with his legs firmly crossed. "Show a bit of respect for a gentleman, can't you? Besides, Miss Sarah's got to go home now so we can all get on with our work."

In the carriage, on the way back to the shop, Sarah could not resist telling the coachman that she heard Mr Mendel threatened with a castration and didn't know what it was or why Mr Mendel looked so afraid of the woman who picked up a pair of tailor's scissors and said it. She watched with interest as the man blanched and pulled his leather apron hard across his lap before telling her sternly that it was not a suitable matter for a gentleman to discuss with a young lady. Sarah sat back in the bouncing carriage, and was reflecting on her new found knowledge of a man's cowardice where his bollocks are concerned, when they reached the corner of Beak Street and she saw a milling crowd among the carts and carriages outside Mrs Pendleton's shop. Through the racketing noise, she heard a woman's high pitched scream of horror and knew with a deadly certainty it was Mrs Pendleton.

In an instant, she was out of the coach and running to the shop and Marie, only to be caught up in the arms of a constable. "You can't go through there miss," he said. "There's been a nasty accident."

She stiffened, unable to struggle. With her heart pounding, she whispered. "I live in the soap shop over there with Mrs Pendleton. Me and my baby girl. What accident?" Over the constable's shoulder, she could see a dishevelled and wildly sobbing Mrs Constantine being lifted and pitched head first into a Black Maria. Through the terrible buzzing that threatened to split her head wide open, she could hear the policeman saying. "It might not have been your little girl, my luvvy. Keep your heart up. Keep your heart up."

The Black Maria moved through the crowd past Sarah. Her hand bled where she came to life and struck at it and blood was on the constable's hand where he caught her back before she could strike again. There was more blood when the small still bundle that had been Marie was brought to her in another policeman's arms. She opened her mouth to scream but no sound escaped her closed throat. Almost retching in her desperate reach for air, she heard the policeman who held the bundle ask, "Is it yours, ma'am?" The crowd surged and spilled round her and Mrs Pendleton stood by. With more blood yet, Sarah saw. Splashing from Mrs Pendleton's mouth where Mrs Constantine had struck her before snatching up the terrified child, running into the street and dashing her to the ground beneath a cart.

"I couldn't stop her, Sarah," Mrs Pendleton was gabbling through her torn lips and loosened teeth. "I couldn't stop her. Oh Sarah, Sarah."

Lost in a welter of blood, unable to understand anything from what she heard and saw, Sarah could only repeat the constable's words. "Is it mine?"

It was then, putting her hand out to touch Marie's curly, red gold hair, she saw the blooded track of an iron clad cart wheel across the flattened mess the child's chest had become. And was able to shriek once before her eyes rolled up in their sockets and she fainted.

Sarah Fowkes woke in a hospital ward after a repeated nightmare of seeing Marie thrown down before a cart and being too late to reach her before she was crushed to death by a creaking wheel. Sarah's shrieks and thrashing limbs when she remembered it was not a nightmare, had her leeched for the hysteria. When that treatment proved ineffective and it was decided by the doctor she had become a lunatic, the nurses bound her to the metal frame of the bed while twenty or so drops of laudanum were administered to quieten her in preparation for her transfer to the asylum in Colney Hatch Lane. In her weakened state, she wet herself and worse. An Inspector of Police who came to speak to her about the tragedy, shook his head and walked away from the sight and smell of her. There was no doubt in his or anyone else in the hospital's mind that the experience of having her dead baby brought to her in the street had driven the poor girl beyond any hope of recovery.

Mr Constantine came to the hospital in time to save her. Accompanied by his own doctor and ignoring the odious smell that rose from her, he took the hand of the semi-conscious girl and said distinctly, "Do you know me, Sarah?"

"Mr Constantine," she mumbled, narrowing her eyes and peering at him sideways in an attempt to focus on his face. "My little Marie is dead."

"I know it, my poor dear. My grandson, Timothy, is also dead."

"Both babbies dead? It's very hard, Mr Constantine."

"It is very hard, Sarah. The doctors in the hospital here think you are not strong enough to bear it. They think you are mad. Are you mad, Sarah?"

"No," said Mr Constantine's doctor before the confused girl could formulate an answer. "She is perfectly sane and rational. I think we should have her washed and take her back to my hospital. Let her rest for a time. Then she can go back to Mrs Pendleton and start work again. I promise you, Mr Constantine, that will be the best medicine anyone could give her."

Two months later, Sarah Fowkes, a little thinner and dressed in severe black, stood in her usual place behind the counter of Mrs Pendleton's shop, selling soaps and perfumes, giving the customers advice when she was required to, otherwise speaking little and smiling less, her face giving nothing of her emotional state away. A few weeks later, she began stealing money, both from Mrs Pendleton and from any customer careless enough to leave her bag unattended. Then a ring disappeared. When challenged, Sarah loudly protested her innocence, saying it was like the last time a woman swore she'd left a ring on the counter, but Nora Pendleton, knowing better, did her best to placate the outraged lady and later, told Mr Constantine she was sorry for the girl, no one could be sorrier, but she had become untrustworthy and would have to go.

Mr Constantine, himself grown shaky since the double tragedy and his wife's impending trial for the murder of the infant Marie Fowkes, thumped his walking stick on the floor and pleaded tearfully for Mrs Pendleton to give the girl another chance. To please him, she did, after warning a non-repentant Sarah it was the only chance she would ever get. For a time things improved and Nora, believing the phase Sarah had gone through was over, was taken completely unawares by her own sudden illness some weeks later. The piercing headache and dizziness she had woken up with persisted as she groped her way down the stairs, through the shop, and on to the pavement where she and Sarah were to pull down the shop blinds against the spattering rain. As her knees gave way and she fell to the ground, the last thing Nora Pendleton was to see in this life was the sudden blaze of triumph that flared in Sarah's dark eyes.

During the years that passed after Mrs Pendleton's sudden death from food poisoning, the business underwent a subtle change. While soaps and perfumes were still being sold in the shop, the treatment rooms upstairs had also become a convenient place for lovers to meet, their assignations arranged through Madame Sarah who, when their rumpling was done and they returned to her red-faced and happy with their adventures, was not above indulging in a little blackmail to increase her fortune. Then, there were the lonely ones, usually widowed in middle age, who watched what there was to see with envy and some hope.

Chapter Six

Prosecuting counsel William Shanklin, shook his head disparagingly at the notes in his hand, returned them to the table at his side while pushing his spectacles even higher up the bridge of his nose, and then spent some little time regarding the witness with a strange mixture of sympathy and exasperation.

"Mrs Tombrin," he said at last. "I want the gentlemen of the jury to be absolutely clear on the point we are making. You are telling this court that you gave a considerable sum of money to Sarah Fowkes on the understanding that the man she introduced to you as Lord Charles Beniton, a man who wrote letters to you which were sometimes signed Thomas and sometimes signed William, had made you an offer of marriage. Am I correct?"

Two spots of red appeared high on Mrs Tombrin's pale cheeks and she bit her thin lower lip before nodding her head in agreement. "Yes sir, that is quite correct."

"And the letters you received from this gentleman ordered you to have a number of quite expensive beauty treatments from this same Sarah Fowkes before the wedding could take place. Is that also correct?"

"In one of the letters I received from Lord Beniton, he asked me to have treatments before our wedding, yes," the witness replied in a low voice.

"But madam," Shanklin protested, with a spread of his hands, "if this be so, do you not think you were somewhat naive in accepting such a proposition?"

Mrs Tombrin hesitated and then said shamefacedly, "Yes sir, the way you have put it all together proves I was naive.

I formed an attachment for a man I understood to be a gentleman of quality and I had been given every possible encouragement to believe he had fallen in love with me. I have been lonely since the death of my husband. I felt the want of companionship and the protection I had become accustomed to enjoying in the past. That is why I closed my eyes to the manner of Lord Beniton's courtship. I hoped things would come right once we were married."

Shanklin waited for her to wipe a tear from her eye and said gently, "It was a laudable ambition, madam, and a very natural one. My aim is to show you were taken advantage of, Mrs Tombrin, not that you are guilty of any wrong-doing. Tell me, when you had paid for the treatments you received, were there any other demands on your purse?"

"Yes there were," Mrs Tombrin replied bitterly. "Most certainly there were more demands upon my purse. Madame Sarah told me she would get together my trousseau for our marriage. I ordered clothes and lace and jewellery and then I executed a bond and gave it to her. The articles were delivered to Madame Sarah's shop and I have never had any of them. I also gave her other sums of money which I understood were to be for the benefit of Lord Charles Beniton. I parted with the money on the representations made to me by Madame Sarah on his behalf."

"Thank you Mrs Tombrin. Now, madam, we know the marriage did not take place. Will you please tell the court what happened to prevent it?"

Mrs Tombrin took a sip of water and drew a shaky breath before saying, "Madame Sarah told me we were to go to a livery stable to select a carriage for my wedding to Lord Beniton. She said it had to be done in good time, so that his coat of arms could be painted on the door panels. It seems I mistook the day she told me we were to go, for when I approached the shop, I saw Madame Sarah on the doorstep talking to my poor dear friend, Mrs Carlisle."

Shanklin raised a hand to stop the flow of words.

"You knew Mrs Carlisle well?" he asked.

"Oh yes sir," Mrs Tombrin hurried on eagerly. "I knew her very well. Our husbands were close friends as well as being fellow administrators. They often shared an office when they were serving Her Majesty's government in India. We two families lived close by in Barrackpore and dined with each other at least once each week. And each year, in the high summer, Florence and I travelled to the hills together as companions. We, too, were very good friends and we shared the sorrow of being widowed within a six-month of each other."

"I see. Thank you very much, Mrs Tombrin, that was a very comprehensive answer. Now madam, you say that you approached the shop on the wrong morning, saw your friend Mrs Carlisle on the doorstep, and she was deep in conversation with Sarah Fowkes. What happened next? Did you greet her?"

"I intended to. I tried to. I was delighted to see dear Florence and started forward to speak to her, but before I could say a word to my friend, I heard Madame Sarah calling out 'Wrong day, you have come on the wrong day'. Then she came across the street and put her arm through mine to turn me away from the shop. As she was attempting to do so, she said again and very loudly, that I had come on the wrong day for my treatment, which was not due until the next Wednesday. I was about to remind her that I had not come for treatment but to go to the livery stables with her to order a coach, when I heard Florence call out for me to congratulate her, for she was soon to be married."

"Mrs Carlisle was soon to be married and so were you," Shanklin said slowly. "What a remarkable coincidence. And did you then go forward to congratulate your friend?"

Mrs Tombrin shook her head. Unable to continue for the moment, she accepted a fresh handkerchief from William Shanklin and spent a moment dabbing at her swollen eyes, before saying miserably, "I was not given the opportunity to say anything at all to Florence Carlisle."

"But Mrs Tombrin, you were within speaking distance of your friend and she had just given you the good news that she was to be married. Why did you not congratulate her and tell her that by a happy chance, you too were about to be married?"

"I meant to do so." Mrs Tombrin screwed up Shanklin's handkerchief in a tight knot. "I withdrew my arm from

Madame Sarah's hold on me and turned to speak to Florence but before I could say a word, Madame Sarah struck me on the face and demanded to know why I had insulted her friend, Mrs Carlisle."

"Sarah Fowkes struck you on the face?" Shanklin looked over his shoulder at the woman in the dock with apparent incredulity before turning back to Mrs Tombrin. "And in what way had you insulted Mrs Carlisle?"

"I had not insulted dear Florence in any way, but before I could say that I had not, Madame Sarah ordered me to stay away from her establishment until I had learned my manners. She then left me and quickly took Mrs Carlisle inside her shop. They were speaking together as they went indoors but I could not hear what was being said."

"Now then, madam," Shanklin said firmly. "You had been struck on the face and prevented from speaking to a friend of some years standing. Did you not follow them into the shop and demand an immediate explanation of Sarah Fowkes's extraordinary behaviour?"

"No, I did not."

"But why did you not follow them? It would seem a very natural thing to do."

"Madame Sarah had struck me very hard on the cheek and the look in her eye when she did so, made me afraid for my safety. I could not see the slightest reason for the way she turned on me and I truly thought she had gone mad. I hailed a hansom and went home."

"I see," Shanklin glanced at Sarah Fowkes again before resuming his questioning with, "And have you visited Madame Sarah's establishment since that day?"

"No sir."

"And have you seen Mrs Carlisle since that day?

"No sir. I know only that she was murdered and I know that wicked woman killed her."

Arnold Roberts, the counsel for defence, began to scramble to his feet and Shanklin raised a hand to prevent him from doing so.

"You may not say that, Mrs Tombrin," he told her gently. "That is an opinion and not a fact. You can only tell the court what you know to be true."

"What I know to be true," Mrs Tombrin said bitterly, "is that that woman is a wicked murderer and richly deserves to be hanged."

Arnold Roberts again bounced to his feet to protest. While a defiant and totally unrepentant Mrs Tombrin was being reproved by the judge, the man sitting in the dock shifted uneasily. It was all very well old Alice having it in for Sarah, Charlie Bennet was thinking, but whatever good she thought she was doing him by it, it wasn't going to work. If Sarah was found guilty, the finger of the jury would be pointing at him too. His neck would get stretched at the same time as hers because he was her accomplice. Everyone would say they were in the business together. Rightly, too. They had been together almost from the moment he went to her shop and asked for the return of Mrs Avery's jewels. The memory of his first meeting with Sarah Fowkes and what it had led to, made him drop his head and become even more afraid of the consequences of murdering Florence Carlisle. Within minutes, the wildness of the thoughts churning through his mind caused Charlie Bennet to close his eyes and begin to caress his aching forehead with trembling fingers.

His fingers had trembled in much the same way on the night he got to Sarah's shop and, finding it locked and bolted against him, used his knuckles to knock on the shuttered door. There was no answer but imagining he could hear some movement from behind the shutters, he rapped harder and almost jumped out of his skin when a woman's voice asked sharply who was out there and what did they mean by knocking people up at this hour? Whoever she was, the woman sounded angry enough to make Charlie want to turn tail and run, but the memory of his boasting to Annie and Mrs Avery stopped him.

"I'm here on behalf of one of your clients, Madame Sarah," he said as firmly as he could. "Mrs Avery sent me to say she is quite certain she mislaid some jewellery when she had treatment on your premises. She is prepared to pay a fair reward to anyone who can find her jewels for her."

"How much of a reward?" asked the voice and Charlie,

now certain that the woman he was speaking to had the jewellery and its return was only a matter of arranging a price, relaxed a little.

"Well now, madam," he said more boldly. "That all depends on how much of the stuff I can take back with me, don't it."

Ignoring his truculence, the woman behind the door said, "All right, I'll have a look around for her. Come back tomorrow morning when the shop is open."

Hearing retreating footsteps, Charlie raised his voice. "I'm sorry," he called out, "but tomorrow morning won't do. The reward is offered because Mrs Avery particularly wants her jewellery back tonight."

The footsteps returned and there came a low chuckle. "Before Mr Avery puts in an appearance, eh?"

"It's as much for your sake as it is for hers, ma'am," Charlie said hastily. "If she is forced to tell him she left her rings and necklace here, it'll be him on your doorstep within the next hour or two, not me. Mrs Avery knows what his temper is like and she wants to save trouble all round."

"All right. Stand back under the street lamp where I can see you."

Charlie stepped backwards into the dim pool of light, while the bolts were being drawn and, when the door was half way open, stared at the shapely figure of the woman standing before him. At first her face was in shadow but when she led the way into the shop and, after closing the door behind them, turned to face him, he almost forgot what he'd come for.

'Gawd above, but she's a beauty,' he thought, licking his suddenly dry lips. His disappointments at Mrs Avery's, what with Annie acting the tease and then with Mrs Avery not going off to the theatre as expected, had left him frustrated and he knew women found him attractive. Squaring his shoulders, he made a slight bow and smiled down at her, preening a little when he could see her appraisal of him was no less thorough.

"Well?" she asked, breaking the silence. "How much is Mrs Avery offering for her valuable jewellery."

"Fifty if it's all there, ma'am," he said, keeping his voice low and looking deep into her long-lashed, almost midnight blue eyes. "Mrs Avery told me you couldn't find them the first time of asking so I would be only too happy to help you search for the pieces. I wouldn't want you to lose your chance of a fat reward."

Sarah smiled briefly. "I wouldn't go upstairs to look in the dressing-table drawer for fifty pounds, never mind starting a search through a building this size. You go back to your friend Mrs Avery and tell her she's out of luck unless she can find two hundred."

Charlie scratched his head and managed to look thoughtful. "I think I might be able to find you a hundred, ma'am. Why don't we have a drink together and talk about it?"

She came closer and he could smell the perfume on her hair. "I said two hundred pounds or you can get out of here. Unless you think you've got something else I might be interested in?"

Charlie's hopes rose and he said fervently, "I do, ma'am. Oh I've got something else I could give you all right."

"I thought your mind was running along that road the minute I clapped eyes on you." Sarah's tone was casual but there was nothing casual about the long points on the pair of scissors in her hand. "So we'll get one thing straight before we talk any more about Mrs Avery and her cheapjack jewels. I've been knocked to the floor by a man one time and I didn't like what he chose to do to me. The next one who tries gets hurt first. Is that understood?"

Charlie stepped back and raised his hands in surrender. "Understood, of course, ma'am. But you said any man who tried to hurt you would get hurt back. I wouldn't have hurt you. I never did any harm to a woman in my life."

"I'm pleased to hear it," said Sarah Fowkes. "Now come into the back parlour and tell me how much that stupid old crow really gave you."

An hour and a half later, Charlie tapped lightly on Mrs Avery's door, put the jewellery into her clutching hands, and had wheedled his way into her bed ten minutes after that. She was tearful, grateful, astonished by the request, and more than willing to let him have his way with her. She was no more attractive to him than when he first met her but it was Sarah's idea for him to do it.

"You get used to having a rumple with the old ones," he could hear her telling him as he almost reluctantly stroked Mrs Avery's flabby breast and trailed his hand down over her stomach to her crotch. Sarah said she had two or three old crones who came in regularly. She told him their tongues were hanging out for a nice bit of meat like he'd got. He had to smile when he kneed Mrs Avery's plump thighs apart, inserted his nice bit of meat, and heard her start to whimper like a puppy. For the sort of money Sarah was talking about paying him, he'd be happy to shove it up anything.

"Oh my dear, dear God!" Mrs Avery almost shrieked when Charlie gripped her heavy buttocks with both hands and pulled her hard against him for his final thrust and throbbing release.

"Oh my dear, dear God," she repeated softly when he relaxed his hold on her and rolled to one side. "Charlie, do you really find me desirable?"

Charlie Bennet lay on his back and looked at the ceiling. "I said I did, didn't I?" he replied. "To tell you the honest truth, I thought I was only sorry for you at first, but once I had met your Madame Sarah and found out what that black hearted woman was doing to make you so unhappy; well, honest to God, Mrs Avery, I wanted to raise my hand and strike her down for it. That's when I knew I must be in love with you and I can prove it too. Your fine friend, Madame Sarah, refused to hand over your jewels for less than two hundred and fifty pounds and rather than have you disappointed again, I went home to get a hundred of my own to make up what you gave me. And you listen here, Mrs Avery, ma'am. I don't want you to even think of giving the money back. It took all my savings but I did it for you because I love you so much."

"Oh my dear, dear man." Mrs Avery smiled softly and raised a hand to caress his shoulder. "All in the one evening, you have brought my jewellery back from that horrid thief and made me feel like a young woman again. You can't possibly ask me to accept your money too. Tomorrow morning, Annie will bring an envelope to the shop for you."

After the lovemaking, her face had grown rosy and her greying hair had become loose and tumbled about her shoulders. Despite the tears in her soft brown eyes, she looked happy enough to be almost pretty.

Charlie leaned over and kissed her full on the lips. 'Silly old goose' he thought almost affectionately, as she threw her arms round his neck and returned the kiss with enthusiasm. 'That Sarah's dead right. This lark is going to be easy money.'

Annie brought him the first wages he earned as a prostitute at eleven thirty the next morning.

"Here's the money and I don't know what you did to the missus," the girl said, laughing up at him as she handed over the sealed package. "My lady was up and singing like a lark this morning. I know she must have been happy to get her jewels back, but she was acting so giddy, I couldn't help thinking something else had happened to her. Come on Charlie Bennet, what did you do to my Mrs Avery?"

Charlie tucked the money away and grinned down at her. "You come back when you're a big, grown-up girl, Annie Barnes, and I might show you."

Annie's smile disappeared as though wiped from her face. In a shocked voice, she almost whispered, "You never did that? Not with a daft old woman like her? I think you're disgusting."

Charlie shrugged as she turned away sharply and began to run down the street. He watched her brush heedlessly by a heavily built woman who stopped to look after her and tut loudly. Charlie held the door open for the generously proportioned woman when she approached him, smiled politely, and murmured, "Good morning madam, and what would madam care to see this morning?" Thinking of all the possible answers she might have given him had she been one of Sarah's customers, made him smile the wider as he led her to a counter and, when she raised her head to look up at him and smile in turn, it was all he could do not to laugh in the silly old cat's face.

His first encounter with one of Madame Sarah's clients took place the following evening. As arranged, he was sitting in the parlour behind the shop, apparently reading his newspaper with great interest, when she walked in with an elderly woman dressed soberly in black. Following instructions, Charlie put down the paper and got to his feet.

"Still here, Mr Bennet?" Sarah said, sounding a little surprised but pleased. "What a happy chance. Now I can introduce you to Mrs Lane. Isabella, my dear, the young scoundrel who stands before you, is Mr Charlie Bennet. He has enough time on his hands to get into all kinds of mischief if someone doesn't keep a stern eye on him. I believe a woman of your experience might do very well for the position of his keeper, don't you?"

"How do you do, Mrs Lane," Charlie said, bowing over the lady's hand. "I hope you'll believe I'm not as bad as Madame Sarah chooses to paint me."

"How do you do, Mr Bennet," Mrs Lane replied with a cool nod. "As to how bad you are, I have always found my friend Sarah a most reliable source of information. I think I will have to watch you very carefully."

Sarah laughed lightly. "In that case, Isabella, my dear, I will leave him in your charge. You can start watching over him as soon as you've a mind to."

Left alone with Isabella Lane, who was small, heavily painted for the occasion, and clearly even older than Mrs Avery, Charlie was not sure what he was supposed to do or say next. Surely she didn't want a rumple with him at her age? She'd likely split in two. He was thinking of the horrified expression on Annie's face when she called him disgusting and turned to run away, when Mrs Lane said coyly. "Madame Sarah tells me you are a very strong young man, Mr Bennet. I remember that my husband would come home from his office so eager for love, he would pick me up in his arms and run with me up the stairs to our bedroom. Do you think you are as strong as my husband?"

Charlie bowed. "And carry you upstairs, Mrs Lane? Why yes, I think I can carry you up to the bedroom if you would like me to."

"I must say I would like that very much."

She smelt faintly musty as he held her against his shoulder. Her eyes were closed and her cold nose nuzzled his cheek as she whispered. "Closer, Mr Bennet, hold me closer to you, my dearest heart."

'Well, would you ever believe such a thing?' Charlie wondered while he carried her up the stairs and into the bedroom Sarah had shown him earlier, 'the randy old bitch is as hot as a griddle cake.'

Isabella Lane was trembling when he helped to unfasten her hooks and ribbons, though whether from desire or fear of what was to come, he couldn't tell. When the last of her undergarments was about to fall to the floor, she clutched them to her and asked him to turn his back while she got into the bed. She lay quite still with the bedclothes drawn up to her chin, watching him strip. He saw her eyes widen when he took off his long underpants, revealing his manhood in much the same way he had once revealed it to Lieutenant Holland. Silently, she moved back the covers to make room for him and, when he lay beside her, he found her to be even tinier than he imagined.

Putting an arm beneath her thin, bony shoulders, he began to gently caress her small breasts and, as he did so, he whispered, "Why, you're not much more than a tiny sparrow, Mrs Lane. Are you sure you want to do this with me? I don't want to hurt you."

"Other men have entered there," she said, pinching his leg, "I should think there's room enough for anything you have to offer."

He tried not to think about the other men who had entered there as he began to earn his money and found that visualising Annie Barnes bumping her fresh little body up and down beneath him helped. His breath became harsher and, as he plunged deeper and deeper into the hot-wet cleft between Isabella Lane's narrow shanks, he was mouthing. "Annie, Annie, Annie, Annie," until with his final plunge, he was spent and looked down to see, instead of the fourteen year old's cheeky grin, Isabella's face beneath him, her painted cheeks blotchy and furrowed, her eyes screwed tight. Shocked, he stayed rigid and staring above her, but when her eyes opened to regard him with some suspicion, he managed to smile warmly and, as Sarah instructed, tell her she was wonderful and it had been like making love to a young girl.

"Really, Mr Bennet?" she asked, some wariness remaining in her eyes.

"You were wonderful," Charlie repeated firmly. "And to tell you the truth, Mrs Lane. If you would allow me a little time to recover myself, I would be more than happy to repeat the exercise."

Convinced, Isabella Lane laughed aloud. "Repeat the exercise?" she crowed happily. "Sarah told me you were once a soldier, Mr Bennet. If I had known sooner how soldiers take their exercise, I would have been an army wife sooner than a banker's."

Charlie laughed with her and put a hand on her thigh, the fingers curled between her legs. "Oh yes ma'am," he whispered in her ear, "that was one of our regular exercises all right and this is how the sergeant major taught us to do one of the others. One two three, one! One two three, one!"

"Stop it! For the love of God, stop it!" Isabella shrieked, clutching at his probing fingers with both hands. "That will be quite enough for today, Mr Bennet. You will just have to contain yourself until we meet again."

"I will if I must," Charlie said passionately as he gathered up his clothes and walked bare arsed to the door, "but you taught me a trick or two today, Isabella Lane, and it isn't going to be easy to wait for the next time."

"Ooh, you naughty man," she was happily simpering when he left the room and closed the door behind him. An hour or so later, he was sitting with his newspaper in Sarah's parlour, when she came in with a tall angular woman at her side.

"Still here Mr Bennet?" she said as he stood up to make his bow. "What a happy chance. Now I can introduce you to Mrs Parker. Mellie, my dear, this is Mr Bennet."

Within a short time, the exercise had become a routine. Four weekly visits to Sarah's shop with one or two of her clients coming in for a rumple on each visit. Charlie smiled warmly at all the various shapes and sizes of women brought into the parlour to be introduced to him. He learned to be gentle with the shy, lonely ones and accept philosophically the scratches and occasional bites from the women who wanted to receive and give back rougher treatment. Whoever they were, once he was in bed with one of them, he acted on Sarah's instruction to make her feel she was the only woman he could ever want to be with. Kissing them full on their lips, rousing them by stroking their breasts and loins, his only curiosity being the size and plumpness of the buttocks he hefted towards himself when he entered them. In time, Charlie Bennet became a practised lover. Without the slightest idea of who lay beneath him, he worked each of them into a frenzy while he thought of rumpling little Annie Barnes until her back teeth rattled or, when he dared, doing the same or more to Sarah Fowkes.

He never knew what the ladies paid Sarah for his services. She gave him ten pounds for each evening he was there, which, in his book, made him a very wealthy man. He made the mistake of giving up his situation at Montague's, as much to avoid the attentions of Mrs Harries as for any other reason, and soon found time hanging heavy on his hands. His lodgings in Baker Street were cheap and plain. He bought some new furniture and curtains to make himself comfortable and found that apart from clothes and the occasional visit to the barber shop, there was very little else to spend his money on. His experience when he sold Holland's shirts to an East End pawnbroker and was dragged out of a public bar to get beaten up in an alley, had kept him off drinking alone and, since leaving the army, he had made no new friends. His solitary visits to the music hall and theatres, though enjoyable enough for an evening, soon began to pall and if he couldn't have Annie Barnes or Sarah Fowkes, the last thing in the world he wanted was the company of another woman. In his increasing isolation, he began to think back to his time as Mr Holland's batman with real affection and had almost decided to change his name, re-enlist in another regiment, and take the chance to see the world as a serving soldier, when he received a proposal of marriage.

Taken completely by surprise, he lifted his head from the woman's fleshy shoulder and said, "Would you say that again please, Mrs Walsh?"

Fanny Walsh, who until that moment had been yet another Annie for him to ravage, smiled up at him nervously.

"The last time we were together in this bed, Mr Bennet," she said hesitantly, "you made me think you were growing

e

fond of me. Whether or not that is so, I have become very fond of you. If you want another reason for my suggestion that we should marry, it has always been my ambition to travel but I would be terrified of travelling alone. I think we might suit each other very well as husband and wife."

Charlie sat up in the bed and looked at her properly. She was, like the majority of the women Sarah introduced him to, plain and well on the wrong side of forty, but she must have taken a real fancy to him if she had been thinking about getting married. And by chance, he'd only been thinking the night before about how much he wanted to see the world.

"I said I like you and I wouldn't lie to a lady about a thing like that," he replied eagerly, bearing in mind Sarah's injunction to tell them anything they want to hear. "To tell you the honest truth, Mrs Walsh, I would marry you in a minute, but I can't afford to take you travelling. Not on my sort of money."

Fanny put a hand on his chest and looked up at him. "I am well provided for, Mr Bennet," she said simply. "My funds will take us anywhere we want to go."

"Let me think about it," said Charlie. "I'd like to get married too, especially to you, Mrs Walsh, but it's a big step to take."

Before she could speak again, he pulled the bedclothes back and began to caress her body. She wasn't young but the breasts he stroked were firm, the nipples rosy and erect beneath his fingers. The belly his hand slid down when her breathing quickened and became uneven, was smooth and gently rounded down to where he could feel the curl of her pubic hair and the swell of her heavy thighs. Annie Barnes for once forgotten, he became eager for sex with Fanny Walsh.

"Oh Fanny," he murmured as he entered her hard and she grunted her response as she began to move with and for him and call him her dearest love. "Fanny, Fanny, Fanny."

Marrying the woman was an impossible idea, of course. When Charlie told Sarah about it later on in the evening, he expected her to laugh and make some sarcastic remark about the randy old cow fancying herself as a bride, but she didn't.

Instead, she looked at him thoughtfully and said. "Don't refuse her. Not yet anyway. Let her think you're ready to go along with it and tell her you'll visit her at home and have a talk about it. There's money to be made here."

"I'm not stealing nothing from her house," Charlie replied, thinking of Mrs Avery's jewels. "I don't want any of that sort of aggravation, thank you."

Sarah gave him a sideways glance. "I never said you should steal anything from her house, did I? There's easier ways of making money out of these women than lifting a few gew-gaws."

Charlie shook his head vehemently. "What I do for them ain't any bloody easier. You should just see 'em at it," he declared with enough feeling to force a reluctant smile from Sarah. Encouraged, he got to his feet and grinned back. "I'm not saying it would be hard work with you, Miss Sarah. I think it would be wonderful with you." But Sarah Fowkes was not listening.

"Love letters," she said thoughtfully. "That ought to do it. Tell her you're willing to marry her soon and we'll get her to write you some love letters."

At his suggestion, he visited Mrs Walsh the following Wednesday at three o'clock in the afternoon.

"I thought it would be nice for us to relax over a cup of tea and perhaps a slice of cake before we talk," she said after she took his coat and hat and moved into his arms for a kiss. "I sent my servants out for the afternoon. We won't be disturbed."

"That will be capital, thank you," said Charlie, sitting on a low sofa and stretching his long legs out before him. Looking around the heavily furnished room appreciatively, he added, "I say, Mrs Walsh, this is the life, isn't it."

Mrs Walsh shrugged. "You must call me Fanny and I'm very glad you think so. It's been a terribly lonely life for me, these past four years."

At once he was by her side. Primed by Sarah, he took her plump hand in his own and said eagerly, "I know, but it doesn't have to go on being lonely, Fanny. I've thought over what you said to me and if you still want us to get married, I'll be very proud to be your husband."

Fanny Walsh looked at him doubtfully. "Yes, certainly I want us to be married, but I've been thinking too. I have no illusions about my appearance and there is some considerable difference in our ages. Charlie, my heart has been broken once before by a gentleman who protested his love for me. If, like him, you are merely fortune hunting, you will be treating me cruelly. Most cruelly."

She turned her head away and looked down. Charlie raised her hand and spread the fingers to kiss them one by one.

"Fortune hunting?" he repeated, and was about to say that marriage to a woman like her would be fortune enough but, remembering Sarah's injunction not to spread the butter too thick to be swallowed, he said quietly, "I suppose I am fortune hunting in a way. Being given the chance to live in a beautiful house like this and to travel the world with you, would be like winning a fortune by gambling on the tables to an ordinary man like me. As to the rest of it. I know I'm a little younger than you but as I told you, I like you very much. Fanny, I do think we would be happy together."

"Would we, Charlie?" she asked, turning quickly to look into his eyes. "I can't tell you how much I want to believe we will be happy."

He looked at her plump, heavy jowls and baggy eyes and assured her they would be as happy as a man and wife could be.

'It will be like having a pet mastiff,' he was thinking when he took her again in his arms and, by the time he went back to report the conversation to Sarah, Fanny Walsh and he had spent more than an hour in her bed where, between their kissing and love-making, they agreed to marry quietly in three months time.

For the following two or three weeks, Charlie Bennet became a regular afternoon visitor to Fanny's home but, after telling her that pressure of business prevented him from seeing her as often as he would like, he stayed away for days at a time and letters were exchanged instead. Letters in which they poured out their love and their need for each other. Regrettably and inevitably, in addition to achieving the desired effect of having a neat bundle of Fanny's letters locked away in Sarah's dressing-table drawer, his absences were making his fiancée suspicious. After receiving some very evasive answers in return to her questions, Fanny Walsh took to watching Madame Sarah's shop from the far corner of Beak Street. On the next occasion Charlie called on her, there was no tea tray on the small table that stood by the sofa and she stepped back when he attempted to take her in his arms.

"Fanny?" he said, dropping his arms awkwardly to his sides. "Fanny my dear, is there anything wrong?"

"Of course something is wrong," she said bitterly, "when a woman must wait two weeks to see the man she is to marry and then finds he has been spending his time in Madame Sarah's shop."

"But I wrote to you. Surely you got my letters?"

"Letters are cold comfort when I must read them knowing you are in bed with one of your other women."

"But Fanny," he protested. "It's nothing like that."

"Is it not?" Fanny replied. "Then what were you doing there all yesterday afternoon and evening?"

"That's good," said Sarah, when he reported the conversation to her. "It's time the matter came to a head. Go back tomorrow and tell her that, in view of her suspicions, you now know you cannot make her happy. For her sake, you intend to release her from the engagement. Then you can tell her you would like to have your letters returned and that you intended to return hers like any gentleman should, but they've disappeared from your writing desk. Say you suspect me of having purloined them. Tell her I've been behaving very oddly since you became engaged to marry her and stopped serving my clients. You can also tell her that I seem to have got very spiteful and jealous. You think I might want paying for the letters. There's no need to mention any particular sum of money."

Charlie squared his shoulders while he stood on Fanny Walsh's doorstep, waiting for her to open the door. The last afternoon he had spent with her had been most uncomfortable and he looked forward to telling her the engagement was over. For her part, Fanny narrowed her eyes and started to nag at him the moment he walked into the drawing-room, asking which of his women he had been with before deigning to pay his fiancée a visit. But when, instead of his usual protestations of innocence, he merely waited for her to finish what she was saying, her voice faltered and began to die away.

"Well?" she asked at last, in a voice which revealed a genuine heartbreak. "What have you got to say to me? Why have you become so cold-hearted?"

"I don't think I can make you happy any more," Charlie began, but before he could continue she threw her arms round him and sobbed.

"No Charlie, please. Please don't say you mean to leave me now. It's too cruel. I can't live if I lose you. Don't you see it's only the fear of losing you that makes me say the things I do?"

Half smothered by her grip, Charlie paid scant attention to her words. Continuing the rehearsed speech, he asked for the return of his letters and told her about the problem of her own letters being missing, probably held by Sarah, who had become jealous. He hardly noticed her release him and begin to listen more carefully. He had just got to telling her about Sarah probably wanting money, when Fanny said, "Blackmail. I suppose I should have known. The pair of you are in it together."

She pushed him away and, facing him squarely, said with quiet venom, "You are dirt and so is your henchwoman. But you can go back and tell her your attempt to blackmail me has been a waste of time. What do I care what you do with my letters or who might publish them? The two of you can't hurt me any more than you already have. You'll get no money from me, not now or ever. You had best get out of my house now, before I strike you."

Charlie blinked at her nervously. Knowing the plot had somehow gone wrong but unwilling to leave the thing up in the air, he said hastily, "But Fanny, you don't understand. Those letters were private. Between you and me. I'm sure I can lay my hands on them for you."

"I'm quite sure you can, for a price," Fanny said, her

face blotchy with emotion and her voice strained. "I don't want them. I have asked you to leave my house."

"No, wait just a minute . . . "

There was no time for Charlie to say more. Fanny Walsh, a little short of his height but a good deal broader and heavier, had clenched her fists and begun raining blows on his head and shoulders.

"For the love of Jesus!" he yelped as he fell back against the door and raised his hands to protect his face, "Fanny, for God's sake, stop it. You're hurting me!"

"Good. I want to hurt you," she was gasping breathlessly while she followed him and continued to punch at his head. In genuine fear of being hurt, he shot out a hand to grab a flailing fist and succeeded only in hitting her shoulder. Spinning round, Fanny Walsh lost balance and, before the horrified man could do anything to prevent it, tottered and fell heavily by the fireplace. To lay still, her breathing stentorian, and her eyes tightly closed.

"Oh my gawd," groaned Charlie, dropping to his knees beside her and taking her hand to pat it. "Fanny, get up. I didn't mean to hurt you." But Fanny Walsh's eyes remained closed. Her teeth, locked tight on her tongue, became red and dribbled blood from the corner of her part open mouth, and her face had become florid. Not knowing what else to do, he was continuing to pat her hand and wait for her to recover her senses, when her heavy breathing became a series of short grunting snores and stopped.

Some fifteen minutes later, a badly shaken, ashen faced Charlie Bennet sat in Sarah's parlour, she listening quietly enough while he gabbled his story. Over and again, he told her that he hadn't meant for Fanny to fall down and get hurt. He was only trying to save himself from getting a walloping. Now she was dead on the floor. When he began to repeat the story for the fourth or fifth time, Sarah leaned across the table and slapped him hard across the face.

"Did you remember to pick up the letters you wrote before you came away from the house?" she asked in the total silence that followed the slap. "We don't want the policemen coming round here asking silly questions, do we?"

Charlie put a trembling hand to his cheek and stared at

her. "I-I didn't think about the letters," he stammered. "She was dead. I told you she was dead. When I saw her stop breathing, I ran away."

Sarah sniffed. "Then you'll have to run back and get the letters, won't you. You said she gives her servants the rest of the day off whenever you're there. They won't be back to find her for an hour or two yet."

Charlie staggered to his feet, his face distorted with fear. "Go back inside that house? I couldn't do it, Madame Sarah. I could never go back and look at her again."

Sarah Fowkes got to her feet, took the lapels of his coat in both fists and shook him hard.

"You are going back to get those letters, Charlie Bennet," she said very distinctly as she released him. "And to make sure you do it right this time, I'm coming with you."

Chapter Seven

William Shanklin fluttered through his sheaf of papers for the last time, thanked Mrs Tombrin for the clear manner in which she gave her evidence, told her he had no further questions for her at this time but she might be recalled by him, and asked her to stay in the witness-box for the benefit of his learned friend, Mr Arnold Roberts, who also had the right to question her.

"Now then, Madam," Shanklin added with a smile, "there is absolutely no need for you to fear Mr Roberts. You know you have told the truth and counsel for the defence can only bully you if you allow him to."

"Really, my lord!" protested Arnold Roberts as he scrambled to his feet. "He turns the witness against me and I have not yet spoken a word to her."

William Shanklin bobbed up again. "My lord," he said, twitching anxiously at his robe. "Mrs Tombrin is a lady of excellent reputation who feels she has suffered much at the hands of the prisoners in the dock. I would not have her further humiliated by unfair and painful questioning without at least warning her of the defence's probable tactics."

Arnold Roberts threw his notes on the table and his hands in the air. "My lord, this simply will not do! If I cannot ask pertinent questions before the witness is instructed in how to answer them, how can your lordship conduct a fair trial?"

"I am sorry, my lord," Shanklin interrupted with a disarming smile and bow. "I was merely trying to assist you."

"You, Mr Shanklin, will assist me best by sitting down," said the judge, and turning to Arnold Roberts, added acidly, "and you sir, will assist me best by asking your questions and leaving the conduct of the trial to me."

Roberts bowed and gave up the unequal struggle with a muttered, "As your lordship pleases." He then turned to a wary Mrs Tombrin and said, "Madam, I hope you know that you have no reason to fear me."

"I know I am guilty of no wrong-doing, whatever you may say to the contrary."

The counsel smiled and said placatingly, "Now, now, my dear Mrs Tombrin, you know perfectly well that no such suggestion has been made. Let me first ask you one or two questions about the man in the dock. The man who you have testified, made you an offer of marriage because he had fallen deeply in love with you."

"He wrote a letter to me saying he loved me."

"So you have said to this court. Now, Mrs Tombrin, let us look at this young man as he sits in the dock. He is on trial for his life and in my opinion, he looks as worried and drawn as a man could possibly be. I put it to you, Mrs Tombrin, that at this moment we are seeing Charles Bennet at his worst? Would you agree with me?"

Mrs Tombrin looked dutifully at Charlie's bowed head and shoulders and said sulkily, "He does not look well. Are you blaming me for that?"

"Quite so," said Shanklin, getting to his feet. "My lord, I can see no purpose in the question."

"Mr Roberts?" asked the judge.

"I merely want the witness to estimate his age, my lord."

"To what end?"

"To point to the unlikelihood of his alleged proposal of marriage, my lord."

The judge shook his head doubtfully but waved to Roberts to carry on.

"Thank you my lord. Now Mrs Tombrin, despite his cares, Mr Bennet seems quite young to me. I would say about thirty years of age. Would you agree with my estimate?"

"Yes, I imagine so."

Arnold Roberts smiled at the witness and briskly rubbed

his hands as though they needed warming. "Thank you Mrs Tombrin, we are in full agreement thus far. I am certain we will get along famously. Now madam, we come to question two. Would you think it impertinent of me to ask your age? A rough approximation will do."

Mrs Tombrin flushed angrily. "I should think it most impertinent and ungentlemanly of you to ask such a question and I will not answer it. I was married for twenty-three years when my husband passed away and that was three years ago."

"I must apologise for any offence I may have caused you, Mrs Tombrin. That will do very well for an answer. Now ma'am, according to our agreed estimate, when you married your husband twenty-six years ago, the defendant was not much more than a babe in arms. I would respectfully suggest you are nearer the age to be a mother to Mr Bennet than his bride."

"Lord Beniton made me an offer," Mrs Tombrin said stiffly. "He wrote me a letter saying he loved me and he wanted to be married."

"Ah yes, the letters. He wrote a letter telling you he loved you, he wrote a letter ordering you to give money to Sarah Fowkes, and he wrote yet another letter to say you would be the recipient of his mother's jewels. That is what you have told this court, is it not?"

"Yes it is. That is what he wrote in his letters to me."

Roberts looked about the court as though in search of something and then said, "But where is the proof of these letters, Mrs Tombrin? Why were they not bound in a pink satin ribbon and kept beneath your pillow as I understand lover's letters invariably are? You have not produced a single letter signed in his or any other name."

"Madame Sarah kept the letters and I explained the reason for the different signatures."

But madam, you have not explained the reason to my satisfaction. In all my many years at the bar, I have never heard of a woman cheerfully handing over anything as personal as a love letter to a third party for safe-keeping. I have to tell you now, Mrs Tombrin, that unless you produce a piece of correspondence you can prove to be Mr Bennet's handiwork, you will not have proved the existence of the letters to the jury's satisfaction either."

Sarah Fowkes was forced to bite the inside of her cheek. Even in the present circumstances, it was difficult to prevent a sardonic smile from reaching her lips. Writing letters that couldn't be traced back to her and Charlie was a lesson learned the hardest way imaginable. It was taught to her on the night she dragged Charlie along the poorly lit back streets of Pimlico in their hurried return to Fanny Walsh's house. They had to recover the letters written to Fanny before the dead woman's servants returned. Letters bearing Charlie's signature and the protestations of love that would almost certainly incriminate them the moment the body was found. When they got to the house and found that Charlie had allowed the front door to slam behind him as he made his escape, she made him break a side window to let them in.

They walked quickly through the hall, Charlie stopping dead outside the drawing-room and looking at Sarah with pleading eyes. Ignoring the plea, she opened the door without hesitation and pulled him through to see the fire had burned low. In the flickering light, Fanny Walsh, who had no mark on her apart from a thin streak of dried blood on the side of her chin, could have been asleep. Sarah looked down at the body without curiosity, turned away to glance round the room, and asked, "Do you know where she kept your letters?"

"No I don't," Charlie whispered hoarsely, his eyes averted.

Sarah laughed acidly. "You're not in church and I don't suppose your sweetheart can hear what we're saying about her. You get upstairs and look for her writing desk and if there's a cash box in it, bring that too. I'm going to look down here. And be sharp, will you? We don't want any of the servants walking in on us."

The search through the rooms, hurried through in about ten minutes, produced nothing. An increasingly panicky Charlie brought down some papers and money he found in Fanny's dressing-table drawer, but there was no desk and the letters were nowhere to be found.

"Then there's only one thing left to be done," Sarah said firmly. "You get that fire built up."

While Charlie, after a puzzled look at her, emptied the brass coal scuttle and poked at the fire till it began to roar up the chimney, she picked up a lamp from a side table and opened the oil reservoir to spill most of the contents over Fanny's skirts, the nearby plush covered sofa, and the bottom of the curtains. After which, she splashed the remaining oil in the fireplace and threw the lamp hard down on to the floor by Fanny's side. Waiting only to be sure the flames were spreading fast, Sarah took Charlie's arm and dragged the horrified man to the front door.

Chalk faced, trembling, and in no fit state to go back to his rooms in Baker Street, Charlie spent the night in the bedroom usually reserved for sex with Sarah's customers. Several times during the long dark hours, he started up from a fitful doze, remembering that Fanny Walsh, who he had last seen with flames licking at her boots and skirts, had been one of them. The following morning, unshaven and with bloodshot, haunted eyes, he walked heavily into the kitchen and slumped in a chair. Sarah, as fresh and darkly beautiful as ever, scowled at him.

"You're not going to be much use to my ladies if you can't make yourself look more presentable than that," she snapped. "You'd best have a cup of tea and then get back upstairs and clean yourself up. Here, while you drink it, have a look at this."

Charlie gulped at the tea and picked up the newspaper. 'Horrible conflagration in Pimlico', he read, 'Yesterday afternoon, it is reported, a lady died in a gruesome accident in Pimlico. The unfortunate victim, named by our correspondent as Mrs Fanny Walsh, a widow well known and respected in the neighbourhood in which she resided, was found dead and horribly disfigured by a fire which partly consumed her body. The discoverer, Mrs Amy Wheeler, who was employed as Mrs Walsh's cook housekeeper, returned home at six o'clock last night to prepare her mistress's supper. Mrs Wheeler, who had been visiting her sister during the afternoon, let herself in through the back door and immediately smelled smoke. On hurrying upstairs she found the sitting-room ablaze and her mistress dead among the flames, a broken lamp on the floor by her side. Mrs Walsh, who according to the cook, had been showing signs of considerable strain and distress recently, evidently had a fainting fit and had fallen into the fireplace, the lamp she held breaking and spilling its contents as she did so.

'From Mrs Wheeler's observations, it would seem that a quantity of spilled oil reached the fire in the grate and the flames which leapt out to meet the unhappy Mrs Walsh, found her lying helpless before them. Although the outside of the building is not much damaged, most of the inside rooms and both the main and the servant's staircases are virtually burned out. So far as can be ascertained, no other person was on the premises at the time of the unfortunate accident and, after a thorough investigation by Inspector Stephens of the Metropolitan Police, we are able to report that foul play is not suspected.'

"So there you are, Charlie Bennet," said Sarah, after she watched him read it through twice. "Thanks to me, you wriggled off the hook this time. You lost your head and caused the death of that woman and no one will ever know you did it." Charlie felt he could have said it was thanks to her, he got involved with Fanny Walsh and wrote the stupid bloody letters in the first place, but at that moment the relief was so great, he could not speak. For one thing, he had spent the better part of his night expecting a loud knock on the outside shutters, the heavy tread of policemen's boots on the stair, and the rattle of the chains he'd be led off to the gallows in.

The knowledge he had escaped a summary execution was almost too much for him. Drawing a deep, shaky breath, he pushed away the newspaper as though it too, was contaminated by the death of Fanny Walsh, and dropped his head in his hands. Through a strange jumble of noises in his head, he listened to Sarah Fowkes telling him of the mistakes he had made and what a waste of her time the whole business had been. When she had done with scolding, she told him how different it would be when the next old biddy who looked like falling in love with him, came along.

When that happened, she said softly, he was going to be the one to suggest marriage. Nor would there be any more stupid letters going backwards and forwards. None that were written in his hand anyway.

She had another brilliant idea too. Thanks to his army officer, he could speak well enough when he chose. The next time they got the chance, he was going to be Lord Bennet, down on his luck and looking for a chance to pass on his title to a wealthy wife. Who would, of course, be expected to rescue his lordship's impoverished estates before the wedding could take place. The old crones would jump at the chance of becoming Lady Bennet and by the time they find out they'd been made fools of, they'll be glad enough to forget the money they paid over and keep quiet about it. And if there was one that said she wouldn't keep quiet, she'd better look out for herself because she'd have Sarah Fowkes to deal with and no one gets the better of Sarah Fowkes. Not any more.

While an enthusiastic Sarah put the memory of Fanny Walsh behind her and spoke about her schemes and the fortune they were going to make, Charlie raised his head dully to look at her. She sat on the other side of the table, her hands clasped round a raised knee, her head thrown back to show the long line of her throat and her lovely profile. Quite suddenly, he realised he no longer lusted after her. What she wanted him to do to these women terrified him and at that moment, he wanted nothing so much as to put his hands round that perfect throat and rid himself of her forever. While he stared and tensed as though preparing to attack, Sarah turned her head and smiled brilliantly at him.

"Bennet isn't going to do it for us," she said, her eyes sparkling with laughter. "It's nothing like gentlemanly enough. We'll make you a Beniton. Lord Charles Beniton and you'd best remember to stick to the smart way of talking you learnt."

Amelia Hinks was a thin, almost emaciated, spinster who lost her mother when she was nine years old. She had been cared for by a succession of more or less well-meaning aunts until she, in her turn, was called on to care for her father when he retired from the army. Being kept by the Colonel on what he called short rations and a pretty damn tight rein, she always assumed they were poor but when he died, she found herself the sole owner of a large estate in Sussex and the possessor of a considerable sum of money she had no idea what to do with.

Abraham Newman, the country solicitor who told her of her good fortune, and a man almost as unworldly as herself, suggested to the suddenly terrified Amelia that it might be best if she let herself be taken in hand by a sensible lady. One who could advise her on dress and manners. Not some wild amateur who would simply help her spend money to no avail, but a professional lady who would charge a fair price for introducing her to society and teaching her how to make the best advantage of her new situation. For example, he told her, there was an interesting advertisement in the *Daily Telegraph* of that very morning. One that his lady wife, Mrs Newman, had told him she meant to cut out for her own future reference. He unfolded the newspaper, turned it towards Amelia, and indicated the place with a bony, ink-stained, forefinger.

"Here it is, Miss Hinks," he said. "I would think the help of this lady is the very thing you need." Amelia, who was nearly fifty years old and had spent most of her adult evenings darning by the dim light of a single, turned down oil lamp or a candle, peered shortsightedly at the advertisement. It began 'I can make you beautiful for life'.

"My dear Miss Hinks," Sarah said when Amelia first visited her and was ushered into the parlour to take tea, "my clients are not permitted to apologise for their appearance or their unworldliness. I am here to help ladies like yourself." She put out a hand to touch Amelia's thin, sallow cheek. "You already have the benefit of a fine skin and good bones. It will give me a good deal of personal satisfaction to help you become a lady others will admire. A woman of charm, who will not only be beautiful for the rest of her life, but will also be welcome among the leading members of London society. Many of whom, I'm happy to tell you, Miss Hinks, I number among my closest friends." She touched Amelia's cheek once more and gently traced the soft little jaw-line with a finger. "You see, my dear Amelia, I like you already and in no time at all, you will grow to like me and we shall be firm friends. I am a woman who will do anything for her friends."

Amelia blinked nervously and, almost twisting her fingers in a knot, said in as determined a voice as she could manage, "You are very kind, Madame Sarah. I would indeed treasure a friend like you but I hope you will not let our friendship get in the way of our business arrangement. I am fully able to pay you for your kind attentions."

"I know that you are, my dear," Sarah beamed at her, "and it's very good and sensible of you to remind me of it. Sometimes I meet a lady I take such a great fancy to, I quite forget I am keeping a shop."

"I shall not let you forget it in my case," said Amelia, sufficiently relaxed to return the smile and show her dingy teeth.

"What a sweet smile you have, Amelia," Sarah laughed. "It really lights up your face. My dear girl, you must always smile. That's the way to catch a man and keep him."

Amelia blushed to the roots of her hair. "A man," she whispered incredulously. "Oh, my dear Madame Sarah, what on earth would I do with a man? I should be terrified of him."

She met the tall, fair-haired young gentleman on her third visit to Madame Sarah's establishment. He raised his hat when they were introduced, bowed over her hand with a murmuring greeting, and left.

"I have never met a lord before," Amelia said, more than a little worried. "Should I have curtsied?"

"Certainly not to Lord Beniton, my dear," Sarah said dismissively. "He's of no importance at all. The poor young man hasn't a penny."

"Oh dear. And he has such a noble face. I pity him if he is impoverished."

"My dear Amelia, offering pity to a stranger proves how

good natured you are, but I wouldn't waste your sympathy on Charles Beniton. Nor, I suggest, should you have too much to do with him. He is on the lookout for a wealthy wife who he hopes will restore his family fortune and all he has to offer in return is his title and his mother's jewellery."

"His mother's jewellery?" Amelia raised her eyebrows. "But how very intriguing. Why can't he sell the jewellery if money is such a problem?"

"My question exactly and it seems he cannot bring himself to do so. He said it was his mother's dying wish that he should marry and present her jewel box to her unknown but beloved daughter, the new Lady Beniton."

"How romantic you make it all sound," sighed Amelia Hinks, who a few weeks earlier would hardly have known the meaning of the word.

The next time she called on Madame Sarah, she had an appointment to take a bath. An experience she enjoyed more perhaps than she should, for the bath water was heavily scented and Sarah, in her attendance, was very free with her hands. Amelia, who had never been touched so intimately before, closed her eyes and had some difficulty in controlling her breathing and keeping herself from responding to the gently insistent fingering without a moan of pure animal pleasure. At last it was over. Dressed in her new evening gown, to make quite certain of the fit, and with her face delicately painted by Sarah, who went downstairs ahead of her, she walked into the shop and found Lord Beniton, who was also formally dressed, sitting by the counter.

Apparently not seeing her enter, he frowned and said unhappily, "It really is the most confounded nuisance, Sarah. I went to no end of trouble to arrange this evening and now my cousin has let me down. I think it's too bad of her, I really do."

"Your cousin has a fever, Lord Beniton," Sarah replied coldly. "You can hardly blame her for not feeling well enough to go to the theatre. The poor girl can hardly be looking her best."

"But what in Heaven's name am I to do? I hate to dine alone and where's the pleasure in seeing a show on one's own?"

Sarah shrugged her elegant shoulders. "Then you had best tear up your tickets, my dear young man, and stop making such a fuss about them."

"Oh very well. It seems a great pity, but if I must."

Charlie, contriving to look miserable, took an envelope from an inside pocket and held it between his fingers, preparatory to tearing it across.

"No, Beniton, stop a moment," said Sarah, looking at Amelia, who stood hesitating in the doorway. "I have such a splendid idea."

"Pardon?" asked Charlie, looking up and getting to his feet to make a bow as the blushing Miss Hinks came a little further into the shop. "What idea?"

"Here is a lady who might have the evening free, and if there's one thing I do know about you, Charles Beniton, it's that I can rely on you to behave towards her like a gentleman if she will condescend to accompany you."

"To dinner at Romano's and the show at the Novelty?" Charlie said, while he too gazed at the suddenly scarlet-faced Amelia. "Oh surely not. It would be too much to ask."

"You could find the courage to try before you tear up your silly reservations, couldn't you?"

"That's true, I suppose."

Charlie crossed the shop floor and took Amelia's trembling hand in his. "My dear Miss Hinks," he said, not relinquishing her fingers. "I have a splendid table for dinner and two reservations for the theatre and thanks to my cousin's very inconvenient ill health, no companion to share it with. Won't you please take pity on me, Miss Hinks? I would count it a very great kindness if you were to do so."

Amelia, desperately wanting to go with him but not daring to say yes, looked helplessly at Sarah, who smiled back at her and said, "I should go, my dear, if only to spare me another fit of his sulks. Make sure he gives you an excellent dinner and if you find the theatre a bore, insist on being taken home at once. That will teach him a lesson."

"Very well," said Amelia in a high, frightened voice. "If Lord Beniton wishes me to accompany him, I shall be most happy to do so."

"Now I call that jolly kind of you, Miss Hinks," Charlie said warmly. "The evening's saved. Or will be if you drop this Lord Beniton stuff and call me Charles. You will call me Charles, won't you?" He smiled and gently squeezed Amelia's fingers, making her blush more furiously than ever.

"If you wish me to do so, Charles," she whispered meekly.

For Amelia, the evening passed in an agony of fear and joy as she sat opposite the handsome young Lord Beniton in the restaurant, trying to nibble her food and sip the wine he chose for her as elegantly as the bare shouldered, almost, she thought, bare breasted young women she saw at the tables round her. Some of whom eyed her in turn, doubtless envying Amelia her handsome and attentive companion. The play at the theatre meant little enough to her but she enjoyed watching Charles throw back his head and laugh and from time to time, enjoyed even more the light pressure of his hand on her arm and hearing him whisper in her ear, "Jolly clever that, don't you think, Amelia?" Once, she turned her head to answer and, feeling his beautifully golden moustache brush her cheek, saw the blue of his eyes and the nearness of his lips. Light-headed from the heady red wine she drank at dinner, Amelia Hinks had to fight an inner battle to stop herself swaying towards him.

"I don't think I've enjoyed an evening more or had a more delightful companion," Charlie told Amelia when he took her back to her rooms in Beale Street. "I will tell you the truth, Miss Amelia, even if you think me wicked for it. I'm quite pleased my cousin decided to become ill and take to her bed. I just hope you don't feel you have wasted your time. You must be keeping very occupied while you are in London."

"Only on some financial matters to do with my father's estate and my visits to Madame Sarah," she replied shyly. "I have to tell you, Charles, this has been my first ever meal in a restaurant and my first visit to a real theatre."

"And the first evening you've spent with me," Charlie said warmly. "My goodness, what a lot of firsts. I hope there'll be more of all of them."

"You are very good to say so, Charles, and it has been very

exciting for me, but tonight's outing was due to your cousin's illness and I hope the lady soon recovers her health. I am a very simple countrywoman brought up in a small Sussex town. Hardly a fitting companion for Lord Beniton, I think."

Charles Beniton raised his eyebrows. "Did you not say you enjoyed the evening?"

"It was a wonderful evening," Amelia Hinks said wistfully. "One I shall remember for the rest of my life."

"My dear Amelia," Charlie said when he left her on her doorstep. "I'm quite sure I shall remember it too."

Amelia Hinks put the back of the hand he kissed against her cheek while she stood at her window to watch him hail a cab and be driven smartly away. When she got into her narrow bed and pulled the bedclothes fully up to her chin, she could not help but turn her face into the pillow and cry herself to sleep for her wasted life.

The following morning Madame Sarah greeted Amelia with a kiss on her cheek. "You've just missed Lord Beniton," she announced cheerfully. "And I must say you are a clever woman to have left him so confused. I don't think that young man is likely to trouble you again."

"C-confused?" stammered Amelia. "But how so? I made myself as agreeable as I possibly could and as far as I could tell, he enjoyed the evening."

"There you are and that's the point of it!" Sarah laughed and put her hands on Amelia's shoulders to give her a gentle shake. "He enjoyed the evening very much indeed. He thought you enjoyed it too until you told him you wouldn't waste time on him again and ordered him to wait until his cousin's health improves."

"But Sarah, I told him only that I was a countrywoman and not fitted for society as he would understand it. In any case, I was quite sure it was only politeness that made him suggest we might go to the theatre again."

Sarah dropped her hands from Amelia's shoulders and led the way into the parlour. Pouring her a cup of tea, she said, "Oh dear, I think perhaps I frightened you off the man. I had no idea you would take me so seriously."

"I-I don't think I understand."

"My dear Amelia, when I told you Lord Beniton was

merely a fortune hunter I did you both an injustice. With my help, you are becoming an exceedingly attractive woman. Charles Beniton has fallen in love with you and if you seek happiness, it doesn't do to be too cautious in these matters. You might let your chances slip by you."

Amelia put down her cup and was forced to search in her cuff for a handkerchief. "Sarah," she said through her tears, "last night was the happiest evening I have had in my lifetime. I cannot believe that Lord Beniton could have felt any more than a passing attraction for me but if he allowed me to, I should be his willing slave for life."

"Then I should dry your eyes and keep your London rooms a few weeks longer," Sarah said, taking Amelia's hand and starting to play with her fingers. "I can smell a great romance coming for you, Mistress Hinks, and there's nothing I like better than playing Cupid."

The next time Charlie and Amelia went out together, he took her to Richmond and they sat side by side on the river bank, companionably eating a packed lunch of cold chicken and ham while they watched the small boats criss crossing the Thames as their sails caught and lost the gusting breezes. Amelia was watching one craft heel over and almost capsize, when Charlie caught her hand and pressed it, first against his heart, and then to his lips.

"I love you so much, Melly," he said despairingly. "If my father had not squandered the family fortune, I swear I would beg you to marry me at once. The truth is, my dearest, I cannot. Perhaps you were right and we shouldn't go on seeing each other. I am not able to marry for love, my dear heart. I have a duty to marry a lady with money, and I must behave honourably, whatever I might think of her."

He released her hand and bowed his head, and Amelia gave in to the temptation to touch his fair hair. "I have some money, Charles," she said simply. "It may not be enough for your needs but if you could love me as I love you, every penny of it is yours."

Charlie raised his head to look at her. "You have money, Amelia? How wonderful that sounds. But I couldn't ask it of you, my love. You hardly know me."

"I have come into something over forty thousand pounds,

Charles, and not an idea what to do with it all. If you would teach me, I should be so happy."

"My darling Amelia," said Charlie Bennet, holding his lady close enough to his heart to make the company of a passing boat whoop their approval. "We shall make each other so happy. I can hardly wait for the day."

The marriage ceremony was quietly performed in a private chapel in the road behind Sarah's shop. Sarah and a friend of Charles being the only witnesses. A blissfully happy Amelia, Lady Beniton, kissed Sarah after she signed the register and thanked her over and over again for her goodness.

"I have spent my life looking for a sister," she told her, taking Sarah's hand to kiss it, "and I thank God I found her in you." The happy couple departed for their honeymoon cruise that same afternoon, Sarah coming on board the ship to speed their departure with a last kiss for Amelia. After dinner, served in their cabin at Lord Beniton's request because he wanted to share his lovely bride with no one, they walked the deck arm in arm in the moonlight. Passing a life-boat, Charlie said urgently. "Come behind here with me, my darling. I can't wait another moment for a kiss."

Lord and Lady Beniton were on deck when the ship anchored at Finisterre to pick up passengers and a packet of mail. A message was waiting for his lordship to say his ailing cousin was dying and he must return to England at once. Charles read it carefully and then handed the slip of paper to the darkly beautiful woman at his side.

"I'm so sorry, my dear," he said quietly. "It seems that the remainder of our honeymoon cruise will have to be post-poned."

"There'll be other cruises," said Sarah, smiling up at him. "I can wait."

Some three weeks later, the naked and part eaten body of a woman was found by the crew of a fishing smack in the waters off Cape Finisterre. Whatever caused her death had destroyed her face so completely, she was quite beyond recognition. The fishermen sighed, crossed themselves, and said a prayer for her soul. Then they dropped her back in the water for the fishes to eat.

Chapter Eight

Arnold Roberts walked across the court to face the jury, shrugged as though those gentlemen too would understand the difficulty of dealing with an obdurate and difficult female witness, and then turned back to Mrs Tombrin.

"Suppose I were to put it to you in these words, madam," he said wearily. "You became acquainted with Mr Bennet while you were having a course of treatments in an establishment owned and managed by Sarah Fowkes. Is that plain enough for you?"

"It is as plain as what I have said to you. I did not know him then as Mr Bennet."

"Madam!" The sudden rasp in the counsel's voice made Mrs Tombrin jump and press a hand against her breast. "You persist in playing your silly tricks with words while two people sit in that dock with their very lives at stake. I can assure you most positively that his lordship and the officers of the court and every man and woman in the public gallery knows the name of the man in the dock. It is Charles Bennet. Every news sheet in the country has been full of his name for weeks. Are you really telling this court that you are the only person in all of Great Britain who does not know the prisoner's name is Charles Bennet?"

Mrs Tombrin pressed her hands together. "N-no sir," she said hurriedly. "I know perfectly well that his name is Bennet. I was merely trying to explain . . ."

"Spare me your convoluted explanations, madam. If you answer my questions truthfully and without indulging in these pointless prevarications, we shall arrive at the explanation soon enough. Now, if you will kindly answer the

f

first question I asked, we will proceed to the second. Did you become acquainted with Charles Bennet while having treatments in Sarah Fowkes's shop?"

"Yes I did."

"At last, at last. At long last." For the benefit of the jury, Roberts clowned a sigh of relief and nodded to them, as though he and they knew he was dealing with a slippery customer but he had the better of her. Arnold Roberts would not let these good men and true be made fools of.

"Now tell me this, Mrs Tombrin," he went on silkily, "having met this young man during your course of treatments, you became enamoured of him, did you not?"

"I thought he loved me."

"No madam," Roberts shook his head and sighed. "Do please listen to my questions. I am not asking you to tell the court what you thought. I am asking you to tell us what you did. You fell hopelessly in love with Mr Bennet, did you not?"

Mrs Tombrin's thin cheeks coloured. "Yes. I loved him," she admitted.

"Quite so, and having fallen in love, you concocted this foolish prank of writing letters to yourself and pretending they came from your imagined lover."

Mrs Tombrin clenched her fists and glared at the counsel. "Certainly not," she snapped, her voice strained and high-pitched. "I did not write those letters to myself. Madame Sarah gave them to me and said they were from Lord Beniton."

"So you have told this court," retorted the unabashed Roberts, "but even if you were correct in what you say, how did you know the letters came from him? Was it from your own personal and intimate knowledge of his handwriting?"

"No. I knew they came from Lord Beniton because Madame Sarah said they did. I told you it was she who gave them to me."

"You did and I assure you the point has not been lost on me. Nor will it be forgotten, Mrs Tombrin. For the moment, however, let us stay with Mr Bennet. Did you not say in answer to a question from my learned friend, the counsel for the prosecution, that the man known to you as Lord Beniton wrote you several letters? I can look at my notes if your memory needs refreshing on the point."

Mrs Tombrin began to look trapped. "Well, no sir. Of course I remember what I said. I told Mr Shanklin that Lord Beniton had written to me and Madame Sarah had handed me the letters to read, but . . ."

"No buts, Mrs Tombrin. This is not the moment for buts. Are you now telling the court that, despite your earlier evidence, you have no way of knowing if Lord Beniton wrote those letters to you?"

"Well yes," the witness admitted, "I suppose I must be saying that.

"You suppose you must be saying that," Roberts repeated slowly. He frowned sorrowfully at her and continued. "Then you begin to see how dangerous giving evidence in a court of law can be, Mrs Tombrin, and how certain one has to be of one's facts. Especially when I tell you that Charles Bennet denies all knowledge of the letters you so emphatically insisted he sent you. Will you now accept the possibility that he might be telling the truth and you have misled the court?"

Mrs Tombrin looked at Charlie before conceding the possibility with, "I suppose I must accept what you say. It is possible that Mr Bennet did not write the letters."

"Thank you, Mrs Tombrin. And now, when I tell you the other defendant, Sarah Fowkes, also swears she knows nothing of the mysterious letters you claim she gave you, will you also accept that possibility?"

"Never. She is lying if she says she did not give me the letters."

"Is she? Or is it you who perjure yourself, Mrs Tombrin? I have caught you out in one piece of false accounting. Why not two?"

'Or three, or four, or forty-four, what the hell difference does it make?' Sarah shifted slightly on the hard wooden bench while she watched a half hysterical Mrs Tombrin spill most of her glass of water over her shoes and deny vehemently that she had deliberately misled the court.

*　　*　　*　　*

'We made a mistake,' she thought bitterly, 'we should have killed them both while we had the chance.' For the moment she could visualise the dead Mrs Tombrin lying at her feet, mouth gaping open and blood streaming from a gaping wound in the old bitch's head. Then she turned away to glance at Charlie, seeing he was beginning to look drawn and loose lipped.

He wouldn't have had the stomach for it, she told herself. He's already scared silly enough to crack.

Certainly, Charlie Bennet had no stomach for what they did on the night they beat Amelia Hinks to death behind a lifeboat, smashed in her face to stop her being known if she was found, and dropped her pathetically thin and naked body into the sea.

He rushed back to the cabin and collapsed on the floor, whimpering like a whipped child when he suddenly realised he was still clutching Amelia's blood splattered clothes in both hands. Convulsively, he threw them away from him and Sarah, a slight smile on her lips and her colour higher than usual, picked them up and began to step across his legs to stuff them into the bottom of a cabin trunk.

She stiffened when she felt his hand on her ankle but said quietly, "You've got blood all over those hands, Charlie Bennet. You'd better let go of me and get yourself washed. If you look sharp about it. I'll pour you a drink."

White-faced, Charlie looked at his hands, gasped with horror, and scrambled for the wash-basin. When he was scrubbed and certain there was no more blood on him, he drank the brandy gratefully and asked Sarah to put her arms round him to steady his nerves.

"I'm cold. I can't stop shaking," he whined miserably. "Besides, we're supposed to be Lord and Lady Beniton on our honeymoon ain't we. I ought to be in bed with you for when the steward comes in. It's what he'll expect."

"The only thing that comes in my bed tonight are my scissors," Sarah said, pushing him hard away. "You can sleep on the chair and get in next to me when the steward knocks on the door tomorrow morning. And if you try any of your bleeding nonsense then, you'll cop it. Is that understood?" And on Charlie's sulky nod, "Well, that's all right then."

Clutching the brandy bottle to his chest, Charlie sat by the dressing-table, feet planted wide to balance against the slight roll of the ship, grateful to the beat of the engines taking him further and further away from the horror of Amelia's accusing eyes in her smashed face. The sea was quiet, but the sounds of water gently lapping the side of the ship did little to calm his jangled nerves. He spent the night with his time divided between looking in the mirror and seeing himself as a murderer, and taking ever deeper swigs from his bottle of brandy. By morning the bottle was empty and he was sitting bleary-eyed and leaning to one side, hating Sarah for her ability to forget the thing they had done together. She must be a mad woman, he decided, looking at her curled in sleep, the pointed tip of her forefinger in her mouth. A few hours earlier, when he was holding Amelia's arms behind her back and watching Sarah keep hitting the old girl through the blur of splashing blood in his eyes, he could see she was enjoying the savage work she was engaged on. Quite suddenly, he knew she was being revenged on Amelia Hinks for some dark reason of her own. Something he could know nothing about.

In the morning, when the steward tapped on the cabin door and wheeled in a trolley, he got into the narrow bed beside Sarah and felt the warm pressure of her thigh against his own. She kept her head turned away, her face hidden by a sweep of her loosened hair, while the steward set out their breakfast. After the man had wished them *bon appetit* and left, Charlie got out of the bed without looking at her, though he knew she had turned to lie on her back and stretch her arms above her head. At any other time, the sudden lift of her breasts and the shadow of her nipples through the sheer silk of her nightgown, would have roused him to near frenzy, but after the way she killed Amelia, lying beside her had roused nothing in him but revulsion. At that moment, he could no more have made love to Sarah Fowkes than he could have mounted a serpent.

For her part, Sarah looked at him curiously once or twice while they made a pretence of eating their porridge and mutton chops and waited for the ship to reach Finisterre and the pre-arranged letter that was to call them back to England. She had expected much more of an effort at love-making from him and, though she had sworn often enough that she would kill any man who tried to take her by force, she had been stimulated by the murder and, she was forced to admit, excited by Charlie's presence in the bed. Feeling the warm strength of his thigh against her own had stirred feelings in her she had not previously allowed herself to be aware of.

Maybe, she was thinking while she pushed the stodgy food around on her plate, she had been too hard on him. Perhaps too hard on herself too. Sarah Fowkes and Charlie Bennet were partners after all. Their continuing safety depended on each other and rejecting him might have been a mistake she would regret one day. Making a snap decision, she leaned towards him and said softly, "Charlie, that bastard who raped me hurt me very badly." A dishevelled Charlie put down his second brandy bottle and gazed deep into Sarah's eyes.

"Can't say I blame him," he said.

Sarah's appetite for killing seemed to grow from that time on and Charlie, who carried on whoring for her in addition to his involvement in the murders she arranged, was soon beyond caring. Two more victims quickly followed Amelia Hinks, both believing until their last moment that they had become Lady Beniton. Sarah grew wealthy on the proceeds and more bitter, though nothing of her rancour showed in her face. Charlie, whose drinking she could no longer keep in check, grew plumper, though he kept his good looks and something of his military bearing. He was a little more than twenty-seven years old when Sarah brought Mrs Tombrin into the parlour to meet him as the impoverished Lord Beniton. Two weeks later, deciding it would add a little spice to play two fish at once, she introduced him to Mrs Carlisle.

Florence Carlisle was undeniably fat. She sweated freely, bathed less often than she should, and a distinct odour of stale perspiration hung about her when she entered the shop and came close to Sarah.

"I've seen your advertisement," she puffed as she heaved

her bulk on to one of the shop's gold painted chairs. "Name's Carlisle. Don't know what you can do for me but now that I'm back in England, I wouldn't mind being made a bit more presentable, even if I don't know who for."

Her small, china-blue eyes disappeared into her fat cheeks as she began to wheeze with laughter and appeared again to stare when Sarah said without flinching, "But my dear Mrs Carlisle, you have beautiful hair and a lovely smile. That is more than enough to start with. And I'll give you one piece of advice for no payment at all. Always smile at the people you meet. It makes you look very agreeable and believe me, that's the best way to find a man to be presentable for."

Charlie, who since the incident in the ship's cabin usually managed not to look directly at Sarah, couldn't help but stare at her after Florence had bobbed a creaky curtsey in answer to his bow and left the premises.

"She farted," he said in disgust. "She's so fat, I don't suppose she even knew she was doing it. You must be going soft in the head if you think you can make a woman like that believe a man could fall in love with her. She must know she's past the age for that sort of thing."

"Past the age for it, is she?" Sarah's voice was cold. "Well if she is, you won't have to worry about her, will you? Keep off that bottle and come here early tomorrow evening. Florence Carlisle won't be the first plump goose to make a fool of herself over you, or want to be Lady Beniton when she learns you're down on your luck.

Charlie shrugged awkwardly. "Maybe it's time we changed that name. She'd be the fifth of them."

Sarah smiled reflectively. "It's been a lucky enough name till now. You play your part properly and it'll go on being lucky. We won't have to change it yet awhile, my lord."

"Lord Beniton admires me, you say?" wheezed Florence Carlisle as she settled on the gold chair by the counter, making it squeak a loud protest. "He must want a good deal of flesh for his money."

Sarah smiled fondly at her and replied, "That is very clever of you, my dear Mrs Carlisle. The thing of it is, Lord

Beniton has no money at all and he tells me, his creditors are pressing him very hard. To tell you the plain truth, Florence, the young man is after a wealthy wife and is prepared to sell himself and his title to any lady with a large enough bankbook to offer in exchange."

"Is he now? Well, that at least is honest but I can't say I approve of the dissolute classes. My late husband, Mr Carlisle, worked pretty damn hard for his money in the Colonial Service and has left me comfortably off. I mean to keep my fortune to please myself with, Madame Sarah. You may tell his lordship that I am not flattered by his admiration of my bank balance, however sincere it may be. He would do better to look for his saviour elsewhere."

Sarah sighed gently and patted the back of Florence's plump hand. "Of course," she murmured, "I expect you are right to refuse him. I mention it only because I know what it is like to lose a loved one and have to spend my nights with only a pillow for company. I too have cried myself to sleep, Mrs Carlisle."

Florence stared at her. "A woman with your looks? Good God, madam. I would not have thought you were ever left alone!"

"Oh, but I am left alone," Sarah replied quietly. "Such suitors as I had soon realised they could not match the standard set by my dear Harry, who died so tragically young. I discouraged them then and now they have given up the chase. Florence my dear, we have only known each other for two or three weeks but I already think of you as a dear friend. Do not let false pride make you lonely. Being alone for the rest of her life is a dreadful prospect for a woman to look forward to."

"Huh," snorted Florence, without much conviction. "You may be right but I am used to living with a steady going gentleman who knows what he must do to earn his bread. I certainly don't want to marry a young scallywag like Lord Beniton."

Sarah laughed. "And why should you marry Beniton? You are growing more beautiful every day and in another few weeks, Florence Carlisle will be able to choose any gentleman she fancies."

The next day, when Mrs Carlisle squeezed through the shop door and made for her chair by the counter, Charlie was sitting on it and having what appeared to be an animated conversation with Sarah. Breaking off in mid-sentence when he saw Florence approach, he stood up and bowed.

"I beg your pardon, Mrs Carlisle," he said formally. "Madame Sarah has told me you do not wish to speak to me. I would do better to come back when you have finished your business."

He looked so doleful when he picked up his tall hat and made to step past her, she put a hand on his sleeve and said gruffly, "There is no need to leave because I have come into the shop, Lord Beniton. I don't mind in the least bit talking to you. You seem to be a very pleasant young man. I told Madame Sarah only that I am not at all interested in marrying a title."

Charlie smiled complacently and smoothed his moustache with a licked forefinger. "When a lady becomes married to me, Mrs Carlisle, she will find she has married a man, not merely a title."

Sarah chuckled softly. "I think he is telling you he has hot blood, Mrs Carlisle. I told you he admires you."

Florence looked first at her and then at Charlie. "I am not accustomed to being admired," she confessed in total honesty. "I have not the slightest notion what I am to do with a man who admires me."

Charlie took Florence to dinner at the Trocadero the following evening. She was uncomfortable and red faced in her new, and for her, far too low cut gown. The boning pinched savagely below her heavily powdered and generously exposed upper breasts and in the excessive warmth of the crowded dining-rooms, they and her meaty shoulders were soon red and blotchy with heat. Dabbing at her flushed cheeks with a crumpled lace-edged handkerchief, she looked at the extremely personable young man on the other side of the table. He was drumming the table-cloth gently with long, well manicured fingers, and studying the wine list with some care. As she watched him she wondered, despite his professed admiration, what he could possibly want from her other than money.

Nothing at all, she had decided grimly when he looked up to meet her eyes, smile into them and say, "This is really very good of you, Mrs Carlisle. I hope I may be allowed to say you look quite charming in that dress. I imagine Madame Sarah might have suggested blue. It is your colour."

"It doesn't stop me being so fat and awkward," she grumbled discontentedly. "You look so handsome in your tails, Beniton, it makes me wish I made you a more suitable companion, if only for this evening."

Charlie seized the moment and put on his earnest look. "It isn't only for this evening if I have anything to do with it, Mrs Carlisle. As for appearances, Madame Sarah is a wonder with a lady's appearance and in any case, I always think the way one looks is largely a matter of bearing and having confidence in oneself."

Florence chuckled. "That's all very well for a man to say. A fat man can be called a fine figure and grow a moustache. Tell a man he's enormous and he'll probably take it as a compliment. How do you think a woman feels when she sees what I have to look at in my mirror every morning?"

Smiling even more widely, Charlie leaned across the table to pat her hand. "I hope that very soon now, she will feel it's the start of a new day. I hope she will look out of her window to see the sun is shining on the meadow, the birds are singing in the trees, and someone she knows, wants nothing better than to make her happy for the rest of her life." He was quite pleased with his little homily until he saw the way she was looking at him. "I am something of a romantic," he finished lamely.

Knowing he had overplayed his hand, Charlie said little more than the occasional pleasantry during the rest of the evening, received more grunts than replies in response, and was glad when the time came for him to plant a kiss on her fat wrist and leave her on her doorstep.

"It was a waste of a good dinner," he reported to Sarah when he got back to the shop. "That fat old sow is never going to believe I want to marry her, whether she's got money or not."

"She's got money all right," Sarah said slowly, "I can smell it on her. She needs getting at in a different way, that's all. You get on home and let me think about it."

Florence Carlisle came straight to the point when she walked into the shop two mornings later. Ignoring Sarah's gay "Good morning, my dear Mrs Carlisle," she said grimly:

"I've come in for some more of the perfumed soaps you sold me last week. I'll take sufficient to last a month or thereabouts. I'm going to visit a cousin in Yorkshire. London is no place for me."

Sarah looked concerned but turned obediently to bring down four tablets of the scented soap from a shelf behind her. "These should be more than sufficient for a month," she said quietly. "I'll put them in a box for you. I must say I shall be quite sorry to see you go, Mrs Carlisle. I was beginning to think you were happy here in London."

Florence sniffed dismissively. "So did I before I came near to making a fool of myself over that damn fortune hunting friend of yours. It must have looked very easy to him. Silly old widder woman with money. Handsome young man comes along and offers to sell his title and himself along with it. I'm an old India hand who should know better, but I damn near fell for the trick. If the swine hadn't been sitting with me in a restaurant full of lovely young women when he began making pretty speeches about my supposed charms, I might have too. I suppose it was a clever enough scheme. It certainly made me see that you London folk are too smart for me."

Sarah lifted her shoulders in a delicate shrug but did not answer at once. She took her time arranging the soaps in the box and tying the package carefully, and then said, "Young men do make pretty speeches to the ladies they are spending an evening with, it is true. I'm sorry to have been the one to introduce him to you." She held up a hand when Florence began to speak and went on, "No, Mrs Carlisle, now that I have found the courage to speak of it, please let me finish what I have to say. I should not be telling you because I am sworn to secrecy, but since you are leaving London because of Charles Beniton, I hate to think of you going away angry with him."

"I don't know that I am angry with him."

Sarah came round from behind her counter to stand

close by Florence. "Oh but you must not pretend to me, Mrs Carlisle. You are angry and disappointed. I can see it in your eyes but you are wrong to feel so bitter. The truth is, Lord Charles Beniton had a very unhappy affair with a lady who probably looked exactly like the young women you saw in the restaurant. The girl was very silly and ignorant of men's ways. She may not have meant the affair to turn out as it did, but whether she did or not, she came between him and his best friend and the friend called him out. Beniton shot him dead and had to escape to France, where he was forced to live quietly until the scandal died down. The scandal cost him his friend, his commission in the Life Guards, and even his mother, for she died of a broken heart before he could come back to England to comfort her. Oh, my dear Mrs Carlisle, does it really surprise you to find he does not care for beautiful young women and that he thinks of them as dangerous and treacherous minxes? I must tell you that knowing his history as I do, it does not surprise me in the least. He told me you made him think of his mother as she was in happier times, when he was young and without cares, and they would go to the theatre together. Particularly when you were wearing your blue gown which was also her favourite colour. As things are, I think it's as well you are going as far away as Yorkshire, Mrs Carlisle. I felt it right to explain his behaviour to you but I would not want to think about the pain it would give Charles Beniton if he were to discover you know his sad story."

Florence Carlisle swallowed noisily, picked up the small package of soaps and put them down again.

"Madame Sarah . . . " she began.

"Ah no," interrupted Sarah Fowkes as she sensed victory. "Not another word please, dear Mrs Carlisle. I said I was sorry I introduced him to you and so I am. To be perfectly honest with you, madam, my sorrow is much more for his sake than yours. Nevertheless, I can't help feeling guilty about you too. It will make me happy if you will accept these soaps as a memento of my little shop. That way, you might at least have one kind thought of me, if not of my poor friend, Lord Beniton."

"Sarah," Mrs Carlisle protested. "I couldn't possibly

accept the soaps as a gift."

"But you must." Sarah's voice broke and for a moment she seemed unable to continue but, recovering herself with an effort, she said quickly, "Take them and go, my dear. I expect Charles Beniton in shortly and I think he has suffered enough from your rejection of him, don't you?"

Florence looked at the package of soaps but did not pick it up. Settling herself on the loudly protesting gold chair, she said firmly, "Sarah, since you expect Beniton to come in here this morning, perhaps you'll allow me to wait and thank him for my very nice dinner."

"Oh, but my dear," said Sarah, putting a hand to her cheek and looking contrite. "I would never have told you his sad story if I thought you might meet him again."

"There's no need for you to worry your head about that," Florence Carlisle grunted happily. "You told me his secret and you can trust me to keep it."

The wedding was arranged for the following month. Charlie, who had been warned off making flowery speeches by Sarah, managed not to tell Florence she made him the happiest man in the world. Smiling his warm, practised smile while they had tea in her rooms, speaking of the settlement she would make on him and the family jewels he would then be in a position to bestow on her, he wondered how Sarah meant this one to die and, for the first time, would not have minded having a hand in the killing. His smile deepened while he imagined strangling her, digging his fingers ever deeper into the creases of her disgustingly fat throat. Florence returned the smile, making him laugh out loud. She reddened a little and said, almost coyly, "You remind me so much of the way my dear husband would laugh at me in the early days of our marriage and I always knew what activity he had in mind. Charles, I think of you as my husband now. You don't have to wait for our wedding night if your need is urgent."

Doing his best to look eager for love, Charlie stripped off in front of her and, almost floundering on her vast belly, rested his chin on her shoulder and forced his way between the mounds of flesh until he found himself deep inside her. Feeling her convulsive upward thrust to meet him, he began working as rhythmically as he could until her fingers gripped hard on his buttocks and held him tight against her. Usually, making love to the women he and Sarah were soon to kill excited him but with Florence, the lumpy blubberiness of her bloated pink body disgusted him. Hating her for the disappointment he felt, he was forced to revert to his old trick of closing his eyes and trying to visualise Annie but to his surprise, he could only see Sarah as she lay on her back in the ship's cabin with her arms above her head, her lovely breasts thrusting against the almost sheer nightgown, her mouth half open, inviting him to take her.

"Sarah, Sarah, Sarah!" he was almost panting as he plunged deeper and finished with a gasping shudder, feeling Florence's grip on his buttocks relax.

"I'll never doubt you again," Florence said softly. "I know you love me. Nobody could make love to a woman the way you did, and not love her."

"Of course they couldn't," panted an almost breathless Charlie. "You must know I love you very much." The knowledge that whenever she invited him to, he would have to mount that gross body again was a revolting thought but it would soon be over and he and Sarah would be rid of her. Thinking about her impending death made him feel better and he raised a hand to stroke her face in sympathy.

"Your fingers are so gentle," Florence wheezed happily. "I know we will be happy together. Stay with me tonight and I will let you love me again.

Spending his nights with Florence Carlisle became a regular practice and an easier one as time went on. She told him the second time they made love that all through her married life she never knew her husband had finished until he rolled off her and began to sneeze. After which, it was easy enough for Charlie to fake orgasm and satisfy her with the knowledge she had pleased him. With the date of the wedding approaching, he became sufficiently relaxed with her to chat about generalities while they ate together and prepared to go to bed. The evening he walked in, dropped his hat on the hallstand, and had her ask him about Mrs Tombrin, who he had arranged to marry two weeks after Florence had been disposed of, came as a complete shock.

"Mrs Tombrin, you say?" he repeated nervously. "I'm very sorry Florence, my love. I don't think I know the lady."

"Possibly not," snapped Florence, "but I know the lady and so does your precious Madame Sarah. She fobbed me off when I wanted to go after Molly this morning by telling me a tale about my poor friend becoming deranged and making a nuisance of herself. Charles, I don't believe a word of it. I know Molly Tombrin and she's as sane a woman as I am. I want you to come to the shop with me and make Sarah give us Mollie's address. I mean to visit her tonight and get to the bottom of this."

"The bottom of what?" Charlie said helplessly. "My dear Florence, I can see you have had an upset but I honestly can't make sense of what you are telling me. Or, for that matter, why on earth Madame Sarah should tell you tales about your friend. Don't you think we could leave the matter rest till the morning? Perhaps if we go to bed soon, have an early night . . ."

"No! Now you are making me think that you are trying to fob me off. Charles, I am worried. Molly and I have been friends for a great many years and I can't believe she said those awful things about me, whatever Sarah says. Charles, you and I are man and wife or as near as two people can be before their wedding. I must know what has happened to Molly and I need your protection to help me find out."

Charlie picked up his hat and gloves from the hallstand and opened the front door. "Very well, old girl," he said firmly. "Of course we must find out what has happened to your old chum. Let us go and call on Madame Sarah."

Chapter Nine

"I did not lie! That woman gave me the letters! She said they were his! She told me he would make me a good husband! She told me he loved me!" At the end of each of her blurting and almost incoherent statements, Mrs Tombrin beat an ineffectual fist on the sill of the witness-box. Arnold Roberts tried to interrupt the flow, failed, and at last turned his back on the hysterical woman and spread his arms wide.

"My lord," he shouted over the hubbub in the courtroom. "I really must protest."

Mr Justice Hughes waved him away and, fixing Mrs Tombrin with a glare, rapped for silence until at last, she became aware of the insistent tapping of his gavel, faltered, and quietened to listen to him.

"Mrs Tombrin," said Mr Hughes, "you are an important witness in this most serious trial for murder. You are to conduct yourself in a proper and fitting manner and you are to confine yourself to answering the counsel's questions. Whatever you may think of a question, or of the manner in which Mr Roberts chooses to ask it, your answer must be straightforward, to the point, and honest. That is the only way you can help the gentlemen of the jury arrive at the truth. Do you understand that?"

Mrs Tombrin nodded and clumsily flopped backwards in the box. Roberts, whose arms remained widespread throughout the judge's remarks, dropped them to his sides and said, "Thank you, my lord, I am obliged."

Turning back to Mrs Tombrin, he bowed slightly and asked, almost casually, "Do you wear spectacles, madam?"

The question was unexpected and a surprised Mrs Tombrin

repeated, "Do I wear spectacles, sir?"

"That is what I asked you, Mrs Tombrin."

"I have a reading glass, if that is what you mean."

"No madam, that is not at all what I mean, but no matter. Mrs Tombrin, once again I am about to question the accuracy of part of the evidence you have given. Before I do so, I want you to understand that I am not trying to belittle you, nor do I accuse you of any misdemeanour. I intend merely to put it to you and the jury that you may have been mistaken in what you claim to have seen. Is that perfectly clear?"

"Yes sir, I think it is."

"Excellent. Now then, Mrs Tombrin, in your signed statement made at the police station, you said you saw the murdered woman, Florence Carlisle, outside the shop owned by Sarah Fowkes and in the company of Sarah Fowkes, with whom she was having some conversation. You have also repeated that statement in this court. Am I correct?"

"Yes sir, that is what I saw."

"And you knew Mrs Carlisle quite well?"

Mrs Tombrin sniffed unhappily and said in a low voice. "I knew Florence Carlisle very well indeed."

"I see."

Roberts walked closer to Mrs Tombrin. Standing immediately before her, he raised a finger and asked, "Were you well enough acquainted with the lady to know what she would be wearing that morning?"

Mrs Tombrin's eyes followed the finger and she hesitated, before saying, "No sir. I had not seen her for some months."

"Rather more than nine months according to your signed statement to the police officer. You came back to England on different ships. In fact, Mrs Tombrin, when you last saw Mrs Carlisle, you were in Bengal, were you not?"

"Well yes, in Barrackpore. She was in the process of selling her bungalow."

"Quite so," Roberts interrupted smoothly. "And on that occasion, she was appropriately dressed for the heat and clear light of a tropical sun rather than muffled up in a coat and hat against the chill and dullness of a murky London morning?"

"Of course she was." Mrs Tombrin allowed herself a flicker

of a smile at the memory. "In Barrackpore the temperature was above ninety degrees."

"Exactly." Roberts smiled in turn and lowered his finger. "Now tell me this, Mrs Tombrin. Did you expect to meet Mrs Carlisle at Madame Sarah's establishment on that day?"

Mrs Tombrin shook her head and replied, "Why no, nothing was further from my thoughts."

"Really?" said Roberts. "Nothing was further from your thoughts than a meeting with Mrs Carlisle?"

"No sir, I knew she was coming to England after me but we had made no arrangement to meet in London. I was under the impression she meant to stay with relatives in Yorkshire."

Arnold Roberts glanced at the jury and shook his head, before saying slowly, "In that case, Mrs Tombrin, you are telling this court that you unexpectedly came across a lady you had not seen for a considerable time, in a place you did not anticipate a meeting with her. She was dressed in garments you had not seen her wear before, and yet you instantly recognised her?"

"Yes, of course I recognised her. Why should I not know an old friend?"

Roberts allowed her counter question to hang in the air for a few moments before asking almost casually, "Was the lady you saw with Sarah Fowkes wearing a hat and overcoat?"

"She was dressed for out of doors, yes."

"Evidence has been given that it was a cool morning. Was the lady's overcoat fastened high and close to the chin?"

"Well yes, I suppose it was."

"The hat now, madam. Large and trimmed? With feathers perhaps?"

Mrs Tombrin began to look distraught. "I do not remember, sir. It was large certainly. Yes, perhaps there were some feathers on it."

"You do not remember. So, if I were to ask you if the lady's face was seen in the clear light of day or if it was partly shadowed by the hat or its feather trimming, you could not answer?"

"No sir, I could not possibly answer such a question after this space of time.

Arnold Roberts put down his notes and thoughtfully rubbed at his clean shaven chin. "Well now, Mrs Tombrin, you have some difficulty in remembering how the lady was dressed and whether or not her face was in clear view, yet you are very positive she was Mrs Carlisle. Is there no room for doubt in your mind?"

"None whatever. Of course it was Florence Carlisle."

"You are quite certain of the fact?"

"Yes I am."

"As certain as you were that Charles Bennet wrote you those letters?"

"Oh but this is quite different. I might not have known Mr Bennet's hand but when I saw Florence Carlisle, I knew her at once."

"And yet you have admitted that you did not see her face clearly and you have agreed the clothes she had on were unfamiliar. Why are you so certain it was her?"

Mrs Tombrin relaxed momentarily and allowed another brief smile to touch her lips. "You did not know my poor friend if you think I needed to see every one of her features to recognise her. She was unmistakably fat and red in the cheeks. In India, I was for ever telling her to eat less or . . . "

Roberts held up his finger. "One moment please, Mrs Tombrin. Before you go on, I want to be perfectly clear about what you are telling the court. Are you saying that you base your identification of this lady, not on her features which you did not see, nor on the unfamiliar clothing she wore, but merely because she was fat and had a red face?"

"I meant nothing of the sort. Florence Carlisle and I were neighbours and friends. I knew her as I would know a sister."

"I see. What colour was her hair?"

"Florence's hair was . . "

"No, not Florence Carlisle. The lady you saw with Sarah Fowkes, please?"

"She was wearing a hat."

"Quite so. And the colour of her eyes?" Mrs Tombrin bit her lip and made no attempt at an answer.

Roberts smiled and said peaceably, "No matter, Mrs Tombrin. If you could not see the colour of the hair beneath a lady's hat, you certainly could not see the colour of her eyes. It seems to me that you saw a fat lady in a shop doorway and because you one time had a neighbour of a similar build, you assumed it was her."

"No, I assumed nothing of the sort. It was Florence Carlisle!"

"Thank you, madam." Roberts turned away to glance at a page of his notes and then said, "Mrs Tombrin, perhaps this is a side issue but I hope his lordship will allow it. When you were neighbours in India, how did your friend, Mrs Carlisle, answer you on the occasions you advised her to eat less?"

"Why, she would laugh and call me an old worrier. She promised she would try to eat less when she got back to dear old England."

"And this advice was repeatedly given by you?"

"Oh yes sir. Many times. I was always concerned for my friend's health and well-being."

"Then I must ask you to consider this, Mrs Tombrin. You had not seen Florence Carlisle for almost a year. If she had taken your advice when she got back to England, she could not possibly have been the woman you saw with Sarah Fowkes, could she?"

Mrs Tombrin began to cry again. Through her tears, she said brokenly, "You are trying to confuse me. I know I saw Florence Carlisle that morning as well as I know that wicked woman slaughtered her as though she were an animal."

She covered her face with her hands and Roberts appealed to the judge. "My Lord, how can I possibly go on with my cross examination in these circumstances? I have no way of knowing if the witness is ill or merely avoiding my questions."

Mr Justice Hughes looked doubtfully at Mrs Tombrin and asked, "Have you many more questions to ask this witness, Mr Roberts?"

"I do have some further questions, my lord. As you were good enough to say to the jury, this lady is the prosecution's most important witness. It is Mrs Tombrin who first reported the disappearance of the murdered woman. It is Mrs Tombrin who claims to have seen her friend Mrs Carlisle in conversation with Sarah Fowkes. And it is Mrs Tombrin who maliciously and I submit, unjustly, accuses my client of murder. In view of the lady's hostility towards Sarah Fowkes, I should like to ask about her own earlier acquaintanceship with the deceased Mrs Carlisle, and possibly others."

The judge sighed audibly, repeated, "And possibly others. Thank you, Mr Roberts." Turning to Mrs Tombrin, he said, "Madam, you have been giving your evidence for some considerable time and I know it has been a great strain on you. Do you feel you can carry on at present?" A tearful Mrs Tombrin shook her head vehemently.

"In that case," said Mr Hughes, "I think we might do well to adjourn until three o'clock this afternoon. It will give you an opportunity to recover your equilibrium. I suggest you have a short conversation with the counsel for the prosecution and then lie down for a while. We can't have you getting ill, you know. When two people's lives are in the balance, Mr Roberts must be given every opportunity to make out the best case he can for them."

"I suppose he does," flared a suddenly furious Mrs Tombrin, "but why does he hope to save them by accusing me? What am I supposed to have done wrong?"

"Ah yes," said Roberts in a curiously gentle voice while he gathered up his robe and sat down. "That is what I mean to discover, no matter how long it may take us."

The accused were taken away separately as the court cleared. Charlie, now seeming to need the support of his gaoler's arm, stumbled slightly in his unlaced boots and massaged his aching forehead with his fingertips as he went. Sarah Fowkes, head high and masking her feelings of disquiet with a slight smile when she was led past the trembling and ashen faced Mrs Tombrin, just as the lady was being helped down from the witness stand by William Shanklin.

Sarah had smiled in much the same way and for much the same reason on the night Charlie brought Florence Carlisle to the door and demanded admittance.

"I'm sorry to disturb you at this late an hour, Madame Sarah," he said politely after she drew back the bolts and stood in the doorway looking at them. "But we are concerned about a friend of Mrs Carlisle's. I have to tell you that my fiancée was very disturbed by the behaviour of a lady she spoke to outside your shop this morning. She has known the lady in question for many years and means to visit her tonight and have the matter out. We have come to you because Mrs Carlisle thinks you may have the lady's address."

"I see," Sarah said briskly as she stepped aside. "Well, you'd better come in and tell me the lady's name. I'll be pleased to help if I can but if she was only a casual customer, I may not know her or where she lives."

"Her name is Mrs Alice Tombrin," Florence said as she stumped into the shop ahead of Charlie, who gave Sarah a warning shake of the head and passed a forefinger across his throat.

"Tombrin?" Sarah repeated doubtfully. "I don't think I know the name."

"You seemed to know her well enough this morning when you prevented her from walking across the road to speak to me."

"I remember there was a slight incident outside the shop this morning," Sarah said smoothly as she turned to face Charlie. "A woman began to curse and swear at us from across the street. My dear Mrs Carlisle, Lord Beniton knows we get lots of drunk rowdies in this district and they're not in the least particular about what they say to me or my clients. I generally turn them away before they come close enough to start begging for money to buy more gin."

"But Sarah," protested the outraged Florence Carlisle. "I heard you tell her she had come on the wrong day for her treatment."

Sarah smiled gently and turned to close the shop door and bolt it.

"You heard me say that to her, did you?" she asked as she came back to face Florence. "Then it seems you are correct and I must know her. Why not take a seat for a few moments whilst I get my treatment book. We will search out your Mrs Tombrin together." Florence nodded briefly and, while she was settling on the chair by the counter, Sarah transferred the smile to Charlie. "You have a long arm, Lord Beniton. Will you save me the trouble of fetching a stool by reaching my treatment book down from its shelf? It's just through here."

Charlie followed Sarah into the parlour and whispered hoarsely. "What are we going to do? We can't let them two meet. Between them, they could finish us off."

"Just shut your mouth and let me think." The returning whisper was savage enough to make him step back a pace and lean against the wall.

"You're right. We can't let her go," Sarah continued in a calmer tone. "Who knows what tricks she might get up to. We'll have to keep her here for now. Get her down in the cellar where you can tie her up and gag her. Then I can think what to do."

"Why not kill her now?"

"Maybe we will. I don't know. We haven't got her money yet."

"Her money?" Charlie repeated stupidly. "That old cow could be the death of the pair of us and you're thinking about her money?"

"Will you shut your mouth?" she hissed. "I said I need time to work it all out, didn't I? Come back in the shop. I know what to do for the time being."

Sarah was laughing as she led the way back into the shop and, leaving Charlie by the door, walked to the counter.

"My dear Mrs Carlisle," she said gaily. "The way the two of you were staring at me when I opened the door must have startled me into forgetting one of my favourite customers. Of course I knew dear Mrs Tombrin. The moment Lord Beniton lifted the treatment book down for me, I remembered her without his having to open it. And I've got the most splendid news for you. She lives close by, just across the yard at the back of the shop. Come through the parlour and into the yard, the pair of you. I'll point out the house."

Florence Carlisle glanced away from Sarah at the heavily bolted shop door and, some sudden instinct making her wary, said, "It is rather late, Madame Sarah. Perhaps Lord Beniton was right when he advised me not to disturb you and told me the matter could be left till morning. If you would be so kind as to write out the address, his lordship and I will call on her tomorrow."

"Come, come, Mrs Carlisle," Sarah said as she came forward

to stand close to the older woman. "If you intended to call on Mrs Tombrin tomorrow, you would have waited until then to call on me. Come along, my dear, it's only a few steps across the backyard."

"Yes, come along, my dear," Charlie repeated encouragingly as he took up his position on the other side of Florence. "We know how you are once you get to worrying. If we don't get this business settled at once, you'll get no sleep tonight and I'll get no peace."

Florence Carlisle pressed her hands together and interlocked her fingers as though she was about to pray. Despite her apparent stolidity, she was a highly imaginative woman and an avid reader of the penny dreadful reports that described in gruesome detail, the bodies of murdered women found in dark alleys or on the wet and greasy steps leading down to the lapping waters of the Thames. The bolted door and the sudden menace of Sarah and Charles standing close on each side of her, made her feel as trapped as those poor souls must have been when they faced their destiny and she trembled with a sudden fear.

"Come on Florence," Charlie said again, less patiently. "Come on old girl. It's got to be done, you know."

Mrs Carlisle couldn't bring herself to ask what it was that had to be done. She could only try to control the tremor in her voice when she heaved herself to her feet, took his arm, and said in a voice that was almost a moan, "Yes, Charles my dear, I suppose it has got to be settled tonight."

Quite unable to move of her own volition, she allowed herself to be guided through the parlour and into the unlit passage beyond.

"Just down these few steps here," said Sarah, opening a door. "Wait at the bottom for me, Mrs Carlisle. I'd quite forgotten how dark it is outside. I'll fetch a lamp to light the rest of the way."

She moved away to return to the parlour and Florence, feeling the menace of the dark, suddenly gabbled, "Don't leave me alone, Charles. Surely you're not going to leave me too?"

"No, of course I'm not going to leave you alone," Charlie's voice was soothing. "You'll be perfectly safe with me. Look,

Florence. There's a chair over there. Why don't you sit down for a few minutes while Sarah goes upstairs to fetch the lamp."

Hearing the note of suppressed excitement in his voice, Florence was filled with horror. Convinced that she was about to be done to death like the poor souls she had read about and trembling even harder, she allowed herself to be taken to the chair and pushed down on to it.

"Ch-Charles. There's no need to think I would make you a bad wife," she began to gabble as her eyes grew accustomed to the dim light and she could see him bend to pick up a length of sash cord. "Please, whatever it is you are thinking of doing with me, I-I beg you not to do it." She sagged in the chair, too terrified to resist when Charlie walked behind her and began to lash her wrists.

"I've got to tie you up, Florence," he said hoarsely. "It's the only thing I can do while Sarah thinks out what we're going to do next."

Florence shook her head violently and tried to look over her shoulder at him. "No, no, you must listen. You've got to think about what you want to do. You've got to know what is best for you. Please don't kill me. I'll give you all the money you could ever want. I haven't made the settlement on you yet. I can make it more. I can make you a wealthy man." Her eyes widened with fear and she shook even harder as Charlie came round the chair to stand before her, ready to stifle her screaming with a piece of rag he held between his hands.

"I know only too well you haven't made the settlement yet. I hear about nothing else from Sarah Fowkes," he muttered. "But it's too late to worry about any of that now."

"No it's not too late," she begged. "Charles, you have to listen to me. It doesn't have to be for nothing. I'll give you anything you need to make you happy. More money than you can imagine. We can go to India. I still have my house in Barrackpore. You can have a wonderful life in India, Charles. You can be a burra sahib. With your own servants to do everything for you. Charles, I don't want to be hurt. Sarah is a wicked woman. You know she is. She has led you into this business but you're a decent man at heart and I know you don't want to kill me. Leave her, Charles. Take me away from here."

Charlie hesitated. Tempted despite himself, by the thought of being a burra sahib in India, he twisted the rag between his fingers, and said, "I couldn't leave Sarah. She knows too much about me."

"Then kill her instead," Florence said quickly, a gleam of hope kindled in her eye. "You'll find me the better bargain. She may get you hanged, Charles, she will never make you rich. Please listen to me before it's too late. Get me away from here. I'll give you everything you ever wanted. You'll be free of her . . . "

The sickening crunch and the almost simultaneous gout of blood that came when Sarah brought the pointed end of the coal hammer down on Florence's head, cut off the rest of her words. Shocked almost out of his senses by the suddenness of the attack, Charlie fell back as blood spattered him and he saw Florence slump forward with the chair, to be followed to the floor by a shrieking Sarah repeatedly bringing the hammer down on her face, a face that was fast becoming little more than a bloody pulp under the frenzy of blows.

"F-for the love of God, st-stop it," Charlie stuttered at last. "Can't you see she's dead? W-why must you go on hitting her?"

The splashy hammering stopped and Sarah, squatting on her haunches beside the dead woman, raised her own blood smeared face and stared up at him.

"Kill Sarah Fowkes instead," she said, mimicking the fear in Florence's voice to perfection. "I'll be the better bargain. She may get you hanged. I can make you rich." She snatched up a hank of Florence's hair and lifted the unrecognisable face towards him. "Have a look at your better bargain, Charlie Bennet. You were going to kill me for her, weren't you? Weren't you?"

Catlike, she rose to her feet and came towards him with the hammer raised. Seeing the bloodlust in her eyes, he shielded his head with his hands and shouted hoarsely, "No Sarah no! I would never have killed you for that fat sow. I swear to God I wouldn't. I was letting her talk on till you came back. She was telling me she had more money and I hoped she might tell where it is, that's all. I swear I wouldn't hurt you. I couldn't hurt you."

"Not much you wouldn't." The hammer missed his head by a fraction and then hung loosely by her side.

"You should see your face," she mocked savagely. "You should just see your face. I ought to do you in, Charlie Bennet, but I need you. I've got a job for you in the morning."

"Anything," gabbled Charlie, his eyes fastened on the blood stained hammer. "I'll do anything for you, Sarah. You know I will."

Sarah's laugh was short but she let the hammer fall to the floor. "Why wouldn't you kill me for her?" she asked. "Is it because you love me so much?"

Charlie grabbed at the straw. "Yes," he gasped. "You know I love you. I've always loved you."

"That horse won't ride, Charlie Bennet. I found out how much you love me on the ship."

"I was mad with the drink, Sarah. I hadn't slept all night. I swear I didn't know what I was saying. Of course I love you. You're the most beautiful woman I've ever seen. I couldn't hurt you. Let's get out of this muck-hole and go upstairs. Give me a chance and I'll prove I love you. Come on Sarah, darling. Get out of them mucky clothes and come upstairs. You'll be trailing blood all over the place."

"Mucky clothes?" Sarah looked down at herself almost dazedly. Her hands, the sleeves and front of her blouse and skirt, and even her shoes were smothered in Florence's blood and worse. Charlie was right. She daren't risk going up to the parlour and through the shop wearing them.

"All right," she conceded. "And you're not much better yourself. We'd best both of us take our clothes off before we go upstairs."

Stripped to her chemise and drawers, she turned to climb the stairs and felt the heat of his naked body close behind her. As it had been on the ship and since, the act of murder had left her excited but unfulfilled and when she reached the parlour, she almost inadvertently put her hand back and found his erection.

"God almighty," he groaned, pulling her to the floor and starting to rip off the rest of her garments. For a moment she welcomed him and began to loosen her drawer strings, and then, almost without a change in conscious thought, she was back among the twisted sheets in her mother's laundry, fifteen years old and fighting for her life with a man who was ripping at her clothes and raping her. Clenching her fists, she struck at him again and again, fighting him off until her bare foot became tangled with the mat and she rolled on to her back, held fast beneath the heavily breathing man.

"Sarah, I've got to," he was muttering as he tried to force her legs apart with his knees to enter her."

"You're trying to kill me again," she sobbed wildly as she fought to push him away. "You filthy bastard, you want to hurt me."

"I got to. You want me to. I can't stop." Charlie's words came in a series of gasps as he finally forced his way between her legs and was deep inside her, ignoring the blows that were falling on his head and shoulders.

"Oh God," moaned Sarah as she felt him enter and was unable to prevent herself from clenching her buttocks and moving to meet him until, feeling him begin to work rhythmically backwards and forwards, her back arched again and again to meet the heat and hardness of his plunge with a glorious heat and sudden wetness of her own.

"Charlie Bennet," she screamed at last, her legs tight round him. "You are no better than a rutting pig!" A moment before he reached his own climax, he opened his eyes to look into Sarah's face. Her lips were parted, she was breathing hard, but she smiled up at him in some sort of mad triumph, unconscious of the smears of Florence Carlisle's blood across her forehead and cheeks. Hastily he closed his eyes and had to think, 'Annie. Annie Annie!' while he held a crazily laughing Sarah Fowkes close in his arms and plunged for his long, shuddering release.

They stood side by side in the bath to wash the blood off each other and, still naked, Sarah clung to him while they got into her bed. They made love twice more during the night and in the morning, while Sarah opened the shop and smilingly dealt with her customers, Charlie went down to the cellar, stripped naked again to save what was left of his clothes, and turned his hand to the task of butchering Florence Carlisle with a saw. It proved more difficult than he expected, but at last he was left with the decapitated torso in one sack and the arms, legs, and head in two others. Late that night, with his hat pulled low over his eyes and a heavy scarf covering his nose and mouth, Charlie heaved the remains of Florence Carlisle into a handcart, wheeled them to a butcher's yard and tipped the sacks into the ditch at the back, where they lay among the rancid fat, mouldy meat, and lazily crawling bluebottles that covered the rotting weeds at the bottom.

When he got back to the shop, the ruined clothes including Florence's, were laboriously cut to pieces and fed to the kitchen boiler. Feeling safe at last, Charlie and Sarah went to bed and lay in each other's arms. Neither of them knowing that Charlie had been seen by a ragged street urchin who'd stopped searching the ditch for a few edible scraps of meat when she heard the handcart approach and tucked herself away in the shadow of the butcher's back door. Nor had either of them seen the gold filigree ring, so deeply embedded in Florence Carlisle's third finger that it was virtually invisible. Or the bloody footprint Sarah left under the parlour mat where they made love on the floor.

Nor indeed, would they have slept so soundly had they known that Mrs Tombrin, no less determined than her friend, Florence Carlisle, to renew their acquaintanceship, had instituted her own enquiries. Beginning at the shipping company's offices, she struck gold at her first attempt. The clerk who had arranged delivery of their heavy baggage, remembered both the ladies quite well and was perfectly happy to hand over Mrs Carlisle's forwarding address. The setbacks began when she called at Florence's rooms in Argyle Street and her friend was not at home. She made three more visits before she went to the police, told of her fears, and described Mrs Carlisle the best way she could. The sergeant at the desk heard her out without interruption and then escorted her to an office where she was asked to repeat the description to a man wearing a quite ordinary herring-bone tweed suit. It was he who asked her to sit down and told her that human remains had been found two days earlier, and they were of a very fat lady.

Mrs Tombrin burst into tears and covered her face with her hands.

"Oh God, I knew it. I knew it," she was sobbing when the detective said:

"That is a very interesting ring you're wearing, Mrs Tombrin. May I ask where you got it?"

"My ring?" flared a suddenly furious Mrs Tombrin. "My dearest friend is dead and you ask about my ring?"

For answer, Detective Sergeant Herrick took a small envelope from his pocket and shook out an identical ring on to his blotter.

"Your ring looks very like this one, madam. It might help to know where they came from."

Molly Tombrin stared at the ring, then took off her own and laid it beside the one she knew to be Florence's. "The Embassy Christmas dinner in '69," she said softly. "All the wives were presented with them. Florence and I always wore ours."

Herrick pulled a sheet of paper towards him, selected a pen with some care, and said, "In that case there seems to be very little doubt in the matter and I am sorry for you in your loss. Suppose I get a cup of tea brought in here for you, Mrs Tombrin, and when you feel able to, you can start telling me all you know about Mrs Carlisle's movements and Madame Sarah's shop."

The following morning, a slim, herring-bone suited man entered Madame Sarah's shop with a constable. Putting his high crowned hat on the counter, he said to the woman standing behind it, "You must be Madame Sarah. I am Detective Sergeant Herrick and this gentleman with me is Constable Haines. We are making enquiries into the disappearance of a lady named Mrs Florence Carlisle and I wonder if you would be good enough to spare me a few minutes of your time."

On entering the parlour with Sarah, Herrick said to the suddenly chalky faced man who dropped his newspaper on the table and was scrambling to his feet, "Ah, how do you do, sir? You must be Lord Charles Beniton."

Chapter Ten

"Thank you my lord, I am feeling much better," Mrs Tombrin assured the judge. "I have been reminded by my good friend, Mr Shanklin, that I will best serve the cause of justice by ignoring that man's bullying tactics and answering each question truthfully. I will not break down again."

"My lord!" Arnold Roberts was at once on his feet, his arms raised high.

Ignoring the counsel's protest, the judge said to Mrs Tombrin, "Your adviser is quite correct, madam. You enjoy the protection of this court and counsel for the defence will be reprimanded if he makes any attempt to press you too hard."

Roberts bowed low. "Thank you very much, my lord," he said sarcastically, "but as the jury has observed, I am doing my best to get the truth from a hostile and extremely unreliable witness."

"Mr Roberts," Mr Justice Hughes replied quietly but very distinctly. "Mrs Tombrin has in my view, answered your questions as fully and as honestly as she can. She has told the court that letters handed to her by Sarah Fowkes were, so far as she could possibly know their source, written by Charles Beniton, otherwise Charles Bennet. She has also told you that she saw the unfortunate Mrs Carlisle, who was a friend of many years standing, in the company of Sarah Fowkes. Before you question her any further on the point, Mr Roberts, allow me to tell you this. If I should happen to see you standing in a shop doorway a year from now, I think I can promise you that I will know you at once, whether you are wearing feathers on your hat or not."

The judge made no attempt to quell the sudden explosion of laughter in the courtroom. When it died away of its own accord, he said to the discomforted Arnold Roberts, "I know you are doing your duty in trying to show the witness may be mistaken in her identification of the lady she saw with Fowkes. You have every right to do so but your questions on the matter have been fully answered and I will allow no more hectoring of the witness. Have I made myself clear?"

Roberts bowed again, his face scarlet. "Perfectly clear, my lord. I thank you. In the circumstances, I have very few additional questions for this witness."

The judge nodded and leaned back in his chair to watch Roberts approach Mrs Tombrin.

"Madam," he said, almost conversationally, "my cross examination seems to have caused you some distress, though I assure you, that was never my intention. Are you normally an excitable lady, given to fits of anger?"

Mrs Tombrin clasped her hands together and said quietly, "No sir, I am not. Not in ordinary circumstances."

"Thank you very much, Mrs Tombrin. Now, on the morning you saw the lady you claim to have recognised as Mrs Carlisle, she was standing on the doorstep of Madame Sarah's shop. Is that correct?"

"Yes it is," Mrs Tombrin said warily. "But I could see very clearly who it was."

"Quite so, but that is not my point. I believe you stood on the opposite side of the street and called out to attract the lady's attention. Is that correct?"

"No, that is not correct. Florence Carlisle called to me first and I tried to answer her."

"But you were standing on the other side of the street when you called out to her, were you not?"

"Yes I was, but . . . "

"The yes will suffice for the moment, thank you, Mrs Tombrin. Now then madam, were there not many occasions on which you took up station on the other side of the street from Madame Sarah's shop and shouted at her and her clients?"

Mrs Tombrin flushed angrily. "No, there were not!" she

snapped. "I have never before been given occasion to raise my voice in a public place and if you are saying I made a habit of doing so, you are a liar."

"Mrs Tombrin . . . " began the judge, a little wearily, but Arnold Roberts was smiling broadly.

"It's of no great importance, my lord," he interrupted. "I think my last question has been answered satisfactorily and I have no more to ask this witness."

"Very well, Mr Roberts. Do you have anything further, Mr Shanklin?" enquired the judge with a lift of his eyebrows.

"Thank you, my lord," said the prosecuting counsel, slowly getting to his feet while Arnold Roberts sat down in a flurry of papers and robe. "Mrs Tombrin, I want only to clear up any possible confusion and make quite sure that your evidence is clear to the court. Is that understood?"

"Yes sir."

"You have been a client of Sarah Fowkes for some weeks, have you not?"

"Yes sir."

"During which time, according to your sworn statement to the police and the evidence you have given in this court, you took certain treatments for which you paid a considerable price, were introduced by Sarah Fowkes to Charles Bennet and were told by her that his name was Lord Charles Beniton?"

"Yes sir. She told me he was Lord Charles Beniton and that he expressed an interest in me."

"After which, you formed an attachment for the young man and you were given the impression by the letters you received and by his demeanour when you were together, that your affection was returned?"

"I thought he loved me, yes."

"Not now?"

"Not now sir. I believe I was misled into behaving very foolishly."

"We are all guilty of behaving foolishly from time to time, Mrs Tombrin. Now let us turn to Mrs Carlisle. You saw a lady with Sarah Fowkes when you were approaching Madame Sarah's shop and you are quite certain that lady was Mrs Carlisle?"

"Quite, quite certain."

"So far as you can be aware, did Mrs Carlisle recognise you?"

Mrs Tombrin rested a fist on the ledge of the witness-box. Pounding it for emphasis, she said loudly, "Of course Florence recognised me! She called out to me. She asked me to congratulate her on her forthcoming marriage."

Shanklin held up a hand to calm her. "And then what happened?" he asked gently.

"I was about to do so and tell her of my own good fortune but Madame Sarah came across the road and prevented me."

"I see. And when you were not allowed to approach your friend, Mrs Carlisle . . . "

"My lord!" roared Arnold Roberts, scrambling to his feet.

Shanklin waved him back imperiously. "A slip of the tongue, my lord. I apologise most sincerely. Mrs Shanklin, when you were not allowed to approach the lady you thought to be Mrs Carlisle, what action did you take?"

"The following morning I went to the shipping company offices and saw the clerk who deals with sending on passenger's heavy luggage. He was good enough to give me Mrs Carlisle's forwarding address. I called at the house she had rented several times during the course of the next two days but she was not at home. I became extremely worried about her and when she was not at home on the following morning, I went to a police station and told an officer that I thought my friend had disappeared and I feared that she may have come to some harm."

"I see. What happened then?"

"The officer asked me to describe Mrs Carlisle and when I had done so, I was escorted to another office, where I was asked to repeat the description by a gentleman who told me he was Sergeant Herrick, a detective. It was he who showed me Florence's ring and it was then I knew my friend had been murdered by that woman."

Shanklin held up his hand to prevent another outburst from Arnold Roberts. "No, Mrs Tombrin," he said firmly. "You can only say what you know to be true and it is certainly true that you friend was murdered. Foully murdered and after that, butchered without mercy in a vain attempt to hide the fact. It is not for you or me to decide who is guilty of that heinous crime. That task, thank God, lies before the jury. You spoke of Mrs Carlisle's ring, which has already been produced in evidence by the police. You said you knew it the moment it was shown to you. Can I ask if it was a common ring? The sort you might find in any good jeweller's shop?"

"No, it is not at all common. I know of very few, all made in India. Florence, Mrs Carlisle, was presented with one at an Embassy dinner and I was given the one I am wearing at the same function. It is its twin."

"Thank you. All that is perfectly clear to me and, I am quite sure, to the gentlemen of the jury." William Shanklin glanced at his notes and looked up to smile broadly at the witness. "Do you know, Mrs Tombrin, I have nothing further to ask you at this time. Thank you very much."

"Thank you, Mrs Tombrin," repeated the judge. "It is my duty to remind you that you are still under oath and can be called back to the stand if any clarification of your previous evidence is required. Do you understand that?"

"Oh yes, my lord. I will not be afraid."

The judge raised a hand to hide a smile and said mildly, "Quite so. You may step down now." Mrs Tombrin nodded graciously and, accepting the arm of a court usher with some style, climbed down from the witness stand to a smattering of applause.

Sarah watched sourly as the small comedy of the tiny Mrs Tombrin being escorted to the back of the court by a giant usher unfolded. 'Just you wait till I get up there to say my piece'. Arnold Roberts had advised her as strongly as he could against taking the stand, saying he was her counsel and it would be far better if he spoke for her, but she insisted.

"Anyone who would have spoken up for me and meant what they were saying is long dead," she told him. "I am the one who can get in the witness-box and say I am an innocent woman, and I mean to do so."

* * * *

She had said she was innocent to the police detective sergeant when he first interviewed her in his office. "I am a seller of soaps and perfumes and I give my expert opinion and treatments for skin disorders," she told him, looking the grey suited and almost grey faced man straight in the eye. "That means I am a respectable business woman and if you've brought me here to tell me that this Mrs Carlisle who was murdered was one of my customers, what of it? I expect she went into lots of shops. Why aren't you talking to her dressmaker or the man who sells her potatoes and cabbages? You've picked the wrong one to talk to in me, sergeant. Customers don't come ten a penny down Beak Street. When I get hold of a client, the last thing I want to do is finish her off."

Sergeant Herrick studied her face while he waited for her to finish speaking, nodded, and looked down to turn a page of his notes. "Before we get on to that, let's start with a Mrs Tombrin," he said slowly. "Tell me, Miss Fowkes. Would you happen to have a customer named Mrs Tombrin?"

"Mrs Tombrin?" Sarah frowned as though considering the question. Then her face cleared and she gave the policeman a dazzling smile. "Oh her. Yes, I know her all right. She's a bit soft in the head. What's up with your Mrs Tombrin? Has she been murdered too?"

Herrick returned the smile. "No," he said easily, "it's nothing like that. Is Mrs Tombrin still one of your customers?"

"No sergeant, she is not. Like I said, she was a good customer once and the truth is, I thought she was quite the lady till she started making a nuisance of herself."

Herrick looked up from his note pad and raised his eyebrows. "Made a nuisance of herself, did she? How did she manage to do that, Miss Fowkes?"

Sarah's smile deepened. "She fell head over heels in love with my gentleman friend, Mr Bennet. She came into the shop one afternoon and told me he had been writing love letters to her and in one of them, he asked her to marry him. I told her she was behaving like a silly fool. Charlie Bennet was much too young and unsettled to want to marry anyone, let alone a daffy old lady like her. What's more, I knew for a fact that he couldn't write anyone a love letter to save his life."

"Are you saying Bennet cannot read or write?" asked Herrick.

"Oh he can read and write after a fashion," Sarah replied, "but he's no scholar."

The sergeant made a note and asked what happened after Mrs Tombrin was told Bennet had not written the love letters she claimed to have received.

"She got herself very worked up," Sarah replied, "and when I told her she was wasting her time going after Charlie, she said that I was jealous of her and trying to ruin her future happiness by preventing her marriage to the gentleman she loved and who loved her. She swore she wasn't going to let me do it and we finished the argument by having a real row. By the end of it, she got herself so excited, she threatened me with violence and I had to ask her to leave my premises. I told her to get out and not bother me or Mr Bennet any more. From that time on, the daft old cow has taken to standing in the street outside the shop and shouting at me every time I show my face."

Herrick made another note, numbered the page, and took a fresh sheet of paper. "Does this shouting of hers happen at any particular time of day?"

"She could be outside the shop at any time of day but it is mostly in the mornings."

The detective made another note, looked up at Sarah and said, "Now, this question of the missing Mrs Carlisle. Are you quite certain that Florence Carlisle is not a name you recognise?"

"No, I don't know any lady with that name. That's not to say she never came into the shop to buy a bar of soap or a bottle of perfume. I would only write down a client's name if she made an appointment for some special treatments."

"I see. So if I were to tell you we found some bars of the soap you sell in Mrs Carlisle's rooms, it wouldn't come as a surprise to you?"

"No, why should it? I sell soap to a lot of people I don't know. And in any case, who is to say it was bought in my shop. I'm not the only one who sells Constantine's perfumes and soaps."

"That is perfectly true," Herrick said. "There are three others in your vicinity and they are being questioned. Would it surprise you to know that two days before she was reported missing, Mrs Carlisle was seen outside your shop?"

"It's like I already told you, sergeant. I don't have any way of knowing if she was there or not. It's a shop. People are coming in and out all day long. She could have been any one of them."

"Mrs Carlisle was a very fat lady. Do you remember a very fat lady visiting your shop on Tuesday of last week?"

Sarah laughed aloud. "Bless you, my dear," she said, her voice artificially high. "Half of my customers are too fat and the best part of what's left think they're too thin. That's what keeps a business like mine going. Trying to turn my customers into whatever they tell me they want to be."

This time Herrick did not return the smile. Instead, he asked quietly, "How do you account for your cellar floor and walls being heavily splashed with blood?"

For once, there was no immediate answer and the detective looked up to study Sarah's face while he repeated the question.

"Oh God Almighty, you found that terrible dog's blood," she said at last, and sighed heavily before going on with, "I'm sorry, Mr Herrick, for the minute I didn't know what you were talking about because I didn't know the mess it made was still down there. Charlie Bennet promised me faithfully he would wash the cellar down after he killed a mad dog in there. I expect you gentlemen came before he had the chance."

Herrick leaned back in his chair, folded his arms, and continued watching her carefully while he said, "Mr Bennet killed a mad dog in your cellar, did he? I'd like to know a little more about that, Miss Fowkes. Why don't you tell me all about the dog?"

"A great big thing it was," said Sarah, her eyes wide. "It got into my backyard somehow or other and it was rushing round and round the place, growling and snapping at everything like it was mad. I tried to get in the yard to let it out the back gate but as soon as I put my nose out of the scullery door, it showed all its teeth and made a rush at my skirts as though he wanted to take a lump out of me."

"Did it really?" said Herrick, shaking his head doubtfully. "I don't think I would have cared to tackle an animal like that. Did you manage to let it out of the yard eventually?"

"Of course not, silly. I wouldn't have had my cellar full of the blood then, would I?"

Sarah smiled brilliantly and Herrick managed to look abashed when he tutted and replied, "Yes of course, you're quite right, Miss Fowkes. And it was the blood in the cellar I wanted to know about, too. Well, if you couldn't manage to let the dog out of the gate when it rushed at you, what on earth did you do?"

"I ran back into the kitchen and shouted for Charlie Bennet to tell him what was happening. He came and had a look at the dog and told me it was all right. I should leave it to him and he would get a lump of poisoned meat prepared. When he had the meat ready, he chucked it into the cellar for the dog to go after it, but it must have been a strong beast because even after it went down there and swallowed every scrap, it kept on growling and making noises. In the end, Charlie went down to take a look and he found the dog was still alive and trying to bite him, so he was forced to cut its throat and it bled a lot. That's where the blood came from."

Herrick wrote in silence for a minute or two and then, without looking up, asked, "What colour was the animal, Miss Fowkes?"

"Colour? Brown, sort of a black and brown mixed."

"I see. Was it a dog or a bitch?"

"Wh-what?" Sarah said, staring at the top of his balding head.

Herrick looked up at her. "There is a difference as I'm sure you know. Was it a dog or a bitch?"

"You listen to me, mister sergeant," Sarah said indignantly. "The next time a mad dog chases you out of your backyard, you can tell me if it's a dog or a bitch. I didn't stop to look, thank you very kindly."

"Not even after it was dead?"

"No, of course I didn't look at it. What do I want to look

at a dead dog for?"

"I don't know the answer to that one either, Miss Fowkes, but in the parlour above the cellar steps, there is a clear mark of a bare foot that has stepped in blood. It is much too small to have been made by Mr Bennet. Can you explain the footprint?"

Sarah shook her head vehemently. "No I can't," she declared, and then, as Herrick took up his pen and prepared to write, added hurriedly, "Oh yes I can. I remember it all clearly now. I was still frightened of the dog and Charlie made me go into the cellar and see for myself it was dead. I slipped on some of the blood and took my shoe off. When I went back upstairs, I must have got some more of the blood on my foot."

Sergeant Herrick held her eye for a moment and, when she did not drop her gaze, asked, "What did you do with the dog after you killed it? It wasn't in the cellar when we searched your premises."

"How would I know what happened to it? Charlie threw it in a ditch somewhere, I expect. What else would you do with a dead dog you want to get rid of?"

"Or a dead woman?" Herrick asked rhetorically. When Sarah made no answer, he nodded to the waiting constable who took Sarah's elbow, preparatory to taking her below to a cell.

"By the way," the detective said conversationally when the pair reached the door. "You must know that very little of your statement agrees with Mr Bennet's. I wonder the two of you didn't get your stories straight when you killed her."

Sarah turned quickly to face him. "Look here, Mr Clever," she said acidly. "I have never killed anyone in my life and that is the plain truth. If Charlie Bennet remembers things any different from the way I do, then I don't know what he might have been up to. You'll just have to take the matter up with him, won't you." The normally impassive constable winked at Herrick over the top of Sarah's head and, as the door closed behind them, the detective pushed the notes away and permitted himself a slight smile of appreciation. She was a cool one all right. Beautiful, cruel, and as hard as a diamond if he was any judge. She didn't even blink when he told her Bennet's statement didn't agree with hers. Herrick had lied, of course. Bennet hadn't been interviewed yet, but she had been lying too. That story about the mad dog had been made up on the spur of the moment, he was positive of it. So positive, that the blood splattered cellar was the subject of the first question he asked Charlie when the prisoner was escorted into his office.

"B-blood?" The shocked man stammered when he repeated the word. "On the cellar f-floor?" Herrick tapped the point of a pen against his teeth and waited without repeating the question. After a few moments, Charlie rubbed the heel of his hand across his forehead.

"Look," he said, "I don't know what blood you're talking about. The shop belongs to Madame Sarah. I don't go down in the cellar and I never saw no blood."

Charlie paused expectantly, and when Herrick did not react, went on pleadingly. "Now listen, guv, I've been thinking about this trouble you got me in here for. It's all got to be a mistake because I don't know a lady called Mrs Carlisle and I've got no reason to have anything to do with her disappearing. Always supposing she really has disappeared and not just gone away like anyone might. I don't think you had any right to keep me in that freezing cold cell all this time and I want to go home this minute."

Herrick put his pen down on the blotter and looked at Charlie. "I dare say you do want to go home," he said, "but a lady has been murdered and you've got a few questions to answer before you can think of going anywhere. Not that I can blame you, Mr Bennet. I had a look round your gaff last night and I must say you do yourself pretty well. How do you make your money?"

"Sarah Fowkes gives me money. I do jobs for her now and again."

"She pays you pretty well for an odd job man, doesn't she, Lord Beniton?"

Charlie half rose from his chair and was unceremoniously pushed back into it by the constable.

"Lord Beniton?" he repeated nervously. "I've never heard of him. You've got it all wrong again. My name is Charlie Bennet."

"But Mrs Tombrin has good reason to know you as Lord Beniton, doesn't she?"

"Mrs Tombrin?" Charlie asked nervously. "I never heard of no one called Mrs Tombrin."

"I see." Sergeant Herrick turned back two or three pages of his notes and tutted as though dissatisfied. "So what you're telling me, Mr Bennet, is that you know nothing about the two ladies called Mrs Carlisle and Mrs Tombrin, and you know nothing about the blood on the floor and walls of Sarah Fowkes's cellar because you've never been down there?"

"That's right. I don't know anything about any of it."

"And no one to the best of your knowledge, has any reason to know you as Lord Beniton?"

"No, they don't. Of course they don't."

"I must tell you that Mrs Tombrin will be given an opportunity to identify you as the man she called Lord Beniton."

"What if she does? It's only the word of a silly old woman against mine."

"A silly old woman, you say, Mr Bennet. If you don't know Mrs Tombrin, what makes you think she is old? I didn't say so."

Charlie lifted his shoulders in a poor attempt at a careless shrug. "I don't know why I thought it. I expect I took it she was one of Madame Sarah's customers. She calls them all silly old women."

"Silly old women the pair of you can make a bit of money from, I imagine?"

"I don't know what you're talking about again. You keep on at me and I don't understand any of it."

Herrick smiled and wagged a finger at Charlie. "Oh I think you know what I mean all right, Mr Bennet. Lonely old woman. Good looking young masher comes along with the promise she can marry a title. There must be money in it. The question is, why did such a pretty little dodge go so wrong it had to end in murder?"

Charlie blanched. "It didn't," he gabbled. "I never murdered no one. I already told you I don't know what you're talking about."

"Really? Well, you'd best take that up with your friend, Sarah Fowkes. I've got her sworn statement to say you went down into the cellar and cut the mad bitch's throat."

Charlie jumped to his feet and brushed off the constable's restraining hand.

"If she says such a thing, she's a bloody liar!" he shouted.

"Then how do you explain the blood in the cellar?"

"I told you I don't know about the blood in the cellar. I've never been down there."

"I've never been down there," Herrick repeated slowly while he wrote it down. His voice sharpening, he looked at Charlie and said, "People who tell lies usually have something to hide, Mr Bennet. Mrs Tombrin has described your appearance accurately and she tells me she knows you as Lord Beniton. Why do you suppose the lady would want to lie about you?"

"I don't know why. How should I know why someone tells lies about me?"

"And Sarah Fowkes has not only said you have been in her cellar, she also told me in a sworn statement that you are responsible for shedding blood down there. Why do you suppose Miss Fowkes would tell lies about you?"

"I don't know," Charlie wailed. "Ask her."

"I expect I will, but right now I'm asking you. Do you think she lied because she killed the poor woman herself and only used you to cart away the remains?"

Charlie caught his breath and gabbled, "I never carted away any remains and like I told you, I don't know why Sarah Fowkes tells lies about me. Ask her."

"But a man answering your description was seen tipping the sacks containing Mrs Carlisle's remains into the ditch behind the abattoir in Gandry Lane. You're surely not going to tell me you know nothing about that too?"

"Oh yes I am. You're all telling lies about me. I don't know why."

"Me as well as Sarah Fowkes and Mrs Tombrin?"

"Everyone," blurted a wild-eyed Charlie Bennet. "You're all telling lies about me."

Herrick dropped the pen, pushed his writing block to one side, and fixing Charlie with a steely grey eye, said bluntly,

"Tell me something, Mr Bennet. Have you ever seen a man hanged?"

Charlie's eyes widened in terror and then closed as he slumped in the chair and began to rub his throbbing temples with the heels of his hands.

"Have I ever seen a man hanged?" he almost groaned. "No, of course I haven't seen a man hanged. What are you asking me a question like that for?"

"I'll tell you what for," said Herrick, beginning to sound exasperated. "In fact, I'm going to tell you something I suggest you think about very carefully, Mr Bennet. The last man I saw hanged was found guilty of a crime he swore he knew nothing about. He swore he had never been there, he'd never seen the body of the victim, and he had none of the victim's money. When it came to standing up in court, he had to keep his mouth shut while the other two defendants put all the blame on him. He couldn't say they were lying without admitting he had been lying too and they committed the crime while he was in the street outside, watching out for any constable who might happen by on his rounds."

Herrick picked up the pen and, pointing it at Charlie's throat, went on. "I took a good look at the man after he stopped kicking the air long enough for the prison doctor to say he was dead and could be taken down. His eyes were popping, his mouth was open, and his tongue was sticking out like he was trying to say something. And do you know what I think he wanted to say, Mr Bennet? I think he had made up his mind to tell the truth at last, only it was too late because by the time he was ready to tell it, he was either strangled or his neck was broken and he was never going to tell anyone the truth again. Now you listen to me, Mr Bennet. The constable is going to take you back to your cell. While you're down there, I want you to think about what I just told you. It's for your own sake."

Charlie's face was ashen when he was taken back to his cell. As the constable swung back the heavy door and silently motioned him inside, he said, "Here, hold on a minute, I've been thinking. Maybe I do know this Mrs Tombrin that sergeant was talking about. Skinny old crow with yellow hair, is she?"

Herrick sat in his chief's office and consulted his notes before saying, "That pair killed Florence Carlisle, I guarantee it. They both admit to knowing Mrs Tombrin, though the man denied it at first. I would guess they were playing the Lord Beniton hook with both the ladies swallowing the bait. It must have come as a terrible shock to Fowkes when Mrs Tombrin came to the shop on the wrong day and she saw that she and Mrs Carlisle knew each other. I think Fowkes decided then one of them had to die quickly or the game was up. It's my guess the victim was Florence Carlisle only because she was the first to voice her suspicions. I'm quite certain too, that Fowkes wasn't just an accessory to murder. She had a hand in the killing. She's already admitted the bloodstained footprint is hers and I don't believe a word of her story about a mad dog. In a nutshell, sir, Fowkes was seen with Mrs Carlisle shortly before the poor lady disappeared and was found murdered. I believe Sarah Fowkes and Charlie Bennet killed her in the cellar below Fowkes's shop. And of course, Bennet answers the description of the man pushing the handcart with the lady's remains."

Inspector Marks shook his head. "You wouldn't believe it of a woman like Fowkes to look at her, would you, but I say you're right. We've got our killers and our friend, Mrs Tombrin, has had a lucky escape."

An hour later, in their separate cells, Sarah Fowkes and Charles Bennet were both charged with the wilful murder of Mrs Florence Carlisle, residing in London and late of Barrackpore, India. Sarah flushed a dark red and said nothing. Charlie fainted.

Chapter Eleven

The judge watched Mrs Tombrin walk slowly to the rear of the court, shook his head, and then looked enquiringly at the prosecuting counsel.

William Shanklin bowed. "Mrs Tombrin was the last of the witnesses for the Crown, my lord."

"Thank you Mr Shanklin. Are you ready to begin your defence, Mr Roberts?"

"Thank you, my lord. I call on Sarah Fowkes to take the stand."

There was a murmur of appreciation mixed with some maliciousness from the well of the court when Sarah, the higher than usual colour in her cheeks only serving to enhance her beauty, obediently rose to her feet. Escorted by a lumpy, heavy shouldered matron, she looked slight and almost girlish as she walked quickly to the witness-box and stepped into it. Looking first at the judge and then round the court, she saw every eye was on her and for the first time since her arrest, felt a sudden thrill of fear. Roberts had told her it was almost unknown for a defendant in a murder trial to take the stand and the crowd knew she was gambling with her life. She knew too, they expected her to lose. She could see them smirking in anticipation of seeing her cut down by Shanklin's questions until she was a broken reed, her guilt self-evident. Then they would have the additional pleasure of watching her have to face up to being condemned to death by hanging. Well, she hadn't lost the fight yet and she didn't mean to lose. She wrenched her eyes away from a thin, vindictively smiling woman in a dark, greasy looking bonnet, and looked down to see the Bible had been placed on the ledge before her. Once more looking at the judge, she placed a hand on its worn cover and repeated the oath in a firm, cool voice.

Arnold Roberts took his time getting to his feet and gathering up his notes before he asked quietly, "You are Sarah Fowkes, the proprietress of a shop known as Madame Sarah in Beak Street, and you reside in the rooms above the premises?"

"Yes, I am Sarah Fowkes and I live over my shop."

"Thank you, Miss Fowkes. Did you know the deceased lady, Mrs Florence Carlisle?"

"No, I did not. Not by name at least. I do not deny she might have been one of my customers."

Roberts glanced towards the jury and made some play of leafing through his notes before turning back to Sarah and saying, "Quite so, thank you again, Miss Fowkes. Now, you have heard the last witness for the prosecution say in evidence that she saw you and Mrs Carlisle in conversation outside your shop. Mrs Tombrin also said that, upon recognising Mrs Carlisle, she called out to her. Did you hear Mrs Tombrin call out?"

"Of course I heard her calling out. The whole street could hear her, the way she was carrying on. She spent half her life out in the street, shouting at me and my clients."

"I see. And on this occasion you heard her quite clearly?"

Sarah nodded and looked towards the back of the court before saying, "Oh yes. She was quite as loud as usual, thank you."

Roberts smiled at a titter from somewhere behind him and went on, "Did she address the lady she thought to be Mrs Carlisle by name?"

"I did not understand her if she did call out a name. As always, her cries made no sense to me."

"A moment if you please, Mr Roberts." The judge's tone was hard edged and Arnold Roberts stepped back at once. As he sat down, Mr Hughes turned to Sarah.

"Miss Fowkes," he said coldly. "Are you telling this court that Mrs Tombrin was in the habit of standing in the street outside your shop premises and calling out unintelligible remarks?"

"Yes sir, that is exactly what I'm saying."

"I wonder you did not call a constable on any of these occasions, Miss Fowkes. Judging by what you are telling us, Mrs Tombrin was making a great nuisance of herself. Her behaviour must have interfered considerably with the smooth running of your business?"

Sarah sighed deeply before she said, "I know it was wrong of me to let it go on but at one time Mrs Tombrin and I were friendly enough. Even when she first started making a racket in the street, I felt sorry for the lady. She had somehow got it into her head that I was her rival in love and had stolen her fiancé. I just hoped that when she got over her disappointment, she would give it up of her own accord and go away."

"I see." The judge looked down to make a note and said, "Mr Roberts?"

"Thank you, my lord." Arnold Roberts got to his feet, came forward to face Sarah, and took up the questioning with, "Miss Fowkes, on the occasion Mrs Tombrin thought she recognised her friend, you are saying you did not hear her call out the name of Mrs Carlisle?"

"No I did not."

Under cover of again searching through his sheaf of documents, Roberts glanced at William Shanklin, who sat with his eyes closed and his short plump legs stretched out before him. There had always been rivalry between the two men and not a little jealousy on the part of Roberts, who felt that Shanklin sucked up to the judges. Usually to his advantage when, like now, they were meeting on opposing sides. Determined to shock the Crown's advocate into paying proper attention to the defence arguments, he asked loudly. "Sarah Fowkes, did you, on or about the night of November 14th, 1881, murder Mrs Florence Carlisle and dismember, or cause to be dismembered, her body?"

Sarah gripped the edge of the witness-box and looked directly at the jury. "Before God, I did no such thing!" she cried passionately. "The very thought of murder is abhorrent to me and besides, what possible reason could I have for doing away with the lady, whoever she was? I am a shopkeeper, not a murderer!"

Shanklin's eyes were open and he was sitting up to study Sarah's face carefully. Satisfied, Roberts raised a hand and said calmly, "Miss Fowkes, I have no wish to distress you any further but you must expect to be questioned in this manner. It is the wilful murder of another human being you are charged with, after all."

"But I am innocent!"

"I believe you wholeheartedly, Miss Fowkes, but the unfortunate Mrs Carlisle was undoubtedly murdered by someone and you must give direct answers to my questions so that the jury can decide on the truth of the matter. Did you have any hand in the subsequent disposal of the remains of Florence Carlisle?"

"No never. I wouldn't have the faintest idea how to do such a thing."

"Few of us would, Miss Fowkes. Few of us would."

Roberts turned to look round the court. There was complete quiet and every eye was on him. Almost swelling with gratification, he continued almost conversationally, "You have stated that you conduct your business in the property you live in?"

"Yes sir, I do. Mostly downstairs in the shop."

"Thank you Miss Fowkes. Now, for the benefit of the jury, will you describe the premises and tell the court how your business is conducted."

"I have a shop and parlour on the lower floor, with a kitchen and scullery at the back. The kitchen has a door leading into a backyard which has a low wall round it and a gate. Above stairs, there is a bathroom and dressing-room for myself and for any of my clients who require a course of treatments. Apart from one more upstairs room used for storage, the top part of the house is my home. As for the business I do. I sell soaps and perfumes in the shop, discuss treatments for ladies privately in the parlour, and give all treatments in the evenings when the shop is closed. The treatments are carried out upstairs."

Roberts nodded. "Thank you, Miss Fowkes, that is very clear and precise. There is a cellar, is there not?"

"Yes there is a cellar but it is too damp for storage and never used."

"And never entered by you, Miss Fowkes?"

"Hardly ever. It is too dark and smelly for me. My coal is stored under cover in the yard."

"According to evidence given by the police witness, Sergeant Herrick, you made a statement saying a mad dog entered your backyard. A dog that was lured into the cellar by your sometime employee, Mr Bennet, and killed by him there. Is what the sergeant says correct?"

Sarah nodded. "Yes it is," she said. "Mr Bennet first tried to kill the dog with a piece of poisoned meat and when that failed, he went into the cellar after the creature and cut its throat."

"You also told the police officer that was one of the very few occasions on which you did enter the cellar and that you did so at the insistence of Mr Bennet."

Sarah squared her shoulders and looked directly at Charlie when she answered. "Yes, he made me go down into the cellar, but it was for my own good. I was hiding in the parlour and very afraid after the dog tried to attack me in the yard. And afterwards, when the animal was in the cellar and Mr Bennet went down after it to put it to death, the awful growling and snapping I could hear, frightened me even more. I am a woman, sir, and I was so distracted by the time Mr Bennet came up from the cellar and told me the dog was dead, I was unable to believe him. 'You are lying to me, Mr Bennet," I told him, 'the dog is alive, I can hear it breathing. At any moment it will come up here and attack me again.' I was weeping so hard that Mr Bennet grew impatient with me. He insisted on my going into the cellar to see the dead animal for myself. I was very reluctant but eventually I allowed him to escort me down the cellar steps and press me forward to inspect the animal."

Sarah clenched her fists and closed her eyes as though the memory was almost too much for her. Roberts came closer and said gently, "I know this is painful for you, but we must know. Was the animal dead?"

"It was," said Sarah, opening her eyes to look again at Charlie. "Its mouth was wide open ready to bite, but it was certainly dead. I had no idea there would be so much blood splashed about the place. I cannot bear the sight of blood and I felt so very faint, I almost slipped and fell as I turned to go back up to the parlour. When I looked down and saw the animal's blood on my slippers, I kicked them off on the cellar steps and went straight to my room. I have not entered the cellar from that day to this."

Her eyes left Charlie's face while Arnold Roberts turned over a page of his notes and said, "The police sergeant has testified there was a bloodstained mark of a woman's foot on the parlour floor and that at first, you denied all knowledge of that mark and the blood he found in the cellar."

Sarah nodded quickly. "When Mr Herrick questioned me, I did not know I had left such a mark. Later I remembered that I found blood on my foot when I got upstairs and got in the bath to scrub myself clean again, so yes, I must have made it. As to the cellar, I knew there had been a deal of blood down there but I thought Mr Bennet had kept his promise to wash the floor after he disposed of the dog. He knew I was terrified of blood."

In the dock, Charlie was forced to raise his hand to hide a grimace. Sarah Fowkes afraid of blood? Christ, but that was rich. Coming from the woman who threatened to cut off his bollocks five minutes after they met! And showed him the pair of scissors she meant to do it with. The wicked bitch loved to see blood. God Almighty, she was laughing like a loony when she was bashing in Amelia Hinks's face behind the lifeboat on the Pride of Plymouth. And what about the way she was screaming for blood when she wouldn't stop smashing at old Florence's head with that bloody coal hammer? And like as not, ready to smash his own turnip in as well. If she hadn't needed him to cut up the body, she might have done it too. And getting so mad with excitement at what she did, they had their first rumple on the parlour floor.

A vision of the blood-streaked Sarah, naked as the day she was born, rolling her belly beneath his own on the parlour floor, stirred his loins unbearably. God, but she was a fiery bitch when she was roused. Pulling him into her with all her strength, fighting him off and at the same time, shrieking with the passion of his thrusting, thrusting, thrusting, until the final surging plunge, which ended with a great shudder from him, Sarah's teeth in his shoulder, and the sharpened points of her fingernails tearing at his bare arse.

He dropped the hand that was covering his mouth and began to stare at the woman standing in the witness-box. He didn't know who she was pretending to be but she wasn't his Madame Sarah any more. This new Sarah Fowkes, slim as a blade in her prim blue, tailor-made suit and white blouse, answered old Robert's questions in a way that could almost make Charlie believe there had been a mad dog in the cellar and he should have done the right thing and washed the blood away after he had cut the brute's throat and thrown it into a ditch. The way she was telling it, this new Sarah was saying he was the cause of the trouble she found herself in over the death of Florence Carlisle. Because if he'd washed the cellar floor and walls like he promised, Sergeant Herrick wouldn't have found any blood in the cellar. As it was, he naturally thought the old lady had been done to death down there. Which, a very confused Charlie had to remind himself, she had been.

His mind in a whirl, Charlie looked down at his shaking hands. It was almost impossible for him to understand any of what was going on. He hadn't been given an opportunity to talk to Sarah since they were arrested and when Roberts visited him on remand, all the counsel said was that he should have kept his mouth shut.

"Bennet, my man," Mr Roberts told him severely. "You have already made my task more difficult by talking much too freely to the police. I am sorry to give you such bad news but you are in deep trouble and must prepare yourself for the worst. Are you a religious man, Bennet?"

Charlie shook his head dumbly.

Roberts tutted. "No? More's the pity. The best advice I can give you is to say your prayers nightly and leave yourself completely in my hands. If any barrister in England can get you off this charge, it is me."

Gathering up his papers, the defence counsel stood up to leave Charlie's cell. "Oh yes," he said almost casually, "one more thing I have to tell you. Very much against my advice, Miss Fowkes will be taking the stand to give evidence on her own behalf. How much help that will be to her, or indeed to your own case when she is cross-examined by William Shanklin, I cannot tell you." That was the last time Charlie was to see Arnold Roberts before being brought into the court and ordered to sit beside Sarah in the dock. He had not the least idea how Roberts meant to defend him and the story the counsel was encouraging Sarah to tell, mystified him even further.

He studied her covertly as she spoke. God almighty, but she was a queer fish. Fire and ice all mixed up together. There was the time he sat in her parlour, waiting for her to bring in one of her clients for him to take upstairs and rumple. The posh newspaper she made him read to impress her customers, bored him and he had put it down to poke around in the coffee table drawer when he came across a silver framed photograph of a little girl of about three. A pretty little thing she was, with a large bow on top of her head and corkscrew curls coming down to her shoulders. She had been photographed sitting good as gold on a studio chair, holding a rag doll against her cheek and smiling into the camera. Intrigued, Charlie was looking at the hand-tinted photograph when Sarah came in, snatched it away from him without a word, and he thought, held it against her breast for a split second before throwing it to the floor. The pain in her eyes when she picked it up again and put it back in the drawer forbade any questioning but Charlie had often wondered who the child might be.

He had wondered too, what happened in her life to turn Sarah so vicious. He knew she had been raped but they never went after men and that couldn't be why she always wanted to kill the women they cheated. It was easy enough to swindle their money out of them and it couldn't be the fear of discovery that made her want to do murder. Amelia and the others wouldn't have told anyone, he was sure of it. He reckoned all he had to do was tell them a tale about his Royal connections preventing his marriage to a commoner, and the daft old biddies would have swallowed it and gone home to cry into their pillows. But when he tried to give the idea to Sarah, adding that it would save having to kill the old girls off, she near enough bit his head off.

She told him he was a fool and going soft in the head. The

women she chose were stupid old cows who deserved to be done in. She was right about them being stupid, especially poor little Amelia with her soft brown eyes, but Charlie never had understood the need for killing. There was a wickedness deep inside Sarah Fowkes that he was incapable of comprehending. He looked at her in the witness-box, listened to her high, clear, and unafraid voice answering the questions Arnold Roberts put to her, and shook his head again. If he couldn't make sense of the answers she gave Roberts, it was no wonder. He couldn't make sense of the questions.

"Tell me, Miss Fowkes," Arnold Roberts was asking now. "Do you know Charles Bennet well?"

For the first time since she entered the witness-box, Sarah seemed to falter. "Pretty well, I think. I have known him for some considerable time I have grown to think of him as my good friend rather than as an employee."

"That does you a good deal of credit, Miss Fowkes, considering that he was dishonourably discharged from his regiment."

"Oh, but Mr Bennet was completely open about that," gushed Sarah. "He was discharged for defending the good name of his officer. The officer who tried to defend him at the court martial."

Roberts smiled pityingly at her. "There was no court martial, Miss Fowkes. I wonder if you would have been so free in offering the hand of friendship, had you known he was discharged ignominiously from the army for stealing shirts from the very officer you speak of?"

"I-I cannot say."

"And that, after he stole the shirts, he sold them and his uniform to a Whitechapel pawnbroker, following that little exercise by getting himself involved in a drunken brawl with a common prostitute and her bully?"

Sarah clasped her hands together tightly and looked very shocked. "If this is so, then Mr Bennet has lied to me. Had I known the truth about him, I would not have had the fellow in my house."

"It is true and proved beyond doubt, Miss Fowkes. I have the papers here and witnesses prepared to swear to them if necessary. It seems your soft heart worked in favour of Charles Bennet as well as Mrs Tombrin. Tell me, did he have a key to the premises?"

"To the back way only. I gave him a key to the padlock on the yard gate and another to the kitchen door."

"Thank you. Once inside the kitchen, would he have free access to the rest of the house?"

Sarah bit her lip and shot a frightened look towards the man in the dock. "The inside doors are not locked at night, if that is what you mean by free access."

"That is precisely what I mean by free access," Roberts replied. "Now then, Miss Fowkes. Since becoming acquainted with Bennet, have you ever had stock stolen from the shelves or the shop counter?"

"On a few occasions yes, but some of the customers are well known to be light fingered, especially the wealthy ladies. I have never found reason to suspect Mr Bennet. Not for a single moment."

"He struck you as an honest man?"

"Most certainly he did."

"He is most certainly plausible, I give you that. You put your trust in him?"

"I had no reason to do otherwise."

The counsel shook his head and watched the jury for its reaction when he said, "No, that is not quite correct, Miss Fowkes. You knew no reason to do otherwise." Roberts had lingered on the word 'knew' and Charlie shifted uneasily on the wooden bench, but was ignored by the officer beside him, who, like the rest of the court, was leaning forward and listening keenly to every word.

"Now then, Miss Fowkes," Roberts said in a sharper tone. "I can see by your demeanour that you do not wish to speak ill of the man you befriended. Nevertheless, it will not help the court understand your part in this matter if you withhold the truth. To your knowledge, did Charles Bennet approach any of your customers on or outside your premises and make assignations with them?"

"Assignations, Mr Roberts? Whatever do you mean?"

"You must not ask me questions, Miss Fowkes. To your knowledge, did Bennet meet with your customers outside your shop?"

"Certainly not to my knowledge. I cannot think of any reason why he should."

"Indeed? Let us suppose that Mrs Tombrin is telling the truth, at least about her own acquaintanceship with Bennet, who she claims to have known as Lord Charles Beniton. Does not that suggest to you that he may have made an approach to the lady?"

"Mrs Tombrin is deluded, sir. I gave her no letters that suggested Mr Bennet might be in love with her."

"I accept that, but what caused her to become deluded in the first instance and how does she come to know him as Lord Beniton?"

Sarah began to look distressed. "I do not know why anyone should call him Lord Beniton. How should I know such a thing?"

"How indeed? Very well Miss Fowkes, perhaps it was not a proper question to ask you and we must leave it for the jury to decide. If Charles Bennet were to bring a woman through your yard and into your parlour at dead of night, would you know of it?"

"Not if I was in my bed, no."

"That is because you sleep in the upper part of the premises?"

"Yes it is. I have already described the setting out of the property to you."

"Indeed you have. If he came into your parlour, he could also gain access to your cellar?"

"My cellar?" Sarah shrugged delicately, her disdain obvious. "Certainly he would have access to the cellar but what could anyone possibly want down there? It is hardly the place for an assignation with a lady, however coarse his appetite."

"That," Roberts said flatly, "depends entirely on the nature of the lady. Or, of course, the purpose of the assignation."

Charlie's eyes widened in shocked realisation of what was being said about him. The business was being done exactly the way Sergeant Herrick said it would. He was made to keep quiet and listen to himself being damned to Hell.

"Here!" he shouted at the judge, trying to get to his feet

against the restraining hand of the gaoler. "Here, you listen to me a minute. That ain't right!"

"Mr Bennet, you will sit down and behave yourself." Mr Hughes said mildly. "If there is one more outburst like that, I will have you taken down."

Charlie heard none of the judge's words. Seeing he had the court's attention at last, he continued his struggle with the gaoler and shouted. "It ain't right, your honour! They're all telling a pack of bleeding lies about me!"

"Take him down," said the judge. "Before he gets completely out of hand."

The court took their eyes off Sarah to watch the violently struggling Charlie being frog-marched away, his howls of protest muffled by a policeman's large hand placed judiciously across his mouth. As soon as the doors closed behind the four men, Roberts apologised for his client's behaviour and turned back to Sarah.

"Please do not be distressed, Miss Fowkes. Some people find the search for truth unpalatable. You said earlier in your evidence that you were surprised, indeed horrified by the amount of blood you found in the cellar when Bennet insisted on you accompanying him down there. Why was that?"

"Only that the dog did not seem anything like as large in death as it had in life and the blood was splashed everywhere. I was surprised to see the animal had bled so much. That is all."

"That is all? Miss Fowkes, what you have just told the court may be the most vital piece of evidence yet."

Left to himself in one of the holding cells below the court, Charlie Bennet threw himself down on the stone flagged floor and crouched against the wall, as far away from the heavy door as he could get. The shock of Sarah's betrayal had made his face become red and blotchy with fear. His head pounded with the certain knowledge that the blame for Florence Carlisle's murder was being laid on him. Roberts was there to save Sarah's neck by seeing him damned. They had made up a story between them that would see him swing while she got off and sailed home free.

God, but they were wicked. They were up there now, her

and that puffed up Roberts, making him out to be a murderer and a thief, saying he enticed women down into Sarah's cellar and did away with them while sweet little Miss Sarah was innocently tucked up in her bed! It was wicked lies and he ought to be up there to tell everyone what they were doing to him. For an instant, he started up to call the warder and then subsided, forcing himself back into the furthest corner of the cell. What was the use? She was cleverer than him, they all were. Charlie Bennet was done for. While he was made to swing on the end of a rope with his life being choked out of him, Madame Sarah would be back inside her shop. No doubt, with some other young fellow sitting in the parlour, all ready to rumple the next one of her customers she brought in.

Charlie rubbed his forehead hard against the dingy, wet wall and wished the man joy of the job, whoever he may be. As for Sarah, would she give him a second thought on the day he swung? No she would not, and no more would anyone else. For a moment, a picture of his father came into his mind, the old man sitting cross-legged on a table and putting down his stitching to read an account of the hanging in his morning newspaper.

"Oh yes, I used to know him quite well," his father was saying as he dropped the paper to pick up two pieces of cloth and smooth them over his thigh in preparation for the needle and thread. "I always used to tell his mother he was no good. I always told her he was born to be hanged." Charlie caught his breath, struck his head against the wall, and began to sob hopelessly.

Above him, the courtroom was still buzzing with the excitement of seeing him dragged away and the judge was rapping for silence. When some semblance of order was restored, Sarah said firmly, "I do not believe Charlie Bennet would take a woman into my cellar and kill her. The idea is quite ridiculous and absurd."

"Is it?" asked Roberts. "You were wrong about him when you first put your trust in him, Miss Fowkes, and you have just seen him being forcibly removed from the court by three officers. We are speaking of a strong and violent man, who was a key holder to your premises. On your own admission, once you were safe in the upper part of the building, you could have no knowledge of any action he may have taken below."

"That is true, but . . ."

"No madam. There are no buts to help Mr Bennet this way. Once you were in bed, a murder might well have been committed in your cellar and you would have known nothing at all about it. But you need not answer me, Miss Fowkes. You have told the court what you can and I have nothing else to ask you at this time."

Arnold Roberts bowed to the judge before seating himself and, at the uplift of the judge's eyebrows, William Shanklin got to his feet and walked across to stand by the witness-box.

"Well, well," he began genially, "it is very good of Mr Roberts to do so much of the prosecution's work for me. And deciding on which one of you is the guilty party too! I tell you, Miss Fowkes, it seems this case is so neatly stitched up, I expect his lordship will send us all home at any moment. However, there are still one or two small points I should like to cover. In your answers to Mr Roberts, you established that when you were upstairs in your bed, you could not know of any dastardly action your co-defendant may have engaged in. Is that correct?"

Sarah nodded stiffly. "Yes. I have said that I could not hear what he might be doing in the lower part of the building from my bedroom."

"Nor could you have heard the frantic shrieks of a lady being done to death in the cellar?"

"I don't know. I think not."

Shanklin nodded as though satisfied. "Quite so. Suppose Charlie Bennet, the monster you invited into your home, Miss Fowkes, loaned the keys to your house to his friend the Whitechapel pawnbroker. You would not have known what villainy that gentleman was about either. Or for that matter, if Bennet had loaned the keys to any of his dubious female acquaintances, you could not have known what they were doing in your cellar, could you?"

At once, Roberts was on his feet to protest. "But all this is mere conjecture, my lord."

Shanklin beamed at him. "Once more I am obliged to my

friend," he said. "He has made my point exactly. Miss Fowkes, if you were safely tucked up in your bed and dreaming the dreams of the pure and innocent, you were in no position to know if an action took place in your cellar or if no action took place in your cellar. Am I correct?"

Sarah hesitated, before saying slowly, "Well yes, I suppose you are."

"In fact, since you could not hear from your bedroom, it follows that you could not know of any action that took place in the cellar unless you had a hand in it. Am I correct in that, Miss Fowkes?"

"No, you are not correct in that. I did not kill the dog. Mr Bennet killed the dog in the cellar. I went down there after it was dead."

"Ah yes, the mad dog we've heard so much about. You said that when you went into the open yard at the back of your shop, you came upon a large and ferocious dog which barked very loudly and rushed at you, intent on doing you harm."

"Yes I did. I was very frightened by it."

"Because of the barking or because of its attempt to bite you?"

"Both of course. What a silly question."

Shanklin smiled again. "Miss Fowkes, it becomes a silly question only when your neighbours saw the animal or heard the commotion it was making. I have to tell you that extensive enquiries have been made and no one can be found who saw a dog behave in the manner you describe or heard any excessive barking."

"I can't be held responsible for that. My yard backs on to a busy street. Like Beak Street, sometimes the traffic passing through is so heavy, it is impossible to hear anything at all."

"Apart from the sound of Mrs Tombrin's voice heaping coals of fire on your head every morning?"

Sarah bit her lower lip. "I don't know how I am to answer that," she said sullenly and Shanklin smiled broadly.

"I can see how difficult it must be for you, Miss Fowkes, so let us stop indulging in conjecture and keep to plain fact. Before you became owner of your shop, you were employed as an assistant to the late owner, Mrs Pendleton, a lady who died of an attack of food poisoning. Yes, Miss Fowkes?"

"Yes."

"Before you were taken up by Mrs Pendleton, you were employed as a wet-nurse in the home of Mr Frank Mason, a man who hanged himself while you were in his employ?"

"Yes I was. It was none of my doing."

"I see. Now a wet-nurse must also be a mother. Miss Fowkes, I have been made aware of the unfortunate circumstances that led to you becoming a mother and have no wish to distress you by dwelling on that aspect of the matter. I understand your daughter did not survive her third year. May I ask if it was illness that carried her off?"

Sarah paled, visibly fighting for control, before she said in a low voice, "My darling child was murdered by a madwoman."

"I know how painful this must be but I understand the madwoman you refer to was Mrs Constantine, Mr Mason's mother-in-law. Is that correct?"

"Yes. As you seem to know only too well."

"And in turn, you made an attempt to get to Mrs Constantine and make an attempt on her life?"

"Who would not? She killed my child."

"Quite so." Shanklin lifted his wig and scratched his head. "To return to Mr Mason's suicide. I understand he killed himself while you were in the house?"

Sarah flashed him a look of pure hatred. "I was in the bedroom with the babies when he had a row with his mother-in-law and did it to himself. It was nothing to do with me."

"Possibly not. A beautiful young woman and an ailing wife in the same house with a healthy young man? It is difficult to know where to lay blame in such matters. The point I am trying to establish, is that you are no stranger to death and violence, Miss Fowkes. In fact, you were no stranger to death and violence before ever you clapped eyes on your accomplice, Charlie Bennet."

In the cell below the court, tieless, and without braces or bootlaces, a weeping Charlie Bennet slowly took off his shirt and threaded it through the lattice of bars that covered the small and very dirty window. Knotting the sleeves round his neck, he threw himself forward, twisting as he fell in a desperate attempt to tighten the noose and strangle himself. Almost immediately, the cell door was flung open, the semi-conscious man hoisted to his knees, and the sleeves were unknotted. Charlie was then dropped back on the floor and a pitcher of icy water was emptied over his head.

Through the black clouds that had gathered in his mind he heard the gaoler say gruffly, "Wake up you silly beggar. We can't have you cheating the hangman, can we?"

Chapter Twelve

The following morning, a pale and totally unnerved Charlie Bennet was brought up to sit alone in the dock, his red-rimmed, frightened eyes fixing on Sarah's face as she too was brought into the courtroom and escorted to her place on the witness stand. A report of Charlie's attempted suicide on the previous afternoon had reached Mr Justice Hughes, who glanced curiously at the man in the dock before nodding to William Shanklin.

Almost bouncing to his feet, Shanklin bowed to the judge, turned to the witness, bowed again, and said gallantly, "I see you are as fresh and as beautiful as ever this morning, Miss Fowkes. You are obviously an excellent recommendation for your treatments. Is that why Mrs Pendleton chose to employ you?"

Sarah shrugged an elegant shoulder. "I was introduced to Mrs Pendleton and she took an interest in me. I cannot say more than that."

"Oh but I'm quite sure you can say much more than that, Miss Fowkes. Who first took you to the lady and introduced you to her?"

"What does it matter? The old gentleman died years ago."

Before Shanklin could reply, Arnold Roberts was also on his feet. "I must say I agree with the witness, my lord. These questions can have no possible relevance to the matter in hand."

"Can there be any relevance to the matter in hand, Mr Shanklin?" the judge enquired.

"I believe it will help the court to better understand the nature of the business Miss Fowkes and her accomplice

Bennet were engaged in, my lord."

"Very well. The witness will answer the question."

"A Mr Constantine introduced me to Mrs Pendleton," said Sarah.

Shanklin nodded. "Your benefactor, of course. In what circumstances did he carry out the introduction?"

"The night his son-in-law died, I was afraid to stay in the house alone. Mr Constantine, who had come to take charge, loaned me the keys to a property he owned next door to his warehouse in Covent Garden. I took my baby there and the next morning he took me to Mrs Pendleton's shop and found me employment."

"Mr Constantine's warehouse supplied perfumes and soaps for Mrs Pendleton to sell. Is that correct?"

"Yes."

"And subsequently to you?"

"Yes."

"And the nature of the business did not change, once it was in your hands?"

"No, why should it change?"

"Why indeed? Mrs Pendleton was known to be a very successful blackmailer of those ladies who did not wish it known by their husbands that they used her services. I imagine she taught you well?"

Sarah shook her head. "Mrs Pendleton taught me how to sell and how to assist those clients who require baths and skin treatments. If she had any private business going on at the same time, I knew nothing of it."

"I must say, Miss Fowkes, I find that rather difficult to believe. I understand that you lived and worked in the same house with Mrs Pendleton until her death."

"I have told you the exact truth, whatever you choose to believe!"

William Shanklin smiled and raised a hand to cup his ear. "There is really no need to raise your voice, Miss Fowkes. His lordship's hearing is excellent and I do pretty well myself. Now Madam, since talking of Mrs Pendleton seems to cause you so much distress, let us leave that aspect of your illustrious career and come nearer the present day. During the course of their investigation into the murder of Florence

Carlisle, the police inspected your treatment book and came across the name of yet another missing client. Do you specialise in making people disappear?"

Sarah met his eyes. "I don't know if any of the other people here can understand you," she said coldly, "but if you want a sensible answer from me, you will have to ask a sensible question."

"Thank you for your direction, Miss Fowkes. I speak of Miss Amelia Hinks. Do you remember Amelia Hinks?"

In the dock, Charlie blanched and groaned audibly. Shanklin swung on his heel to give him a sharp look before returning to Sarah with, "Come, come, Miss Fowkes. The name obviously means a very great deal to your co-defendant. I ask you again. Do you remember Amelia Hinks?"

Sarah shook her head doubtfully. "If the name is in my treatment book, I suppose I must have known the lady and given her some treatments. I'm afraid I cannot call her to mind, nor can I tell you the reason why she came to me for help."

"Whatever the lady's reason, she seems to have made a very poor choice in coming to you, Miss Fowkes."

Sarah's eyes narrowed dangerously. "I am well trained in the art of giving skin treatments," she snapped, "and if any lady has cause to complain of the way I treated her, she doesn't need a man like you to speak up for her, does she? What do you know about the personal treatments I give my clients?"

Shanklin shook his head and laughed ruefully. "You are quite right, Miss Fowkes. I know nothing at all about your treatments for ladies and I stand corrected. I understand from Amelia Hinks's correspondence, that she was about to get married when she came to you for some of those treatments. Does that fact help to refresh your memory?"

"A great many of my clients come for treatments before they get married. Naturally, they want to look their best for their bridegrooms."

"Of course they do. Perhaps in the case of Miss Hinks, the name of her fiancé may help you. It is contained in this letter she wrote to her solicitor."

William Shanklin passed the letter he held to an usher, who

took it to the judge. Nodding, the judge glanced at it and passed it back. Shanklin put on his half moon spectacles and looked at Sarah over the top of them. "I think if I read part of the letter to you, Miss Fowkes, it might assist your recollection of the lady. She seems to have had something in common with Mrs Tombrin. If you can remember her in any way, it might well help us to clear up one aspect of the matter in hand."

Sarah drew a deep breath. "I will try, sir."

"I can ask no more of you," Shanklin replied sombrely. Unfolding the letter, he read slowly. "I know he cannot love me, how could he, he is young and so very handsome. I think I amuse him and he does seem to be genuinely warm towards me. I have no idea what sort of wife I will make but I mean to try to please him and if my small fortune can help to restore Lord Beniton's impoverished estates, for the first time in my life, I will believe I am put in the world for some purpose."

Shanklin returned the letter to the usher and took off his spectacles to wipe them on the edge of his gown. After a careful inspection of the lenses, he returned them to a pocket and said quietly, "So far as police enquiries have been able to ascertain, the phrase 'I will believe I am put here for some purpose' comprise the last words ever written by Amelia Hinks. Her solicitor has received no reply to his letter of congratulation, nor has he heard from her or Lord Beniton in regard to the disposal of the remaining part of her estate. A fact he finds somewhat surprising in view of what Miss Hinks said about his lordship's impoverished finances. I wonder if I have helped you remember Amelia Hinks, Miss Fowkes?"

Sarah hesitated as though she was deep in thought and then shook her head. "No, I am very sorry, but you have not. As I have told you, if her name is in my book, there is no doubt that I gave the lady some treatments. As for her letter, I cannot help you on that either. Not all my clients confide in me."

"Miss Fowkes!" Shanklin thundered. "The court is waiting for a proper answer. Surely you can see the connection between Miss Hinks and Mrs Tombrin?"

"Apart from them both being great letter writers, no I cannot."

There was a ripple of laughter through the court and Shanklin, who was not accustomed to being the butt of someone else's humour, flushed angrily. "I refer, madam, to the plain fact that both ladies were engaged to marry Lord Charles Beniton."

"I do not remember Miss Hinks but in the case of Mrs Tombrin, I cannot say I envy his Lordship."

The laughter, which had swelled at Sarah's last riposte, hushed when Shanklin pointed dramatically at the man in the dock. "I am certain that no one can envy the wretch who sits there. As you know only too well, Sarah Fowkes, your accomplice Charlie Bennet is the infamous Lord Charles Beniton!"

"I know no such thing."

"But I put it to you that you do know! What is more, the two of you succeeded in doing away with Florence Carlisle, Amelia Hinks, and who knows how many others."

"No, you are talking absolute nonsense. None of it is true."

Sarah's chin was raised in defiance, her heightened colour making her beauty even more startling. Shanklin found himself looking deep into her eyes and, thinking he saw a gleam of contempt behind her challenge, he began to lose his temper and shouted, "Yes it is true, Miss Fowkes, and it is only by the grace of God, that Mrs Tombrin is alive to give evidence here today."

Sarah laughed harshly. "I have told you over and over, I don't know your Miss Hinks."

"Then I hope you hang for the murder of Florence Carlisle, madam! For a wickeder woman than you, I have never known!"

"Mr Shanklin!" bellowed the judge over the hubbub and Shanklin sat down heavily. Raising a shaking hand to his forehead, he said, "I apologise most sincerely, my lord. For a moment, I quite lost control of myself."

"You made that very clear, Mr Shanklin. Your last remark is to be struck off the court records and I ask the gentlemen of the jury to disregard it completely. The two defendants stand accused, not condemned, and until such time as the gentlemen of the jury have ended their deliberations, they are to be regarded as innocent. Now sir, I hope I may have repaired some of the damage you have done. Do you have any more questions for this witness?"

Shanklin shook his head. "No my lord, I think not."

"Then I have. Miss Fowkes, understand me in this. You are on trial for your life and facetiousness will not assist in any way. Are you telling this court that although the name of Amelia Hinks appears in your treatment book on no fewer than five occasions, you do not remember the lady at all?"

"I do not remember Miss Hinks, my lord," Sarah replied quietly.

"Or Mrs Carlisle?"

"I do not know the name, my lord."

"And despite a clear parallel between the names Charlie Bennet and Charles Beniton, you do not know Lord Beniton, nor do you know if Bennet adopted the name Beniton for the purpose of cheating some of the women who patronised your business and defrauding them of money?"

"No, my lord."

The judge made a note and nodded dismissively. "Very well. Anything further, Mr Roberts?"

"No, my lord, I have nothing further," said counsel for the defence.

"Thank you. Officer, kindly return the accused to the dock. Are there any more witnesses for the defence, Mr Roberts?"

Arnold Roberts glanced at the apathetic figure of Charlie Bennet and shook his head. "No my lord. I have no other witnesses to call."

"Thank you. Mr Shanklin, are you sufficiently recovered to present your closing arguments to the jury?"

"I believe I am, my lord. With your permission?"

The judge nodded and, settling against the cushioned back of his chair, appeared to study the ceiling of the courtroom as Shanklin rose to his feet and began, "May it please your lordship and gentlemen of the jury, this is no ordinary case of murder you are here to try. This is not a question of a loss of sanity or a sudden fit of rage during some domestic strife. Nor is it murder in any one of those circumstances where it is possible to extend the hand of mercy. This was a wicked murder done purely for profit and greed. It is my duty to prove to you beyond any possible doubt, that the two who stand accused, Sarah Fowkes and her accomplice Charles Bennet, together conspired to cheat Florence Carlisle of her fortune with a promise of a spurious marriage and then do the poor unfortunate lady to death."

Charlie raised his head to watch Shanklin address the jury. The little man was walking up and down in front of the twelve men, their eyes following his waving arms like mesmerised rabbits. Every man jack of them ready and willing to condemn Charlie Bennet for a murder he hadn't done. A murder which would never have happened if it had been up to him. He never killed Florence and he told Sarah not to do Amelia in, didn't he? Maybe it wasn't too late for him even now, whatever Shanklin was saying. If he stood up this minute and said, 'Excuse me, but that's not right. I told her not to kill the women. There was no need to kill anyone. It wasn't my fault she killed the old lady and made me chop her up. She's the wicked one, not me'. Charlie shifted uncomfortably on the bench and flexed his knees, preparatory to getting to his feet, but Shanklin was speaking again and the opportunity was lost.

"Why did they do it?" asked the barrister, pausing in front of the foreman of the jury. "Why, you may ask, should these two take the dreadful risk of doing away with Mrs Carlisle on the shop premises, with all the subsequent problems attached to the disposal of the body, if they planned their activities so well? The answer is, gentlemen, that they had no choice. However clever a plan may be, its perpetrators cannot know everything about their quarry. This time the two intended victims knew each other well and when Mrs Carlisle recognised Mrs Tombrin outside Sarah Fowkes's shop, she signed her own death warrant."

He paused again to consult his notes and Charlie took the opportunity to clear his dry throat and make an attempt to stand, only to be pulled back by his gaoler.

"But that ain't right . . . " he began, and stopped when he

saw the judge's eyes on him.

Unheeding, Shanklin looked up from his papers and went on, "For how were Fowkes and her accomplice Bennet to know that the two ladies they had ensnared were the widows of distinguished members of the diplomatic corps who once served side by side in India? Indeed, in their greed and in their hurry to lay hands on the money and rid themselves of their victims, the criminals did not wish to know anything about the women other than that they were wealthy. Gentlemen of the jury, when those two ladies acknowledged each other in the street outside her shop, it must have come as a dreadful shock to Sarah Fowkes. Can you imagine her feelings when Mrs Carlisle called out to her friend and said she was engaged to be married. At any moment, Mrs Tombrin would cross the road and the two would be close together, congratulating each other on their forthcoming marriages until the dread time came when they discovered they were both engaged to marry the same man! The same Lord Beniton they had met through the good offices of Sarah Fowkes! As sure as fate, the truth was about to come out. What could Fowkes possibly do to prevent it?"

Shanklin paused for effect, looked round to see every eye on him, and nodded towards the dock. "Well, my lord and gentlemen of the jury, as you have seen here in this very courtroom, Sarah Fowkes is as resourceful as she is beautiful. We know exactly what she did and with what speed she responded to danger. Mrs Tombrin has testified how, to her utter surprise and horror, Fowkes hastened across the street to where she was standing and struck her hard upon the face. This at the very moment Mrs Tombrin was about to return her friend's greeting and say that she too, was about to get married. Can it be any wonder that Mrs Tombrin thought Fowkes had taken leave of her senses and fled for the sake of her own safety?"

Sarah, like everyone else in the court, listened to him almost spit out her name every time he used it. The man hated her. That was nothing new. She fed on hate. For him, for Tombrin, for Herrick. Most of all, for Mrs Constantine who she killed over and over again when she murdered Amelia Hinks, Florence and the others. Mrs Constantine, who she would have killed in reality, if the old harridan hadn't gone mad and died a gibbering idiot in a lunatic asylum. Shanklin was looking at her now and, as when he looked at her in the witness-box, there was something in his eye she had not at first recognised. Now she saw he was looking at her with the same helpless longing Frank Mason had in his eyes when he looked at her naked breats as she fed the babies. The dirty minded old sod lusted after her and he couldn't do a thing to stop himself itching. That was why he got his rag out when he was asking those stupid questions. Her heart, which had been beating wildly in the witness-box, began to steady. Somehow feeling safer, Sarah raised an eyebrow, put her head to one side, and slowly licked her lips for him.

Shanklin held her eye a moment longer and, when he turned away, his voice faltered a little before regaining its normal strength. "Fowkes, seeing the ladies knew each other, realised that immediate action had to be taken. There was no time to kill and dispose of them elsewhere, as I believe happened in the case of Amelia Hinks, that sad and childlike lady who gave her trust and her money to those wretches in the dock and received only the utmost cruelty in return. I tell you, gentlemen, there was no dog, no poisoned meat, and there is no loss of memory on the part of Sarah Fowkes. Or for that matter, in the mind of Charlie Bennet. She knows and he knows there was no mad dog to be slaughtered in the cellar below the shop on that evil night. There was only a terrified woman by the name of Florence Carlisle who, I can well imagine, was reduced to begging for her life before one or other of these fiends struck her down and butchered her as though she was an animal to be disposed of in a ditch."

Keeping his back turned squarely to the woman in the dock, he went on, "But, gentlemen, like many criminals, these two were not as clever as they like to think they were. In their haste to rectify one mistake, they made many others. The figure of a strongly built man, with a physique very much like Bennet's own, was observed tipping the dismembered remains of poor Florence Carlisle in a ditch at the back of the butcher's yard and then running off in the direction of Beak Street. Then there was Mrs Tombrin who, having escaped from their clutches, persisted in trying to trace the whereabouts of her friend. She was of great assistance to the police who, until she walked into the police station and told of her suspicions, knew only that they had the butchered remains of a lady, who in life had been fat and wore a golden ring.

"As you have heard in evidence given by the officers concerned, once Mrs Tombrin had pointed the way, the police investigation found blood in the cellar below Fowkes's parlour, pointing to where the foul murder had taken place. Even more important, there was the footprint of Fowkes's bare foot above the cellar steps. A clear imprint, made in the blood of her victim, placing Sarah Fowkes on the very spot where the deed was done and at a time when the blood was freshly spilt. A bloodstained footprint which, in its very nakedness, suggests who knows what lewd and disgusting practices she and Bennet indulged in over the shattered body of Florence Carlisle.

"But we need not concern ourselves with supposition or suggestions. Fowkes and Bennet are together guilty of murder. The sooner the fate they have earned with their wicked deeds, is meted out to them, the sooner the souls of Florence Carlisle and Amelia Hinks will be able to rest in peace. Madame Sarah's shop in Beak Street was the web which ensnared Amelia Hinks, Mrs Tombrin, Florence Carlisle, and who can say how many others? Gentlemen of the jury, I told you of the web. There in the dock sits the spider and her accomplice. I ask you to do your clear duty and find them guilty."

He dropped his accusing finger, gathered his gown around himself and sat down to gnaw at his thumb. As he did so, Charlie dropped his head to stare at his feet and Sarah turned away to gaze stonily at the judge. Arnold Roberts got to his feet and slowly and carefully adjusted his gown while he waited for the smattering of applause that had followed Shanklin's last words to die down. Clearing his throat, he said quietly, "If it please you, my lord and gentlemen of the jury, I must acknowledge that I do not have the rhetoric of a Mr Shanklin but I can be every bit as impassioned, and on behalf of Miss Sarah Fowkes, I intend to be."

He was looking at the dock and, once more, Charlie half raised a hand, as if to remind counsel that he was there to be defended too. Affecting not to see the gesture, Roberts turned to the jury. "Mr Shanklin tells you there was no dog in the backyard or the cellar of Sarah Fowkes's shop. His proof? Simply that it was not seen or heard by the lady's neighbours. If there was no dog barking and snapping because it was not heard or seen, by the same token there was no Mrs Carlisle begging for mercy or screaming, for she too was not seen or heard by Miss Fowkes's neighbours. Only Mrs Tombrin claims to have seen the unhappy Mrs Carlisle in the vicinity of Sarah Fowkes's shop and Mrs Tombrin has, I submit, made it very clear that she is strongly biased against my client and in consequence of that fact alone, a less than reliable witness. But however you might view Mrs Tombrin's evidence in regard to her sighting in the street, you cannot accept Mr Shanklin's fanciful description of the happenings in the cellar, for if no dog was heard, nor was a woman."

One of the jurymen looked puzzled and scratched his sidewhiskers vigorously. Roberts smiled at him and nodded understandingly.

"Of course it's a puzzle," he seemed to be saying to the man. "But all you have to do is trust me. I'll get you out of it." The juryman visibly relaxed and returned the smile with a gap toothed grin of his own as Roberts continued. "Let us now turn for a moment to the sad story you have been told of Miss Amelia Hinks, a story intended to demonstrate the depths of wickedness to which my client, Sarah Fowkes, is prepared to sink. But what do we really know about Miss Hinks? We know only that she has not written to her solicitor and has not been found. True, she may be dead. Equally true, she may be alive. We simply do not know and therefore, she should not figure in any consideration of the guilt or innocence of Sarah Fowkes, or indeed as a pointer to her character."

He turned to point at Sarah as he spoke. "Gentlemen of the jury, I ask you now to look at the two people in the dock and consider their demeanour. Bennet, the very picture of misery and guilty remorse. It is written on his face and in his lack of composure. Miss Fowkes, on the other hand, remains perfectly composed. Certainly there has been a crime committed. Certainly there is guilt here. Certainly Sarah Fowkes saw more blood in that cellar than could have resulted from the slitting of a dog's throat. There is no doubt in my mind that Bennet is a criminal of the worst possible kind. On the other hand, you have seen Sarah Fowkes on the witness stand. You witnessed her courage when she was made to suffer the outrage of the prosecution counsel's outburst. Giving, I submit, the clearest possible demonstration of a lady who has done no wrong."

"No," began Charlie, who only heard the reference to himself. "What he's saying ain't right . . . " He winced, almost doubling up in agony as an elbow dug into his ribs and a heavy boot descended on to his foot. "But it ain't right," he gasped painfully as the boot ground into his instep. The judge rapped twice for silence and, as Charlie's eyes welled with tears and he subsided, Roberts said:

"Gentlemen of the jury, you see before you a lady much maligned. A lady duped by Bennet, perhaps as much duped as the poor women he enticed into her parlour when she was safe abed. She befriended him and like a true friend, she makes a brave attempt to stand by him in his trouble, but I will not have it so. I tear them asunder. I tell you there is no partnership here. Charles Bennet, alias Lord Charles Beniton, made his guilt abundantly clear to me when I interviewed him in his prison cell."

Charlie shook his head and raised a limp hand, but now Roberts was in full flight and no one saw it.

"For Bennet," Roberts said, "I can offer no defence other than the suggestion that he might be mad rather than totally depraved. But Sarah Fowkes is a perfectly respectable business woman. She is a comfortably off lady who learned to put the tragedy and the heartbreak of a lost child behind her and face the bleakness of a future alone. Without the protection of a man. Gentlemen of the jury, for Sarah Fowkes, I ask for your pity and your understanding. It is obvious to us, as men of the world, that she chose unwisely when she allowed Bennet to become her friend and, I suspect, allowed herself to love him. Bennet insinuated himself into her life and then used her premises to stalk his prey from. That shows Sarah Fowkes as too trusting perhaps, even a touch simplistic in the belief that all of the blood she saw and accidentally stepped into in that cellar came from one slaughtered dog, but it does not involve her in the murder of Florence Carlisle or any other missing lady Mr Shanklin cares to pick out from her treatment book. In the name of God and justice, gentlemen of the jury, I beg you to find Sarah Fowkes innocent."

There were genuine tears in the eyes of Arnold Roberts when he turned away from the jury and Sarah gave him a small smile and nod of gratitude when he returned to his seat. Charlie, his face greyer and more drawn than ever, remained in a state of apathy, hardly listening to the judge when he sat upright and began to address the jury. He knew now that Herrick had been right and he should have spoken up earlier. In his fear, Charlie felt his bowels move and had to squeeze the cheeks of his buttocks together to prevent himself from having an accident.

"You have heard the arguments of both counsel," said Mr Justice Hughes, "and highly effective arguments they were. Both prosecution and defence are pleased to agree that Charles Bennet is a lost cause and they differ in the case of Sarah Fowkes. Gentlemen, you are not here to be persuaded by either argument, however skilled in its presentation."

Skilled? Shanklin thought bitterly as he listened. He had lost his temper like a schoolboy. Over an evil-hearted bitch with a pretty face. No, he had to admit, much more than pretty. This woman possessed a rare beauty that made him long to paint her. To capture her on canvas and possess her. Naked of course. On a chaise-longue. Looking at him with her head a little on one side, the tip of her pointed tongue wetting those perfect lips. The way she had looked at him a moment ago. Closing his eyes, he wrenched his thoughts back to his dumpy little wife and his three dumpy daughters, and found no comfort in any of them.

"You are here to decide," the judge was saying, "if Mrs Florence Carlisle was taken into the cellar below Sarah Fowkes's shop, there to be done to death, her body butchered, and her parts disposed of in the most callous way imaginable. To assist you in coming to your decision, you have the evidence of the bloodstained cellar and the certain knowledge that someone or something died in that dark place, not more than three or four days before the police went down there to investigate Mrs Tombrin's suspicions and found blood still fresh enough to have remained sticky in some of the crevices in the wall and floor.

"Should the evidence you have heard make you conclude that Florence Carlisle died in the cellar, you must then consider the possibility that Bennet enticed or forced Mrs Carlisle into the cellar, with Miss Fowkes being completely unaware of what was happening within her own home and shop premises. There to commit the murder and butchery of Mrs Carlisle and dispose of the unfortunate lady's remains, alone and again without the knowledge of Miss Fowkes. To help you in deciding whether or not that was the case, you have Miss Fowkes's statement that her bedroom is too far away to have heard a commotion in the cellar, the undisputed evidence of the keys she entrusted to Bennet, and the plain fact that while Bennet may have needed to defraud or steal the money necessary to keep up his comparatively expensive life-style, Fowkes was acknowledged to be the owner of a successful and lucrative business."

So far so good, Arnold Roberts was thinking as he listened. If there's to be a sting in the tail, it can only be the footprint. He glanced at Shanklin, who was sitting with his eyes closed, and wondered about his outburst. It was strange the way he'd taken against Fowkes. Almost as though he hated the woman. Roberts almost smiled. He didn't hate her. When he was a younger man he'd have fought like hell to get her acquitted, if only for the chance of getting her skirts off at the end of the matter. He bit his lip, frowned studiously, and made himself listen to the rest of the judge's summing up.

"The last possibility you must consider is that the Sarah Fowkes who you have seen giving evidence and who now sits before you in the dock is Bennet's accomplice. A monster who, together with Bennet, conspired to lure lonely women into believing that a penniless nobleman was prepared to bestow his name and title on them for the sake of restoring his impoverished fortune. Then, when the lady's fortune was secure in their hands or, as in the case of Mrs Carlisle, discovery seemed to be imminent, they killed her together. For your assistance in that deliberation, you have Mrs Tombrin's evidence, disputed as unreliable by Mr Roberts, placing Mrs Carlisle outside Sarah Fowkes's shop, the police evidence that no proof can be found to show there was a mad dog on the premises, the fact that Miss Fowkes's bloodstained footprint proves her presence in the vicinity of the cellar at a time when or soon after a death had occurred, and your own good judgement. Gentlemen, I ask you now to retire and consider your verdict."

When the jury filed out, the prisoners taken down to their cells, and the judge retired to his chambers at the side of the court, it seemed to Shanklin that everyone in the entire building let out their breath simultaneously and started to chatter excitedly. For days and hours past, they had heard nothing but the voices of witnesses, the arguments of counsel and the deliberations of the judge. Arm waving and arguing among themselves, they spilled out into the hall and along the rabbit warren of staircases and passages leading out to the streets beyond. Shanklin, still not recovered from his outburst, remained on his seat for a few moments longer. As two heavily built, red-faced men were passing close by him, he heard one of them say. "They got the right 'un in the man, I reckon, but that Sarah Fowkes were never guilty however much that old prosecutor feller had his knife in her. You only had to look at the gal to see that. A pretty little thing like her couldn't hurt a fly."

For a crazy moment, Shanklin saw red and was on his feet, after a man who was twice his size and weight, wanting to drag him back by his collar and argue his case all over again. To prove to the stupid oaf he was a liar and a fool. Of course Sarah Fowkes was guilty and the judge was right to call her a monster. Recovering himself in time, Shanklin fell back on to his seat and mopped his forehead. When he thought of how he behaved when cross-examining that woman, he could hardly believe it of himself. He had been a Queen's counsel for more than twenty years and was at the peak of his professional career. He prided himself on being a cool and dispassionate man. But when he looked deep into the eyes of Sarah Fowkes while she stood in the witness-box and defied him, the stirring in his loins had become unbearable. He hated her, he wanted her desperately, he had lost his head and shouted at her, and he knew if he hadn't proved her guilt to the people sitting in the public gallery, he might not have proved it to the jury. Usually he had a feeling about jurymen but in this case, his mind had clouded and he had no idea how they would decide. It was with a sombre pulling of his long upper lip, that William Shanklin took his place after almost three hours of waiting and watched the twelve jurymen return to the court, the foreman leading the way.

The names of the jurors were called over by the Clerk amid utter silence and upon the foreman being asked if a verdict had been agreed on, the man swallowed noisily and answered, "Yes sir, it has."

"Do you find Charles Bennet guilty of the wilful murder of Florence Carlisle?"

"Yes sir, we find Charles Bennet guilty, my lord."

"And that is the verdict of you all?"

"Yes sir, it is."

"Do you find Sarah Fowkes guilty of the wilful murder of Florence Carlisle?"

The foreman shook his head, half smiled and looked directly at Sarah as he said, "We find Sarah Fowkes not guilty, my lord."

The question, "And that is the verdict of you all?" the judge's acquittal of Sarah, and his signal to the female gaoler that the prisoner Sarah Fowkes was to be taken down for formal discharge from prison, was all lost in a sudden burst of cheering and clapping that made Sarah spin on her heel and look round the court in astonishment before she was hurried away and order was restored.

The court quietened as Mr Justice Hughes lay down his gavel and said to Charlie, "Charles Bennet, you have been found guilty of a heinous crime. Have you anything you wish to say before sentence is passed on you?"

Charlie shook his head and mumbled, "What's the use of

me saying anything? You're all against me. You have been all along."

"I see," said Hughes and, as a small square of black cloth was draped over his wig and Charlie sagged at the knees, added sharply, "Officer, keep him up."

The gaoler gripped Charlie by the arm and, pulling him upright, muttered, "Come on Bennet, face up to it like a man."

Chapter Thirteen

What happened at the end of the trial came as a complete surprise to Sarah. Her spurious popularity among the people who filled the public gallery and the jury's conclusion that Charlie Bennet, whose worst crime in her book was to crumble under pressure like a rotten walnut, had taken advantage of her good nature and naivety, both amused and irritated her. It also, she was quick to realise when she was free of prison and sitting in a hansom on the way back to her home, gave her a fresh start in life. Not at once, of course. The jostling sightseers who overflowed the narrow way that was Beak Street and goggled at the shop where Florence Carlisle had been so cruelly done to death put a stop to any idea of that.

Sarah paid off the cabbie when he was forced to pull up his nag at the edge of the noisy crowd. Keeping her head low, she walked quickly, and she thought unnoticed, around the corner and into the shop through the yard and kitchen. As soon as she was inside she began shivering almost uncontrollably, partly from reaction to being acquitted and set free and partly from the cold and damp that accumulated on her walls and windows during the weeks she spent in prison. Her hand covering her mouth, Sarah went up to the bedroom to take off her hat.

"You ought to have Charlie here to light the fires," she said aloud to her reflection in the mirror. "He's got nothing much to do with himself for the next three or four weeks." Her laugh sounded strained and unnaturally high pitched even to her own ears. She quietened, drew a deep breath, and glanced at the unmade bed. Weak willed though he was, she would have been glad of Charlie's company. The plain truth was she could have done with the comfort of being in his arms. The lunatic abandon with which they made love on the night she killed Florence Carlisle had never been repeated but she had become used to his presence in the bed and the pressure of his big body above her when they made love. Feeling the slight shock of his penetration and her own rising heat as he moved backwards and forwards inside her. Their mutual cleaving together. Heaving to meet him and almost gasping for air when they climaxed with his hands beneath her buttocks. Squeezing. Squeezing. Oh God!

Restlessly, she kneaded her thighs before crossing to the heavily curtained bedroom window to take a peek at the street. News of her release had preceded her and, if it was possible, the milling crowd had grown even more impenetrable and she could hear one or two shouts of "Come on, Sarah my darling! Let's have a look at you, gal!" Realising the interest in her was not likely to lessen for a time, at least not until Charlie had been topped, she shrugged. A few weeks waiting before she re-opened the shop wouldn't matter now. She had plenty of money tucked away. Meantime, there was the question of getting some warmth into the place and laying hold of the food she hadn't thought to buy before coming home. Probably because she had become used to sending Charlie to do the shopping.

Charlie. What would he be thinking now, she wondered while she went downstairs and found enough dry paper and kindling to light the kitchen boiler. It was a stupid question. What would she be thinking if she knew she was going to be topped in a few weeks time? She tried, but she couldn't think of herself in that situation. Being sentenced to death would have meant she had been beaten by Shanklin, and she couldn't imagine losing to that little fat pig any more than she could see herself in a condemned cell with those grim faced women, having to wait for the hangman to come and stretch her pretty neck.

She shrugged again, dismissing any thoughts of being dragged off to her own execution as the flames she fanned began to lick upwards between the black bars of the grate and the glow of their warmth reached her face. It was

Charlie's hard cheese that things had gone wrong for him. When he was topped and forgotten about, she would re-open the shop and go on selling Constantine's soaps and perfumes. Afterwards, when enough time had passed by to make her feel really safe, she might indulge in a little of Mrs Pendleton's gentle blackmail. Which, truth to tell, had never amounted to more than demanding the occasional gift of a few guineas in return for a discreet silence about a client's occasional assignation or odder still, her use of cosmetics.

A glance through the grubby kitchen window showed her the sky was darkening and, although she could still hear the racketing of the crowd in Beak Street, she thought it safe enough to slip out the way she came in and get a bite of supper and something to carry her through the next day. Finding an old cloak of Mrs Pendleton's in the hall cupboard, she put it on, picked up a basket, and went into the yard. To find Mrs Tombrin waiting by the gate.

For a moment, the two women faced each other in silence. it was Mrs Tombrin who spoke first.

"You spoke about this yard in court," she said by way of explanation. "When I saw the crowd in front, I expected you to come out this way. I've been waiting to talk to you."

"Very clever," Sarah sneered, biting back the sudden thrill of fear that ran through her at the sight of her adversary. "But you wasted your time hanging about at my back gate. I've got nothing to say to you."

Mrs Tombrin faced the taller and much younger Sarah Fowkes squarely and said in a low, almost monotonous, voice, "You killed Florence Carlisle and my fiancé, Lord Beniton is to hang for your crime. I will never allow you to forget what you have done."

Sarah shook her head impatiently. "Your fiancé, Lord Beniton? Listen to me, you old fool. There is no Lord Beniton, there never was any Lord Beniton. It was all in your mind."

"If it was all in my mind," Mrs Tombrin replied bitterly, "you put it there. It was you who told me he wanted to marry me. It was you who gave me his letters."

Sarah shrugged. "That's your story. No one believed you when you told it in court. Who do you think is going to believe you now?"

Mrs Tombrin took a step closer. "If my fiancé dies for your crime, I will be revenged on you."

"Now you listen to me," Sarah snapped. "Charlie Bennet is going to be topped, you can make your mind up to it. When he is and things have quietened down a bit, I'm going to be opening the shop and earning my living like any other respectable woman in business. If I catch you skulking round here making a nuisance of yourself then, just remember the judge said he was surprised I didn't fetch a constable last time. I promise you this, Mrs Tombrin, if you do make a nuisance of yourself, I mean to give you in charge. It would be the natural thing to do.

Whether or not it was because of her threat, Sarah could not know, but Alice Tombrin had melted away in the dusk before she finished speaking. Fighting down the feeling she was still being watched, she walked through to the market and bought a hot meat pie and mash but, although she felt hungry enough when she got back indoors and laid her supper out in the parlour, the food did not taste as it should. In the end, she left the best part of it and went to bed, thinking she would be all right in the morning. She was having a fit of the shivers because the house was still freezing cold and that old crone had given her a fright turning up at the gate the way she had. Sarah got into the bed, her feet and hands like ice. She pulled her pillow up to cover her head and huddled in a tight ball beneath her covers.

Constable Robert Marsh looked anxious as he sat facing Sergeant Herrick. "Fowkes came out of the backyard gate carrying a basket," he reported, "and I was just about to follow her when Mrs Tombrin bobbed up. Fowkes had such a shock when she saw her, she near jumped out of her skin. And I only just had time to duck back in a doorway. I'm sorry, sergeant. I had no way of knowing Mrs Tombrin would be there."

Herrick dropped his pen on to his blotter and chuckled. "I'm not sorry," he said. "If Mrs Tombrin has unsettled Fowkes, that's all to the good. She'll be less likely to think you're telling a cock-and-bull story when you turn up at her shop door."

"So long as she don't remember the real steward."

"You know better than that," grunted Herrick. "All a passenger ever remembers of a ship's steward is a white coat and gold buttons. In her present state of mind, she'll swallow it, you see if she don't. Besides, when I spoke to Bennet about Amelia Hinks yesterday, I couldn't get much sense out of him but I tripped him into saying Fowkes wasn't looking at the steward when he came into the cabin."

"How is he taking it now?" asked Marsh, without too much interest.

Herrick grinned wolfishly. "Coming unstitched. Trying to hide in the corner of the cell. I told him to straighten himself up and take what he had coming to him like a man."

It was advice a near demented Charlie Bennet was to hear often during his remaining three weeks of life. He heard it while he stumbled round the prison yard alone, taking his exercise after the other prisoners had been returned to their cells. He heard it when he crouched in the corner of the cell furthest from the dreaded door to the execution chamber and burst into one of his regular fits of wild sobbing, and he heard it again when, after a week of being a man condemned to death, he became incontinent and continually soiled his clothes.

Sixteen days before Bennet was to die, Sarah was downstairs in the shop wondering whether she dare take down the shutters and open the door, if not for trade, to let a little daylight in so she could clean the floor and see to the dust on the shelves. The crowd she saw gathered in the street on the day of her acquittal had thinned to the occasional goggle-eyed passer-by and even she, when she ventured out in the evenings, had become rather less of a curiosity about the market stalls and the local shops. On the other hand, she had twice more seen Mrs Tombrin standing below the street lamp and she knew, as the date of Charlie's execution drew near, the mob would again be pressed against her shop door.

"Best not open up again until it's all done with," she

was deciding, when she was startled by a heavy knock at the door.

At first she ignored the summons, thinking it was probably mischief making children, but when it came again, she called out sharply, "The shop is closed. Get away from here."

"No, ma'am, not just yet," said a man's voice. "I want to have a few words with you, Lady Beniton, and if you don't want any more trouble from the police, you might do well to listen to me." The tone of the man's voice did not sound particularly threatening but for the moment, Sarah was too stunned at being addressed as Lady Beniton to take in the rest of what he was saying. When she did not answer at once, the knock was repeated, this time heavily enough to rattle the shutters. The noise was loud enough to clear her mind and, thinking she saw daylight, Sarah grew angry.

"You can go on back to your Mrs Tombrin and tell her whatever game she's playing, it isn't going to work. I'm not afraid of anything that old hag reckons she can do, or anything you imagine you can do either."

"This has got nothing to do with any Mrs Tombrin," the voice returned. "This is about the two different Lady Benitons I saw on board the old Plymouth."

"Wait there a minute," Sarah said, clenching her fists and fighting back the impulse to scream abuse at the man. Taking her time unfastening the bolts, she wondered how much money he wanted. It had to be money or he wouldn't be leaning against the shop door now. He would have gone straight to the police with whatever he thought he could tell them about two Lady Benitons and the cruise ship. She shook her head, made herself take a slow deep breath, and pulled back the last of the bolts to swing the door open.

"Come in," she said, "I don't know who you are or what you want of me, but I won't be shouted at be people standing on my doorstep."

The man, clean chinned, neatly side-whiskered, and tall, looked younger than she expected when he pulled off his peaked cap and stepped through into the shop. "Bertram Wheeler at your service, Miss Fowkes," he said diffidently. "Till lately, steward on the Pride of Plymouth. You might remember seeing me setting out your breakfast one fine morning, or of course, you might not have seen me, you were so busy pretending to be Lady Beniton at the time."

Sarah shook her head and put her hand in her apron pocket. With the handles of her scissors securely looped between her fingers, she said quietly, "I have never seen you before and I don't forget the people I see. If you think you know me, you are quite mistaken, Mr Wheeler."

Taking a crumpled copy of the *Daily Sketch* from the back skirt pocket of his heavy topcoat, Marsh occupied himself with smoothing it out on the shop counter. While he was doing so, he said conversationally enough, "All I wanted to tell you, Miss Fowkes, is that on the day the cruise started, I was stepping out of the cabin when Lord and Lady Beniton came down the passageway following behind their baggage. She had her hat pushed back off her face, he was walking alongside her and holding her arm, and I thought to myself she's the one with the money and he's the one with the looks."

The man paused to look round and smile deprecatingly at Sarah, before going on. "I was more than a mite jealous of him at the time, ma'am. Old biddy, lots of brass. I reckoned he was going to see her off nice and quiet in a year or two and settle down in a nice comfortable berth for the rest of his life. Which is exactly what I have always looked for a chance to do. Anyway, we drop anchor at Finisterre and I'm up on deck for a breath of air and a sight of the dockside when the deck officer calls me over. Wheeler, he says, Lord and Lady Beniton have had some sad news and will be disembarking immediately. Yes sir, I says, before coming over to give you a salute and ask if I should go down right away and pack, so as you'd know who to leave a sovereign for. But when I got nearer to you, Miss Fowkes, and saw how Lady Beniton had all of a sudden grown thirty years younger and become a great beauty with it, I thought better of the sov and kept out of your way. I've met enough wrong 'uns to know when I should smell a rat and I didn't want to end up where the other Lady Beniton ended up, did I?"

He paused once more, continuing to smooth the creases out of the newspaper and obviously waiting for Sarah to speak. She said nothing but seeing the artist's sketches of her and Charlie below those of William Shanklin and Arnold Roberts, made her catch her breath and shoot him a glance of pure venom. Appearing not to notice and with the newspaper flattened to his satisfaction, he turned the page toward her in some triumph. "There. See what I mean?"

"No," Sarah said coldly. "I do not see what you mean and I've no idea why you think I would be interested in what you have said to me. If you've finished now, I'll let you out."

"Come on now, Miss Fowkes," Marsh began to bluster loudly. "Of course you can see what I mean. It's plain enough in the paper, ain't it?"

Listening to the man, Sarah's mood changed and she almost smiled. He was a common little sneak thief and so like Charlie it was almost comical. If things didn't go their way at once, men like them went to pieces and said the first stupid thing they could lay their tongues to. She narrowed her eyes slightly and listened while he carried on trying to bully her into submission with, "I'm talking about Amelia Hinks, Miss Fowkes, that's who. As soon as I read about the court case and saw you and Bennet pictured, I knew what must have happened on that cruise ship. It was Amelia Hinks who got on board at the start of the cruise and it was you who got off at the end of it. I can swear it as a fact and I mean to do so if I must. It ain't that I want to, Miss Fowkes. I'd do anything for a lady like you ordinarily, honest I would, but it's my conscience that bothers me and won't let me rest, you see."

Sarah was forced to turn away to hide her face. His last plea was so much a Charlie-ism she almost warmed to the fool sufficiently to ask how much it would cost to set his conscience at rest.

Don't you be the fool, she warned herself. This one ain't Charlie and you don't know which way the cat might jump. But he wasn't a bad looking man and, though he seemed to have put two and two together neatly enough to make trouble in plenty, she could sense that she wasn't in any immediate danger.

"I am about to brew a pot of tea," she said, moving towards the back of the shop. "Come into the parlour and have a cup with me." He was virtually the first man she had been alone with since the trial and as she led the way, she was very conscious of his closeness behind her. After a few minutes spent in preparation, she sat pouring the tea and, in wondering what she was going to do with him, found herself also wondering what he'd be like in bed and if that would be the answer.

"Now, Mr Wheeler," she said, after sipping her tea delicately and returning her cup to its saucer. "I have told you that I don't know what you're talking about and I don't. A lady named Miss Hinks was made a good deal of in court. They said she could not be found and tried to prove I knew something about her disappearance. When my counsel questioned the police witnesses, they couldn't even prove she had disappeared. You would be wasting your time taking that tale to the police and the only reason I haven't told you to go and find it out for yourself, is because I suspect you are really here because you have lost your position as a ship's steward."

Marsh nodded and put down his own cup. "That's about the right of it, Miss Fowkes," he said earnestly. "I've been washed up on shore for nigh on two months and I'm in danger of losing my lodgings if I don't come up with some money soon."

"And that's why you chose to come here and blackmail me? Do you not think I have suffered enough over the past few weeks? Don't you know how much it hurts a woman to discover that the man she befriended and trusted, deceived her and thought so little of her, he almost got her put to death for a murder she knew nothing about? Oh, I have learned that men are cruel, Mr Wheeler, but this too? It is too much to bear."

An hour later, Marsh was back in Herrick's office. "If you're quite certain about her being a killer, sergeant, she ought to be performing at the Empire. When she made her little speech and called me cruel and started dabbing at her eyes with her pretty little wipe, she damn near had me in tears with her."

Herrick reddened and glared at the constable. "I'm certain

she's the killer all right and don't you start feeling sorry for her. For one thing Bennet's not the man to have committed a murder on his own and for another, she was lying like a bloody trooper about the dog in the yard and we both knew she was doing it. That woman is laughing up her sleeve at me and I won't have it. How did you leave matters?"

Marsh grinned across the desk. "She gave me a five pound note to keep me getting thrown out of my lodgings and I'm to go back tomorrow evening at six. When I told her I didn't know when I could repay her, she said she might be able to find some work for me. She didn't say what form the work might take."

"You be careful, my lad," said Herrick. "Don't forget where Bennet has ended up."

Sarah smiled when she let Marsh in. "You're a good timekeeper, Mr Wheeler," she said. "I like that and although I thought I would never trust a man again, I wonder if I might be able to trust you. Can I put my trust in you, Mr Wheeler?"

Marsh lay a hand on his heart. "As God above knows me, Miss Fowkes, if a man is straight with Bert Wheeler, Bert Wheeler is as straight back."

Sarah's smile deepened a little. "I am a woman, Mr Wheeler, I hope your rule applies to me?"

"I can see you're a woman, ma'am," he said fervently. "And a very lovely woman you are. To you the rule applies twice over, I swear it."

Sarah laughed aloud and opened a small drawer below the shop counter. "Then here you are, Mr Wheeler. These are the keys to the kitchen door and the padlock on the gate at the back of the yard. Charlie Bennet used to go out that way in the evening and fetch a pie and mash or a bit of fish for us to share. If you'll do the same for us now, I can tell you about the rest of his duties while we eat our supper."

Marsh went out the way he was instructed and, on his way to the market, muttered the one word required to the constable he passed on the corner. Knowing that Herrick would soon know he was settled in with Fowkes, he was smiling when he got back to the parlour and saw she had laid out knives, forks and glasses.

"That looks really lovely, ma'am," he said. "Every bit as tidy as I set the meal out in the cabin."

Sarah met his eyes. "What cabin would that be, Mr Wheeler?"

"None as you would know of, Miss Fowkes," he said hastily. "My being an ex-steward, your table reminded me of what a table properly set out should look like, that's all."

"I'm glad you find me so efficient, Mr Wheeler. Shall we eat?"

"Yes please, ma'am. I'm starved."

He could feel Sarah's eyes on him, while he cut through the pie crust and shovelled a forkful of the steaming meat and potato filling into his mouth. She ate delicately, he noticed, separating the meat and cutting it small, putting a piece in her mouth and chewing slowly, before swallowing. Knowing what he did of her history, he was thinking, 'That's a trick you didn't pick up in your old ma's laundry, my girl,' when he realised she was speaking to him. Putting down his knife and managing to swallow most of the wadge in his mouth, he said, "I'm sorry, ma'am. I didn't catch what you were saying."

"I was saying that you are not to be shocked when I tell you of Charlie Bennet's other duties. You're not to be greedy either. Greed led him to committing murder and now he's about to end his life on the gallows. If you are satisfied to do only what I asked him to do, you will be well paid for nothing very arduous."

Marsh pricked up his ears and managed to look amused. "You said I am not to be shocked, ma'am? I wouldn't think anything said by a lady like you would shock a man like me."

"It might. When my business was thriving, I had ladies who came here wanting my treatments for their skin and some other ladies who wanted the additional sort of treatments they could only get from a gentleman, if you understand my meaning?"

Marsh looked puzzled. "I think I might know what you

mean, ma'am. An escort duty perhaps."

Sarah favoured him with a smile that barely showed her teeth. "You can escort them to the bedroom upstairs, yes, and then you get on and do your other duty. Just shut your eyes like Charlie did and think you are rumpling your best lady friend."

"I ain't got any lady friend, Miss Fowkes."

Sarah stood up and raised her skirts to above her knees. "Think of me when you're doing it then. Would thinking of me get you excited enough for the work."

Marsh feasted his eyes on her rounded calves. "Oh yes, Miss Fowkes, thoughts of you certainly would."

"Then you call me Madame Sarah in front of the clients and Sarah when we're alone. You keep up your lodgings for the sake of appearances but you can spend your nights here. Would you like to stay here tonight? There's only me to keep you company."

Marsh managed not to look more surprised than he needed to. Knowing he'd have to report in and thanking God there was no need to tell the sergeant everything, he said gallantly. "I couldn't wish for any better company, Sarah, but I'll have to come back for it. It would be best to go home and eat a bit of my landlady's supper and let her think I went to bed early. Otherwise she'll raise the dust trying to find out what's become of me."

"You're right," said Sarah. "We must be careful. Keep the keys and come back as soon as you can."

An hour after making his report to Sergeant Herrick and giving him a wax impression of the kitchen door key, Marsh slipped into bed beside a naked Sarah Fowkes and with his lips on hers, stroked her loosened hair, ran his fingers over her breasts, found her erect nipples and, unable to wait any longer, mounted her.

'Just something I forgot to mention in my report, sergeant,' he was thinking when he put his hand beneath to stroke her buttocks and feel them clench and lift to meet his neat, regular thrusting.

During the days that followed, Marsh scrubbed out and whitewashed the cellar, bought and occasionally prepared food, made efficient and enjoyable love to his mistress, and had nothing at all to report to Herrick, who was becoming increasingly impatient. Sarah seldom let him out of her sight but when he saw an opportunity, he searched for any papers that might link her with the death of Amelia Hinks or the acquisition of her fortune. He found nothing. From time to time, he tried chatting over a meal about his sexual exploits with female passengers on the various cruise ships he had served on but there was no response from Sarah other than a sideways glance from under her long eyelashes. Knowing Herrick was on the point of calling him off and, unwilling to lose Sarah and her home comforts until he must, he became careless and she caught him trying to force the drawer lock on the table in the parlour.

Marsh pretended to lose his temper. "We never go anywhere," he shouted defiantly when she challenged him. "And you ain't paid me any money, neither. I felt like having an evening out and a drink or two. Locked drawers mean money, don't they?"

Sarah relaxed her grip on the scissors and took her hand out of her pocket. "If you wanted money, you could have asked for it," she said quietly.

Not knowing how else to handle the situation, Marsh continued to shout, "I've never asked a woman for money in my life. It's very demeaning."

"Is it?" she asked bitterly. "I suppose you think it more manly to steal from one?"

He stepped away from the table and leaned against the wall. "I'm sorry, Sarah," he said weakly, "honest I am. I've done my best to hold it in since I've been here with you but the truth is, I'm a man who needs to get out for a dram now and again. I was getting desperate for a real drink, that's all."

"I see." Sarah looked at him and found him more like Charlie than ever in his need for drink, even in his trying to force the drawer which contained nothing but Marie's framed photograph. Despite her suspicions being roused, it was a comforting thought. Considering that Charlie, who had less than a week to live, had been on her mind.

"You were wasting your time," she said. "There's nothing in that drawer but some old receipts and other papers to do

with the shop. If you want to go out on your own, I'll get you some money."

"It's not like that," Marsh said penitently. "If you would come out with me, Sarah, we could have a good blow-out in a restaurant and I wouldn't have more than half a bottle, I promise."

"Give me fifteen minutes," said Sarah. "And leave that bloody drawer alone while you're waiting."

Marsh kept away from the table while he waited for Sarah to dress for outdoors. He knew the constable walking his beat would see them leave and, if Herrick wasn't involved in anything else, he'd be in the shop doing his own bit of snooping. When he first brought a constable in to investigate Mrs Tombrin's suspicions, the sergeant was only concerned with Florence Carlisle, but now, if there was anything to be found in connection with Amelia Hinks or anyone else, Herrick would nose it out. Then his liaison with Sarah would be at an end. Marsh shrugged. It had been pleasant enough while it lasted but he was a good looking fellow and he'd had as good sex with others who were younger and always available when you knew where to look. He was smiling gently over the memory of a thirteen-year-old runaway he'd arrested and deflowered inside the railway arch before taking to the police station, when Sarah came in and he allowed his smile to grow wider.

"You look very beautiful, Sarah," he said. "It will be a real honour to be seen out with you."

He carefully locked the kitchen door behind them and they crossed the yard together, the hand he had rested on her sleeve tightening involuntarily when a wild haired Mrs Tombrin loomed up in front of them. Seeing Marsh's hold on Sarah's arm, she let out a screech of triumph.

"I know you," she screamed at him. "I've seen you at the police station. You have come to lock her away?" Before the startled Marsh could speak, Sarah turned in fury, the scissors already in her hand. In an instant, her arm brushed across his front, and the long points were deep in his stomach. As he collapsed sobbing across the wall she was through the gate and kneeling on a thrown down Mrs Tombrin, clawing at the shrieking woman's face until the heavy fist of a uniformed constable knocked her to one side. Hearing the blast of a whistle, Sergeant Herrick came across the road to find her on the ground, semi-conscious and bleeding copiously from a split lip. The two or three hours following saw Sarah Fowkes safely locked away in a cell and the naked body of Constable Marsh in the City of London Morgue.

Before going back to the police station to formally charge her with murder, Herrick paid a last visit to the shop, found the locked drawer in the parlour table, forced it and was disappointed to find within only the framed photograph of a child. Hardly sparing it a glance, he tossed it to one side, pulled out the drawer and turned it over to see if any papers were fastened with tape to the underside. Finding none, he lost interest and dropped the drawer without seeing it land on and splinter the glass in the silver frame as well as dirtying the child's photograph. A day or two later, at Sarah Fowkes's request, the dented frame was found on the parlour floor, the broken glass removed for safety, and the photograph of the smiling little girl given to her to keep. On seeing the damaged frame and the scratched and dirtied photograph of her daughter, Sarah Fowkes, quite suddenly, put her head in her hands and wept for the past.

Had Charlie Bennet kept his sanity during his last hours, he might have guessed there would be people to weep for him after the hangman had finished his work. As it was, he was half carried, half dragged into the room containing the scaffold. Where, in a matter of moments, a hood dropped over his head to hide his swollen, tear-stained face, the rope round his neck was adjusted so the knot lay under his left ear, and the trap door snapped open to let him drop through and into oblivion.

Later, the prison doctor satisfied he was dead, he was taken down and wrapped in a piece of frayed canvas, never to know that Mrs Tombrin, her pale face bruised and showing the marks of recent scratches, was in the forefront of the crowd gathered at the prison gate to read his death notice. By her side stood a grey faced Mrs Avery, Annie Barnes' tearful employer, who, since the trial began, had held herself responsible for being the one who sent Charlie to Madame Sarah in search of her lost jewellery. The women, knowing

nothing of each other's place in Charlie's life, instinctively drawing closer together at the approach of a tall and gently weeping man, dressed for the sake of anonymity, in plain clothes.

Even if he had remained sane, and whatever he might have hoped for in the way of prayers from the two ladies and Lieutenant Holland, the one person Charlie would never have expected to weep for him or to give his death a second thought, was Sarah Fowkes. In that he was quite wrong. Her hair was dishevelled, there were tears on her cheeks, and her mind was full of him when, some four hours after his neck was broken, she was taken from her cell and told by her young, fresh faced counsel, she would do best to plead guilty to the wilful murder of Robert Marsh.

"They're all against you, they really are," he said earnestly, and he never came to understand the reason for Sarah's sudden peals of laughter.